Branded

BRANDED

JOHN A. TURES

OBOL HOUSE
PUBLISHING COMPANY

An imprint of Huntsville Independent Press

2112 Morningside Drive NW, Huntsville, AL, 35810

Obol House can bring authors to your live event.
For more information or to book an event, contact Obol House Publishing Company at +1 (256) 678-0411 or visit our website at:
www.ObolHouse.com

Cover design by Chris Treccani - 3 Dog Creative
Interior design by Chris Treccani - 3 Dog Creative

The text for this book was set in Adobe Garamond Pro.

Manufactured in the United States of America
First Obol House paperback edition December 2024

1 2 3 4 5 6 7 8 9 10

The Library of Congress has cataloged the hardcover edition as follows:

Names: John A. Tures, author.

Title: Branded

LCCN (TBD)
Identifiers: ISBN 979-8-9934325-4-0 (pbk)
ISBN 979-8-9934325-5-7 (hcv)
ISBN 979-8-9934325-3-3 (eBook)

CONTENTS

DEDICATION:

This book is dedicated to my immediate family,
and broader family too.

It's also dedicated to the students, faculty, staff and
administration at LaGrange College

as well as the wonderful people of the city of LaGrange, Georgia.
And thanks to the team at Huntsville Independent Press,
for giving me a shot.

ACKNOWLEDGEMENTS:

It may take a village to raise a child, but it took a family to
help me write this book, from listening to drafts, offering constructive
critiques, and providing emotional support.

Visit Meghan Lacey at [www.meghanlacey.com] to view her portfolio.

BRANDED TRIBUTE PAGE

By John A. Tures

When I started writing *Branded*, COVID-19 was upon us. My wife Beth's school chose to dedicate the Yearbook to her and interviewed me for it. What were we doing during this historic shutdown? My wife was making masks. Our oldest kid Asher was learning the guitar, and our youngest kid Zach was playing online chess. I told the editor I wasn't doing anything different, and column-writing gigs were drying up during the economic downturn. So I decided to use what I knew would be a long pandemic shutdown to write my first ever book of fiction.

I thank Beth, Asher and Zach for patiently listening to my novel, and offering some fun critiques to keep me from taking things too seriously. My mother and sister provided valuable edits and good points for all my chapters. Kim, AJ, Jason, Sophia, Steve, Angie, Dan, Sarah and my dad were there for me all these years, and my mother-in-law Linda, who listened to me read.

Author Michael Bishop, a former writer-in-residence professor at LaGrange College, taught me a thing or two about how to craft the story. Author Sharon Marchisello provided great line-by-line edits and ideas. Atlanta Writers Club's George Weinstein and Kim Conrey gave me chances to meet with agents and publishers. My colleague Jack Slay gave me helpful feedback on my short stories, which helped me with the chapter revisions. Author David Morrell, an early inspiration for me for many of his novels, provided valuable advice via Twitter messenger. Thanks Tim Grahl, Alyssa Matesic and Abbie Emmons for your helpful YouTube videos on writing.

For my critique groups, I thank Laura Kelly Robb, Fred Peace, Edna Littlejohn, Donna Vaal and Stella John for critiques of my early chapters.

Thanks also to Dianne Pearce, Cindy Rosmus, Jim Maxwell, Carlotta Dale, White Cat Publications, Kevin A. Davis, Janet Kuypers, Mark Teppo & Frances Lu-Pai Ippolito, Stephen J. Golds, M. E. Proctor, Gray Wolf, Mark Finnemore, Nathan Pettigrew, Martin Bennett, Kelley York, Margot Kinberg, Nancy Kay, Jill Spinelli, Carol Hightshoe, Seven Story Publishing, The Great Cat, Kell Scott-Reed, Barbara Leonhard, Logan Schreiber, Maria Mazziotti Gillan, Cassandra Arnold, Thomas Page, Shanti Arts, Richard Loller, Rachel Macaulay, Broken Teacup, Mark Antony Rossi, and Jana Begovic, all for publishing short stories of mine.

I owe a debt of gratitude to my undergraduate students, colleagues, staff, and administration at LaGrange College. You inspired the heroes of the story *Branded*, though the names and exact character details are fictional. *Branded* was written for you, as well as my family. Various donors and citizens of LaGrange also provided ideas for a few characters in this story.

Special thanks go to Dwight Satterwhite, Christine Satterwhite and Chuck Kraemer, for reading it and giving feedback. Thanks as well to Evan Kirby, Andrew Cunningham and Chase Moss.

Meghan Lacey did a fabulous job painting the cover art that inspired *Branded*. Commission at https://www.meghanlacey.com/. Her work is amazing!

And last, and definitely not least, *Branded* would not have been published without the team of Joshua Adams at Huntsville Independent Press, as well as Trinity Adams, and editor Samantha Oliver. Thanks for giving me my first novel break, and allowing me to share this with you.

January

CHAPTER 1:

Wednesday, January 8

Dean Franklin Arbell rapped a gavel. "Let the record show that this preliminary tenure hearing for Communications Professor Jackson Pierce has begun… thirty minutes late."

The young academic looked up in surprise. With all of his focus on his academic career, artificial intelligence, and being perfect at this hearing, this was a bad start. "Your email earlier this week said 3:30 p.m.!"

Peach State College's Academic Dean gazed imperiously through glasses at the communications scholar, with wavy hair and glasses. "Check your account, *Assistant* Professor Pierce, to see the most up-to-date communication from my office. Punctuality at official proceedings matters."

Pierce stared incredulously at his tablet, having minimized his PowerPoint presentation to check his email. Sure enough, a message had been sent at 2:55 p.m. calling for a 3 o'clock meeting, even though it was a twenty minute jog from his office in the Communications Department to this cramped room in the administration building. Beads of sweat were trickling down from his forehead, a contrast with Central Georgia's cold temperatures in January.

Wearing a well-tailored suit, Arbell was flanked by two of his toadies that he had brought over from his former university to Peach State College. They were both in administrative positions, something called "Department of Efficiency". Both goons were scrutinizing Jackson's discount rack suit. At least he wore a tie today, one Elena had to fasten for him in a double-Windsor style. Both deacons somberly nodded before their dean during the high priest of higher education's homily on the importance of tenure and the need to restrict it only to a select few.

When he finally came up for air, Dean Arbell held up Professor Pierce's file, a thin set of papers in the manila folder, shockingly smaller than the extensive portfolio he had emailed to the committee. A thought came to him: *Did they not know how to unzip a file?*

Jackson gasped.

Then, he blurted out, "Where's the rest of what I sent to you all earlier this week?"

Arbell responded with a tone usually reserved for a parent who was admonishing a child.

"We only printed what was *relevant* for the tenure committee. And what was left is rather light in length." The Academic Dean flapped the manila folder, as if to emphasize how little there was enclosed.

Politeness would have to take a back seat, as Jackson's job was at stake. "I've published dozens of articles with my undergraduate students…"

"They were newspaper columns, not *academic publications*, so they don't count," Goon #1 shot back.

"And the others weren't in national outlets or among the top three journals in your discipline, so we left them out," the other responded. They were like those cantankerous heckling Muppets, Waldorf and Statler, except these two in the room were younger and lacked any trace of humor.

Jackson squirmed in his stiff wooden seat, which was a sharp contrast to the plush chairs the administrators occupied while sitting across the table. *Where did they get this seat that I've been given?* The communications professor thought to himself. *Did they borrow it from a closed-down elementary school from the 1800s?*

He needed these men to see that he deserved tenure.

"That research we published has helped our students get jobs… *good* jobs! Others get into graduate schools, law school…"

"Where they are someone *else's* success," said the first Department of Efficiency goon.

"But as productive alums, they contribute…"

"…Far less than our corporate donors," The second goon beat back his argument.

"At any rate," Arbell sighed, "I believe this pre-tenure hearing is concluded…"

Jackson couldn't resist rising to his feet. "Wait… what about my teaching evaluations?"

Arbell sniffed indignantly. "Those are an inexact measure of competence in the classroom."

Pierce couldn't believe what he was hearing. "What about my students' grades, their graduation rates…"

"Smells suspiciously like grade inflation." Arbell had an answer for everything.

"Didn't you include my award from this college last year in my file?"

Arbell shook his head. "It's a little more than a *popularity contest* for your students and your friends on the faculty. If you had some sort of *national* award, that might have helped."

If Pierce had taken his blood pressure, it would probably be at dangerous levels.

"What about my service to the college and the community? I've worked on…."

"Community service?" Arbell harrumphed. "Did you get a DUI, professor?"

Pierce found himself standing before the committee, looking around the tiny room, a torture chamber for teachers. "I'm sure the Faculty Tenure Committee members will take my entire record into account before making their decision."

Arbell's eyes flickered with amusement, as if he had been waiting for this moment.

"I'm sure they will, but it won't really matter. Nor will your friendship with this college's president help you. It may have escaped your attention, but the Georgia General Assembly tucked a little provision into the Higher Education Bill last year, giving the Academic Deans of state colleges and universities the power to overrule faculty tenure committees and presidential endorsements when they judge a professor has been *unproductive*. And that's how the three of us see your work here at Peach State College."

The Academic Dean rose and glanced at his two acolytes. "Both of you are excused from this meeting. You…" he pointed at Pierce. "Sit back down. We have a little more to discuss here in this room… in private."

The professor's life came crashing down in less than twenty minutes, as shocking as a thunderclap on a cloudless day. When the door clicked behind the departing administrators, Arbell whirled around, a full grin that students and professors rarely saw.

"This is what you and your wife, the Shakespeare Professor here at PSC, get for opposing my policy of letting students write their papers with artificial intelligence."

The normally talkative teacher was too stunned to reply.

"Now, I know your wife in the English Department has tenure. She received it last year before I arrived or I would have had something to say about that."

As Arbell droned on, Jackson was kicking himself. He and Elena decided it would be best for him to go up for tenure *after* he won his faculty award last year. Both felt he would make a stronger case before the committee this year. She would go first, as she had a better academic record. It would be bad for both to go for tenure in the same year, as husband and wife. Now he needed a miracle just to keep his job.

The Dean decided to twist the knife a little, now that he had plunged it in deeply.

"It will be a huge challenge in this job market to have two young scholars find tenure-track university jobs in their respective fields *at the same college*. Too bad. Perhaps you can tend a bar or drive a truck… you look like a lowlife and frequently dress like one."

Pierce snapped out of his funk. "I'll get that national publication… or win an award that you and your review committee will be impressed with!"

Dean Arbell shook his head. "I doubt even your wife could pull that trick off in one semester, which is all you have before the committee meets and my team reviews their work. It's such a shame, really, that you spent all of your time advising, tutoring, and 'mentoring' your college students. What part of 'publish or perish' did you not understand, *professor*?"

CHAPTER 2:
Friday, January 10

"Pay Attention!"

From a booth high in the Brooklyn auditorium, PPP CEO Jeremiah C. Calhoun scanned the bold cover on the book written by Dr. Edward Edmund Kirby. That distinguished professor, now on Calhoun's company payroll, would provide a lecture that would turn business executive attendees into clients.

Professor Kirby was preaching about a new form of product placement, one that would deliver more profits and market share to Calhoun's company. It would also enable Jeremiah Calhoun to settle a few scores along the way for those who frustrated his prior schemes.

Despite his academic pedigree, Dr. Kirby eased his audience into his lecture with several pop-culture references, as though it was a "Ted Talk."

"Can any one of our distinguished guests remember what James Bond's favorite drink was?"

Many in the audience responded with "Vodka Martini, shaken not stirred."

"And who might this actor be?" Professor Kirby continued. On cue, a heartthrob from the 1950s appeared on the large screen behind him.

"James Dean," the audience replied, with more enthusiasm from the female attendees.

Dr. Kirby smiled. "And you remember what film this picture is from," he said to the most eager of the respondents, a woman with hair a mix of fading-blonde and gray.

"Ah… *East of Eden?*" she stammered, struggling with the spotlight.

"Actually, it's *Rebel Without a Cause*," the professor politely corrected her. "It was made in 1955. And does anyone know what this is?"

"It's a comb," came the snide tone. Calhoun recognized the speaker as the son of a wealthy shipping company CEO. Calhoun smiled, seeing the potential source of future clients.

"Not just any comb," Professor Kirby continued to lecture. "It's an 'Ace Comb.' Produced in 1851, this hard rubber hair-care product occupied the back pocket of some men, but it wasn't until James Dean used it on his locks in that 'rebel film' that sales skyrocketed."

The dark Brooklyn theater became silent. Calhoun was pleased to see his speaker had their full attention.

Kirby shifted to the next slide. "And this film?"

"*E.T...*" most called out, and some added "Reese's Pieces!"

"You anticipated my next question," Professor Kirby admitted. His techie, Ms. Elliot, had swapped the space alien in the movie poster on screen with another image containing the orange, brown, and yellow candies.

"What you may not know is that these sweets weren't the first choice for our famous space alien," Kirby added dramatically. "A deal was offered to Mars Company, the makers of M&Ms. But Mars executives turned down the offer, and Hershey made a bundle with their iconic treats, prominently featured in the movie, firmly placing the product in the minds of children and adults alike."

Now the crowd buzzed with excitement, thinking of the possibilities. "That's right, ladies and gentlemen," Professor Kirby resumed. "The name of the game is product placement. And it's an old one, starting in the Lumiere films of the late 1800s. We all know *Forrest Gump* featured Dr. Pepper and saw the Nokia 7110 in *The Matrix*. Tonight, you'll hear about a plan to take this practice to the next level."

As the images of Tom Hanks with a soda and Keanu Reeves with a cell phone were replaced on the screen with numbers and graphs showing spikes in profits, Dr. Kirby continued his address. "You may ask yourself why product placement even exists, with so many commercials out there. Actually, that's part of the problem."

The reddish-haired scholar adjusted his tie as those in attendance hung on every word. "Traditional ads just aren't working. As I would remind my Ivy League students, an effective commercial should have reach, frequency, awareness, and recall. It must connect with the consumer, and often more than a single time. The potential customer must be aware of the product and be able to recall the rationale for the purchase."

The PowerPoint bullets dissolved, replaced by a series of charts.

"More money than ever is being spent on advertising. But survey assessments of product reach, frequency, awareness, and recall are all down," Kirby gestured at the charts. "And who is responsible?"

An eerily silent pause followed. "*You are!*" Kirby boomed.

Calhoun quietly chuckled. That was how you got them thinking about the bottom line.

"You skip through advertisements, preferring to get a snack or even visit the restroom. Those of you with DVR or Livestream services find additional means of cancelling commercials."

The professor replaced silence with a booming "You just won't '*Pay Attention!*'"

Now the audience laughed, applause followed after Dr. Kirby's catch phrase from the book and lecture title.

Calhoun double-checked his wristwatch. It was time for the post-presentation dealmaking. He exited the control booth, taking the back elevator down so he could reach the stage by the lecture's end.

"But what if the merchandise could be woven into what you will watch? That is a different matter, isn't it?" the distinguished professor asked the attendees. "It's the business of Preston Powell Partnership, for which I am a consultant, when I am not teaching, of course."

Several laughed, perhaps guessing correctly how little time he spent in the classroom.

"Yes, PPP engages in product placement."

He rubbed his eyes before continuing, a deliberate pause that would help material sink in better. "Purchase my latest book, *Pay Attention*, and you'll read stories and lessons about the world of advertisement. Hire the

PPP consulting firm and discover how we can make you and your stockholders rich."

On his way down the elevator from the control booth to the stage, Calhoun could still hear the clapping. It seemed like Kirby's talk was a success. But what he wanted were business leaders with worries bigger than their bank accounts to become future clients.

Kirby waved his right hand to quiet the animated audience. An elderly lady began shushing the crowd, and others followed, ironically hissing louder for silence.

"Businesses have spent nearly $9 billion on the practice, but studies show that product placement isn't connecting with audiences."

"But why are companies failing at product placement?" A voice from the crowd interrupted. It was Ray Maillon, a PPP employee planted by Jeremiah Calhoun.

"My good sir, not every company can do it effectively." Kirby threw up his hands. "A few like PPP make up the lion's share of the profits, while the rest flounder."

"Why?" Maillon pressed.

"It's quite simple," Professor Kirby explained, as if speaking to a struggling student. "Sometimes the placement is too subtle, failing on reach and frequency. Other times, it's just blatant commercialism. Those may produce awareness and recall, but not the purchase. It may even trigger a backlash or possibly a boycott, leaving the product worse off than before. In summary, most attempts at product placement are either too obvious or not obvious enough."

The auditorium was now silent. Calhoun mused that things would never be the same after his vision went into effect.

"What businesses need is the next generation of product placement, where the audience doesn't just see the product, but they can recall the product, want to buy it, and make the purchase," Dr. Kirby explained. "And for those who team up with Preston Powell Partnership, you'll learn about the next generation of product placement, which will earn you the profits and market share you can barely imagine." The audience responded with cheers.

As Kirby signed copies of the book, Calhoun entered the stage. They wouldn't know everything until they signed up to be clients of Preston Powell Partnership, Jeremiah Calhoun concluded. They would learn of his plan to insert products during media broadcasts, and in not-so-subtle ways. Their products wouldn't just be on the news.

They would *be* the news.

Even then, they wouldn't know all of the details. That was something Jeremiah would keep to himself. Those included his plots for revenge, as well as other unsavory parts of his plans. Some people would lose their companies, their good fortune, and their lives, but what did they say about not being able to make an omelet without breaking a few eggs?

Calhoun saw Maillon engage in a conversation with an attendee, assessing him as a potential client. Another company man, Juan Fernandina, was making his way toward a marketing director from a Fortune 500 Company…perhaps there would be more potential for future business? But the real catch was heading the speaker's way.

"Er… Distinguished Prof… ah…"

"Dr. Kirby will suffice. And you are?" he said, though Calhoun and Kirby knew exactly who accosted him. In fact, it was the main purpose of the evening's event.

"Howard Evans, CEO and Founder of SRD," the man with the circular glasses and the dark blue suit managed nervously.

"My company… it's not gone well with the FDA with our latest product, the."

"Why don't you start at the beginning?" Dr. Kirby suggested.

Evans launched into his version of the company story and how he had inherited the pharmaceutical firm from his parents. He added his hopes for filling the niche of sleep aids, adding that his nighttime restlessness encouraged his quest.

"SRD stands for 'Sleep, Rest, Dream,'" and we've developed the NR-120, designed to help people not only get through the night, but also wake up refreshed. But the FDA has kept our drug off the market, claiming something about psychotropic side effects. We're losing market share like crazy to our rivals at Kipenium. By the time our product gets the green light from the government, our pills will be worth less than pennies."

Dr. Kirby feigned sympathy. He knew Jeremiah Calhoun had been searching for a new type of client for this experimental form of product placement, and SRD would be the perfect test case.

Most of the crowd milled around the pre-autographed books in the lobby, so the chances of others overhearing their conversation were slim. Hap Dixon and Oeznik Turosz were guarding both exits, while Vinnie Moro prowled around backstage to ensure there were no eavesdroppers.

Calhoun, the leader of PPP stepped further to greet Evans, shaking the other man's hand. "I'm Jeremiah C. Calhoun. Dr. Kirby is my associate from PPP."

A toothy grin emerged from the attendee as Calhoun continued. "And you're Howard Evans with SRD, yet you have the sleepless nights, as I managed to overhear."

Evans colored a darker shade of pink. "Dr. Kirby has convinced me that your firm can help, but he's also pointed out how tough it is to do a product placement for a product that's not even available."

Calhoun's eyes swept the stage and orchestra to ensure the next words would be limited in exposure. "Have you considered an alternate form of marketing?"

As his client remained tongue-tied, PPP's leader began. "Why don't you visit our firm this week? We can keep the plan confidential while we show you how SRD can bounce back." After Evans took the Preston Powell Partnership card, Calhoun added a line. "And we won't 'rest' until we do!"

"Professor?" a student's voice called out.

Jackson Pierce's hands flew off his head. His face whipped left and right. Six pairs of eyes scrutinized him, each with different facial expressions.

"Huh-wha-?"

"Professor, it's five minutes after our Senior Seminar is supposed to start," Sylvia Wright snapped. With a focus on pre-law, she was often the first to speak and most likely to enforce the rules.

"Are you okay, Dr. Pierce?" John Marshall Bradford III asked, with more than a note of apprehension. They all approached the front of the classroom.

"I have a Tylenol or two, if you need one," Nat Hinton, the school's star wide receiver, eagerly added.

"Is this about your tenure?" Taira Malek offered sympathetically.

Now Professor Pierce was in full-panic mode. "How did you…wait, what makes you say that?"

The Lebanese-born broadcasting major replied. "My work-study job is in the administration building. I overheard Academic Dean Franklin Arbell bragging that if he couldn't get rid of tenure across campus, he'd deny it to anyone going up for it."

All eyes were on the professor, who now morphed into something a shade paler.

"Does that mean you'll be fired, Professor Pierce?" inquired Paul Herrera, a nontraditional student, a veteran of the recent Middle Eastern Wars. He sounded outraged.

The communications instructor, normally one of the chattiest academics on campus, went strangely quiet, opening up the floodgates to a barrage of student questions.

"Is that true?

"They can't do that!"

"Will your wife keep her tenured post in the English Department?"

"Does that mean both of you leave if you don't get tenure?"

Jackson opened his mouth to try and reply to all queries, or even any of them. But nothing came out.

"I..."

Paul stepped forward. "Well, they haven't denied you tenure yet. Maybe you could win a big-time award or publication this semester that'll help you get it."

That got everyone talking rapidly and thinking of ideas. But the communications professor could only shake his head. "Sorry, but publications take too long to write and get through the review stage. It will take until summer to get something even accepted these days. They ignored my campus award. I'm pretty much out of time. Thanks, though...."

The students glanced at Jackson's laptop, projected onto a larger screen, a list of faculty positions outside the state of Georgia. Lone Star College, Anderson University, and the Messinger Institute of Technology.

Nat Hinton locked eyes with Professor Pierce. "If we learned anything from you, it's not to give up. Remember what you told me before the Gator Bowl? I passed those words on to my teammates in the locker room. How do you think we beat Tennessee?"

Surprised, Pierce looked up. He hadn't heard about his role in one of the biggest upsets of the college football season.

Taira jumped in. "Who showed me how to do t-tests so I could pass my final in Dr. McCormick's Math class?"

Others mentioned help with papers, advising assistance, and test prep sessions that Professor Pierce had run.

"And don't forget that presentation of our research that we did at the Georgia Capitol last year," Paul Herrera pointed out. "That'll help us on the job market."

Pierce spread his hands. "I will say that it's been worth it, teaching all of you. You've been some of my best students ever. I only wish…"

"A.I. found something last night online that we'd like to show you," Nat announced.

A sixth student, Alicia Ina Sheehy, parted the Red Sea of classmates as she stepped forward. The slight girl with a pageboy haircut and thick glasses, who often kept a low profile, was being uncharacteristically bold.

Through stutters, she introduced a website that described a state contest, where a winner could go on to a regional version, and eventually a national competition.

As the students excitedly chatted about the event, Jackson Pierce tried to hide his dismay. He knew about such events, but those contests were more for Ivy League schools, other prestigious private colleges, and the flagship state universities, not a public-private hybrid college in Central Georgia like Peach State College.

"The deadline is about a month away," Professor Pierce pointed out.

"We'll do it." Paul insisted. The military veteran was always a go-getter.

"You'll have to go up against the likes of UGA, Georgia Tech, and Emory, and that's even if we make the top four," Jackson Pierce said. "There's also Georgia State, Oglethorpe…"

"You've been trying to inspire us since our first year," Sylvia lectured. "Was it just words you came up with to make us work harder on tests and papers?"

"I meant everything I said, but you'll have to work harder than ever before. And you're seniors. There will be parties, formals…"

Taira put up a hand. "Who came to our sorority's fundraiser?"

"Or cheered loudly at every home game?" Nat added.

Sylvia waved her hand. "Or took us on that field trip to CNN and Fox News?"

"Who advised our student newspaper?"

"Got us published by the *Atlanta Journal-Constitution*?"

With each reminder, blood rushed to Jackson Pierce's face. The animated version of the professor rapidly returned.

"You all are right!" he beamed. "We *could* do this!"

Others started clapping or snapping.

"Now that's the Professor Pierce we know!" Trey exclaimed cheerily.

"But we've got to come up with a killer topic," Professor Pierce said.

Nat laughed. "Guess that Tylenol I gave you must have kicked in."

"Tylenol…" Professor Pierce replied, getting up and pacing around the front of the classroom. "You know, when I was a kid, there was a serial killer who poisoned people in Chicago, adding cyanide to their pills."

The students simply blinked in response. That's it, Professor Pierce thought. They don't know how the poison was administered.

"H-how d-d-did the killer d-do it?" Alicia managed.

"Back then, Tylenol came in capsules, so the guy simply opened them to add the cyanide, then returned them to the package."

"Did they ever catch him?" Sylvia asked. Professor Pierce shook his head.

"Johnson & Johnson's CEO, whose company owns Tylenol, pulled all capsules off the shelves, replacing them with caplets and tamper-proof containers, which you are more familiar with. It cost the company a ton, but it was a good public relations move. It restored their marketing brand over time."

"How do you know so much about this, Dr. Pierce?" Trey asked.

"It was the topic of my Master's thesis."

"Ohhhh…" Several repeated.

"Speaking of brands, Professor, we were watching an O.J. Simpson documentary about the trial," said Sylvia. It was probably her idea if it involved the law.

"Last night's episode was the White Ford Bronco slow-speed chase," Paul added. As a car guy, the veteran would be the one to bring up the iconic vehicle. "You know, Ford was gonna discontinue the Bronco later that year, but after that incident, they kept making them for years afterwards. Now Ford's bringing back the Bronco, thanks to these documentaries about the Simpson case."

"Professor… could we maybe do something with product placement for that contest?" Taira asked.

The words struck Jackson Pierce as though he received a full-body shock.

His students all knew what that meant. "Our professor's back," noted Sylvia Wright.

"Yes… yes! We could make this happen! It's an awesome topic! It would get the judges' attention."

It was the most animated he had felt since that disastrous pre-tenure hearing at the start of the semester. He attacked the whiteboard with a rainbow of markers, a rosary of theories, hypotheses, variables, and assignments.

"Yeah… unfortunately, that's also the same Professor Pierce we all know," Trey whispered to his classmates as they groaned while Jackson excitedly rambled on about a research design and all the work they would have to do.

"We'll all have to receive 'incomplete grades' in our social lives," Taira giggled as their workload began to pile up by a factor of three.

"If we-we make it, do w-we get to go to Savannah?" Alicia asked.

"You get me your best stuff, and we might make the top four, maybe even pull a big upset in that contest over the other Georgia colleges," Professor Pierce added.

"Hey, professor," Nat said as he and his classmates packed their bags at the end of the class. "What if all of those product placement cases were all part of some big conspiracy, you know, to sell Ford Broncos or to hurt Tylenol?"

"There he goes again with those conspiracy theories," Sylvia laughed.

Jackson smiled. "Let's stick with what we actually find and not go off and look for some thriller novel about corporate schemes."

CHAPTER 4:
Monday, January 13

"Any other questions, Miss Adams?"

Britt glared at Jeremiah Calhoun. Her interview did not yield more details about the Preston Powell Partnership CEO, other than what she had learned from his website bio.

"Mr. Calhoun…"

The curly-haired man with the receding hairline interrupted. "Call me Jeremiah, Miss Adams. If we get on friendly terms, perhaps you can call me Jerry in private."

She resisted the urge to roll her eyes again.

"What else can I tell you?" Jeremiah continued. "I came from a good family, gave my clients what they needed, invested the profits well, and saw recessions long before they arrived. Of course, there is a way you can learn so much more about me. I've got a table at 21… the restaurant."

She gasped.

"But… doesn't your bio say you're married?"

"I was. Not anymore, though."

Britt abruptly slammed the laptop down and yanked the cord out from the wall. "I am sorry, Mr. Calhoun, but I have no intention of being your second choice."

"Remember our agreement… the story doesn't run until I see the draft," Calhoun added as she left in a huff, dodging Wallace Bragg, the Chief Operating Officer, as he entered the room.

"How much will she really learn about us?" Calhoun's deputy asked.

Calhoun's smile revealed his teeth. "How much I'm worth, what I own, and what I like, but no trade secrets about PPP."

"So I know your company secrets," Bragg said. "But what about before you came here?"

"You know about my lobbying career?"

Bragg shook his head. "I know the profession, but not how you got started in that business."

"Since you're a partner in the firm, and you're invested in us heavily, I'll tell you. And unlike Miss Adams, you won't have to join me for dinner."

Calhoun walked over to the coffee pot and poured a cup. "Have I ever told you about Magnolia Medical?"

Bragg shifted in his tight suit and nodded. "I know it's one of the leading Southern health care clinics. They've got one in every mid-sized town in Dixie. You work for them?"

The CEO cocked his head to the side. "And against them, too."

Bragg's facial wrinkles doubled. "You switched companies?"

Calhoun smirked. "Years ago, a professor at Clemson told me a tale from the Great Depression, about Prohibition in the South."

"A NASCAR origin story?"

"It's better, Mr. Bragg. It is why booze was banned for so long in the South, despite the fact that folks down in Dixie love their bourbon and beer."

"I assume those self-righteous Southern Baptists were to blame, Jeremiah." Bragg guessed.

"But here's the best part," Calhoun continued. "When those Baptists passed the hat in the service on Sundays to fight legalization efforts in the legislature, guess who put in the most in those churches and revival tents, to outlaw the 'demon drink?'"

Bragg shrugged. "The preacher? The mayor…deacons…I don't know."

The CEO pointed to the small liquor cabinet in the corner. "The bootleggers themselves."

"Wha…"

Calhoun waved his hands. "Think about it, Mr. Bragg. Who benefited the most from keeping alcohol banned? Without Prohibition, everyone would be able to have a legal backyard still. Bootleggers would be out of business! That's why even after FDR ended Prohibition, a bunch of 'dry counties' popped up all over the South, with bootleggers leading the charge."

"I love your story," Bragg admitted. "But what does it have to do with Magnolia Medical?"

"It's what gave me the idea for my start. You see, I grew up in South Carolina, heard the Prohibition tale, and wondered how I could pull a similar stunt and start making money after college. I knew Magnolia Medical's plans, so I created a public relations department to protect them. You see, they'd do *any* procedure, including those that people don't like to talk about, that are often performed in back alleys in big cities."

"Abortion?"

Jeremiah clapped his hands together. "Exactly. Everywhere you'd find a Mag-Med Clinic, the right-to-lifers would be loudly protesting. My job was to keep MMC in business."

"But how… wait, no, you didn't..?"

Calhoun's smile told the tale. "I created a second firm, one separate from my first company, 'Health Cares,' which had Mag-Med as the sole client. My other company was called "JC Corp". You know… J.C.? Jesus Christ? I'd get pro-life money donated to my firm to keep MMC out of towns."

"But how'd you..?"

"I convinced the Chief Ops at Magnolia Medical Center, MMC, that there was money to be made. I'd shake down the Baptists to try and get Magnolia Medical Clinics banned in the South and get MMC money added to the cause to keep their clinics in town. It was a very profitable battle for me."

"I don't see why the health company would give money to the Right-to-Lifers."

"It was simple, really," Calhoun explained. "They had deep enough pockets to afford it. A powerful pro-life group could deter any would-be competition to MMC. The admin at Mag-Med could shake down the investors, citing the threat. They'd hide the cost by charging gals, boyfriends, and dads, even single moms, lots for abortion, as side payments, citing the risk."

Bragg raised his eyebrows. "I'm impressed. Does anyone else know about this?"

"My wife, Gretchen, discovered it while prowling around my computers, looking for any blackmail material she could find to use in divorce court. Never marry an attorney, Wallace."

The financier laughed. PPP's CEO knew Bragg was currently between relationships.

Calhoun's expression went dark. "I had Mr. Dixon follow them on a diving expedition in the Bahamas. It turns out she and the instructor she was sleeping with suffered an equipment malfunction deep in the ocean. Neither had enough air to surface. It was cheaper than court."

Instead of any dismay at the murders, Bragg shrugged his shoulders. "I understand what it's like to not want to split a deal 50-50, Jeremiah."

You do, thought Calhoun. He knew full well the truth about Bragg's former partner, Milo Sharpe, and the suspicious circumstances behind his death. Sharpe had little incentive to take his own life, and Bragg was the chief beneficiary of this surprise suicide.

A young preppie poked his head into the boardroom. "Excuse me, but did I read the email correctly that the Tuesday Weekly has been moved up to Monday?"

Calhoun couldn't hide his irritation. "Looks like you're technically literate, Mr. McLane. You're also five minutes early. Take a seat and let's wait for the others to arrive."

Larry Murray and Kimber Elliot arrived next, speaking in hushed tones. Hap Dixon was there, eyeing the two suspiciously. He gave a nod to Oeznik Turosz, who was also keeping tabs on the junior employees. Darcie Matthews, their news connection who had set up the interview, glided in a little more glamorously dressed, perhaps to take his mind off the gal from *Forbes*? "The Spider" was right on her heels, stalking her as usual. Others would join online.

Calhoun wasted little time. "I'm sure you're all wondering why I called this meeting a day early. Mr. McLane, I assume you have those numbers to show everyone?"

Nervously, McLane stood up and pushed a few buttons on the panel of the mahogany table as Dr. Kirby finally arrived, "fashionably late." A pair of tables appeared on the screens with profits over the last ten years, followed by the second set revealing the last few months' income and future projections.

"And what would you say about our profits, Mr. McLane?"

McLane began haltingly. "PPP is still… technically increasing."

"But at a decreasing rate, Mr. McLane," the CEO interrupted. "And what would happen if we did nothing different?"

Clearly, Chip McLane was nervous at the future projections data. "It would go flat…"

"Our profit margin would eventually be zero, even though rent, salaries, and costs would increase, Mr. McLane. Did they teach you that in economics at your fine college?"

Wallace came to Chip McLane's rescue. "What we should ask is why our slope is not so steep in growth anymore."

"Right, and I want some answers," Calhoun barked.

"As I presented last week, the market for product placement has been saturated," Dr. Kirby pontificated.

"It's the newsrooms," Darcie added. "They've never fully recovered from the last recession. Viewership and ad revenue are down for broadcast, print, and radio."

"Social media and internet-based sources are up," the Spider countered.

For the next five minutes, they all debated what could account for their slowing profit margin.

Finally, Calhoun exploded. "You're too focused on why we're not doing as well as we should, instead of what we're going to *do* about it!"

All quieted down.

"Well, this week you're going to see a new direction this company is going in. And that information is not to leave the room, or your lips, to *anyone*."

Calhoun paused, then continued. "You see, for the last several years, we've owned the product placement market in the news but, like movies and television, even *that* market is getting swamped. Gentlemen and ladies, we're going to move away from seeing our products alongside the news. That's because, from now on, we're offering a new strategy for our clients: the ability of our products to *make* the news."

CHAPTER 5:
Monday, January 13

After class, Professor Jackson Pierce jogged past the grand Alexandria Library, designed to be an architect's recreation of the original version from Egypt. The construction of the building actually predated Peach State College, though the library eventually became the centerpiece of the Central Georgian college town.

Along the way, he exchanged pleasantries with several different students: a soldier, a shift manager from Pyramid Coffee's production facility, and a scientist employed by Taipei Tires.

He waved as he saw Professor Chuck Branigan heading toward him. The professor of counseling was a big backer of the Peach State College Sabers, as evidenced by his trademark silver, black, and white scarf worn at outdoor sporting events.

"Working on that tenure-track application?" his colleague said, accompanied by a sympathetic smile. There were few secrets among the faculty in Ivory Towers.

"In a manner of speaking," he replied. That student project was going to be a make-or-break for his career.

"Well, we're having a spring booster meeting at the Malek Hotel," he explained, "and my car battery died. Can you give me a lift? One of the Athletic Department members is my next-door neighbor, and he can give me a ride home."

"Of course, Chuck."

Jackson squeezed his car into the last space in front of the hotel right on the bustling main square, just below the fountain featuring an armed matron from some Revolutionary War tale. As the two scholars exited the vehicle, a familiar smiling face moved in from the other side of the hotel.

"Good evening Ms. Malek," Professor Pierce said.

"Dr. Pierce, thank you so much for the assignment! I've already checked out three books from the Alexandria Library this afternoon. Can't wait to get started!" Taira Malek bounded to the door of the hotel owned by her parents, just in time to hold it for Dr. Branigan to go inside and also embrace her father, who served as the manager.

Who are you, and where are you holding my student hostage? Jackson thought.

Taira was a smart kid, but not always passionate about research. Most students didn't read articles, much less books. Was the topic as interesting to those seniors as it was to him? Usually being on camera, in social media, or on the campus TV station as a journalist appealed more to his Lebanese-born student.

Sadik Malek, her father, extended his hand for a firm grasp of Jackson's. They had been friends ever since their kids began attending the local K-12 Alexandria Academy. Both had to duck aside as the new and very large American flag, that extended from the hotel's ground level pole, flapped in the spring breeze.

"Think you are showing your patriotism enough, Sadik?" Jackson laughed.

"It's because I love this country so much! The United States took us in when we had to flee the violence in my country and had nothing. Now, I am in charge of the best hotel in the Southeast and serve the Americans who helped me."

A throat cleared. Both men turned to see Senami, arms folded, glaring at her husband.

"There is the matter of the bills, Mr. Manager. And yet you are outside, enjoying the afternoon, talking with Dr. Pierce."

Sadik sighed. "I will take care of it, my dear. But make sure Taira works hard in your class, Professor Pierce. She will be on the nightly news one day." He ducked indoors.

Senami frowned. "I am not sure I approve of our daughter being such a public figure in the future."

"Why?" Jackson wondered aloud. "It's hard to break into the broadcast business, but Taira has a talent for..."

"I am worried about our background," she interrupted.

"Being from Lebanon shouldn't be a problem," Jackson sought to reassure her, though in today's political climate, one could never be sure.

"It is not our country, or our ethnicity," Senami lowered her voice so Jackson had to lean closer to hear the whispers.

Jackson knew about their reasons for fleeing their homeland, the terrible Lebanese Civil War. But he wasn't ready for what Senami began to say.

"A few years ago, we returned home to visit." she explained. "It turns out that Sadik's cousin is now part of Hezbollah. That man's son yelled insults at Taira, saying she was dressed like a whore, and she should be veiled and wearing a hijab. We vowed never to return to Beirut."

"Wow, I had no idea!" Jackson exclaimed. "I don't blame you for wanting to avoid Lebanon. But I don't see how that should affect you three. You are U.S. citizens, right? And Sadik's even more patriotic than most Georgians." He smiled as he gestured to the giant flag, and the red, white, and blue bunting on the balconies.

Senami put her hands on her hips. "And how long will that continue, when someone learns our family secret after our daughter becomes a big name journalist? Hezbollah was behind the killing of your U.S. Marines and embassy workers in Lebanon years ago."

Professor Pierce grimaced. "Well, let me know if anyone gives you any trouble over that. We can get a whole lot of people to vouch for you, Sadik, and Taira."

Taira's mother shook her head. "I know you will, but I would prefer Taira keep a lower profile, maybe get an MBA, work at the hotel, get married, give me grandchildren, and keep quiet. What will happen if she breaks the big story, and others find out about our family?"

Jackson shrugged. What could he say? But while she seemed to accept his promises of help, he now knew that she feared a future with a daughter in journalism.

Senami lowered her eyes. "Taira told us of your struggles. I will also pray that you get that tenure job, and that you and your wife can teach here for many years to come."

Jeez, does everyone in Alexandria know about my predicament? Those thoughts occupied him on the drive home after the booster meeting. Over his shoulder, he glanced at the giant pyramid replica on the border between the city and suburbs. It was the extraordinary headquarters of the production facility for Pyramid Coffee, one of the largest employers in Georgia. The aroma from the winds, which blew from the company across the town, made the town of Alexandria smell like freshly ground coffee beans. That probably explained the numerous coffee shops populated by the PSC students.

Jackson pulled off the main road, into a small subdivision near Lake Satterwhite. At the end of the cul-de-sac, he could see his wife's Toyota Prius was already in the carport. A stray tennis ball lay in the yard, ten feet from the vehicle. Jackson reached down to pluck the ball from the grass. Probably fell out of Isaac's bag after he pulled it from the trunk, part of his son's post-practice routine.

As he turned the key for the front door, the warm smell of dinner overpowered him. What is that concoction Elena's cooking, a mix of vegetables and a starch with some sort of garlicky sauce? But it was his daughter, Vivian, at the stove.

"Wow… what's on the menu tonight, Viv?"

His daughter peered at him owlishly through her huge specs. "Orzo with mushrooms and artichokes!" she declared, then returned to her creation, thankfully stirring with the spatula before dinner would get burned again.

"Don't worry," whispered his wife into his left ear as she ambushed him from behind. "I supervised this time."

Vivian Leigh Pierce did have jet black hair, but there the resemblance to the famous "Gone With The Wind" actresses ended. She would color white or blonde streaks into it, a popular style with kids at the college. His daughter preferred giant goggle-like eyewear to light-framed glasses, as if to emphasize their presence. Almost always wearing an apron or smock, Vivian spent hours on chemistry and biological experiments, at school and at home…and her latest mission appeared to be an attempt to master cooking. Her only limits on studying nature were her militant insistence that no animal be remotely harmed by science. She had formed the first chapter of PETA in town and was president of the Science Club at Alexandria Academy.

His son, Isaac, was in the next room, already playing a VR simulator on the family TV. It was some kind of tennis game. His strokes became those of the characters, but instead of facing Andre Agassi or Serena Williams, one could play Scooby-Doo or Bugs Bunny. Today, it was Yoshi from the world of Mario Bros.

"How was practice?"

His son didn't skip a beat. "Straight sets this time."

"You won?"

"Of course, Dad," Isaac shot back. "Give me a little credit!"

Jackson exhaled, a sigh of relief. He hoped Isaac had reversed his recent slump.

"So… you still have a spot on the team?"

"Coach E said he'll decide after Thursday's practice."

The game sounds were shattered a minute later by shouts. "Isaac Pierce! I told you to get ready for dinner in five minutes, and that was ten minutes ago!" When it came to Elena Pierce's temper, it was wise not to challenge it. Isaac pushed a button on the remote and ducked into the kitchen. The hip new network, USBC's 24-hour news channel, replaced the tennis game on the screen.

"So did the students like your product placement research project you texted me about, Jackson?" his wife asked.

"Nat bolted from the classroom in the direction of the library, and I saw Taira with several books outside their hotel." He checked the ping on his cell phone. "Sylvia just emailed, asking if a particular source is a published one. And the rest have already filed their bibliography sources."

"Well!" Elena was impressed, but also somewhat miffed. "None of my students are that gung-ho on day one."

Her husband smiled. "That's because you haven't had time to show them how fascinating Jane Austen is. They just think she's a relic." He did get an appreciative nod on that remark.

"Hopefully that passion will translate into a win at that contest you texted me about. Then maybe we can still teach at the same college."

"Hon, even if I don't make it here, you can easily…"

"We had to apply to over 200 colleges to land a job in each of our fields!" she reminded him.

"I can always go back to being a reporter," he suggested playfully.

"They don't pay English professors enough to support *two* adults, plus two kids headed for college," Elena pointed out. Isaac and Viv entered the room, each with a pair of dishes.

"Dinner's ready," Viv announced, dishing up the meal and passing the plates around.

"Your students are doing something on product placement?" Isaac queried, handing his dad the evening meal.

"Wha-wait, how did you know?"

Isaac grinned. "These walls… *have ears*," he said in a faux-ominous tone.

"Look!" Viv pointed excitedly at the screen.

"What?" Elena glanced up from her dinner, trying to follow what was on the TV.

"There's half of a Starbucks logo on the cup that the USBC newscaster has at his desk!" Viv insisted with great disgust. "Now it's spread to the news."

"Well, as a matter of fact…" Professor Pierce began, but was interrupted.

"And that story on the ticker… Coca-Cola stock is rising," Isaac contributed, mimicking the opening of a can, forgetting the evening's dinner.

"We are going to study…"

"You can see Paige Glass has got a Treasure & Bond scarf on, and she toys with it between broadcast stories." His wife never missed a beat.

Et tu, Elena?

"As I was going to say," Professor Pierce raised his voice over the din of conversation and clanking of silverware on plates, "we are going to study product placement in the news this semester. And my students are on the case already."

Viv pointed a fork at the screen. "How are you going to collect all that data, Dad? In the last three minutes, we've already seen three product placements."

His daughter brought up a good point. The number of cases they would have to analyze would be enormous.

Suddenly, Jackson began to worry a little about the "golden project" that could save his tenure track application. *Which programs would they watch? How much data would they collect? Would they count the business reports? You couldn't help but talk about corporations when you did that, right? So mainstream news would be covered, but would you count Mick Camden's cup of coffee as a case?*

"…Ford controversy," his son concluded.

"I'm sorry… were you talking about the O.J. Simpson case with the White Ford Bronco?"

"No," Isaac explained. "We were looking up the Firestone Tires and Ford Motor Company controversy. Do you think that's why Taipei Tires moved here?"

"Uh…" Again, his thoughts were interrupted by his cell phone. Instead of his campus email, it was on a message app, from his student Alicia.

"U watchin' the news?"

In some ways, it was easiest to follow A. I. when she was on social media, instead of speed-talking and stuttering.

"Yes," his reply went out.

"USBC?"

"Yes."

"Lots 2 cover."

"You said it."

"I'm on a plan."

CHAPTER 6:
Friday, January 17

"The view from our top floor is one that most can only dream about, right, Mr. Evans?" Jeremiah Calhoun asked.

The other CEO, who had been marveling at the view of the New York City skyline in the morning, spun around and offered his standard greeting. "Howard Evans, Sleep Rest Dream and SRD Company." He extended a handshake. "We met at Dr. Kirby's lecture in Brooklyn. The *Wall Street Journal* yesterday wrote…"

"Yes," Calhoun admitted. "It doesn't look good for NR-120's pill's chances of being approved by the FDA. But you can still win passage."

"Anything…."

Then, the sleep drug manufacturer glanced at the bold number Calhoun indicated on the thick manila paper.

"But…that's a steep figure, Mr. Calhoun…"

"Tell me, Mr. Evans. You're about to be ousted from not just the leadership of SRD if the drug isn't approved, but you've also lost *so much* market share to your rivals at Kipenium that you'll be removed from the board, as well. Unless you gain a lot of it back, in a very short period of time, you will have lost control of the company your father, William, worked so hard to create."

"But…that amount of money…"

"When you regain that market share, Mr. Evans, SRD will make so many profits that no one will miss what we're charging. You'll not only stay on as CEO, but those stock options will be the biggest bonus you've ever seen."

The drug company CEO quietly whispered. "So, how do you do it?"

Calhoun strode past his flat-top desk. "Underneath the invoice for our services is the non-disclosure agreement. You'll have several pages of signatures for that."

A smart businessman would have brought over an attorney to look over the material, or at least read it closely himself. But Evans did neither, as he rapidly scribbled his name on each.

A whisper at the glass door, and his Chief Operating Officer and head of security entered on cue, thanks to a text signal he sent a minute earlier. "These are my associates, Mr. Wallace Bragg and Mr. Hap Dixon."

"Hi," Evans managed to the new entrants. "So how…"

Calhoun took the young CEO by the shoulder and led him to the wall by the door, on the opposite side of the room from the windows and perfect skyline view. On the wall were two large frames, encasing two big black and white picture prints.

"Tell me what you see, Mr. Evans," the PPP CEO Calhoun made his pitch. "Any similarities?"

Evans stooped, squinted a bit. "Looks like a bunch of people drinking booze from a long time ago."

"Any differences?" Calhoun added.

The sleep drug company leader looked closer. "In one painting, they look kind of happy. In the other…not so much."

"Astute as ever, Mr. Evans." Jeremiah Calhoun could turn on the flattery. "The first one, with happy people, as you described it, is titled 'Beer Street.'"

Evans turned to him. "And the other?"

"Gin Lane."

"They look like the same person designed both," Evans guessed.

Calhoun nodded. "Both were done in 1751 by William Hogarth. Beer Street was designed to show the benefits of drinking a good English Ale. By the same token, Gin Lane's purpose was to show the horrors of drinking distilled gin alcohol."

"I certainly don't mind a gin-and-tonic," Hap laughed. Bragg rolled his eyes.

Calhoun continued. "Hogarth and his ally, Magistrate Henry Fielding, were Protestant Moralists who wanted gin outlawed, or at least made scarce."

Evans looked thoroughly confused. "B-but they're both types of alcohol. Why did they show one as better than the other?"

Calhoun, PPP's company leader, stepped forward. "Isn't that the most important question, Mr. Evans? Why would those good Christian people tolerate one type of alcohol and ban another?"

The room remained silent until a new voice joined them.

"Because both artworks were commissioned by the beer industry," began a familiar voice.

Evans looked over. "Dr. Kirby, I did not realize you would be here!"

Professor Edward Edmund Kirby shook the client's hand and then provided the correct answer. He lectured the room about how beer was primarily made from domestic grains, while gin's origins could be from foreign sources.

"It led to the Gin Act of 1752, with hefty taxes on such distilled spirits," E. E. Kirby finally concluded.

"Did it work?"

"How about a 50% reduction in the production of gin, nearly crushing the industry, in merely a year," Calhoun snapped. "It nearly annihilated what had then been called 'The Gin Craze.'"

The room broke out in discussion.

"The government act did that?"

"Didn't you say they had a Gin Act earlier?"

"Maybe they taxed it more."

"Like taxes worked last time."

Jeremiah Calhoun raised his hands for silence. "It wasn't the government's power that broke gin. It was the media of the time, the engraving artist, and the propaganda that did it."

"What?"

"How?"

"The genius of pitting beer against gin was only part of Hogarth's brilliance," Calhoun explained. "He also knew the print media market. Unlike other artists, who charged a lot and produced so few copies, Hogarth reduced his prices for these artworks to a single shilling, which reduced the chances of artist forgery, a plague during that time. Because the artworks were so cheap, his paintings were in every coffee house, tavern, government building, church, and schoolhouse throughout England, making more money than if he charged a big amount for a few artworks. People wouldn't just oppose gin for economic reasons, but for nationalistic, patriotic reasons, and…"

Hap Dixon was now looking at the engraving for himself. "Looks like this lady is letting a kid fall out of her arms, and into the sewer!"

Calhoun returned the focus to his explanation. "That particular character is based on the tale of a lower-class woman who killed her kid to sell those baby clothes for a drink of gin."

Howard Evans gasped.

"Between the taxes, the goodness of drinking an Anglo-Saxon Ale, and the evil of drinking distilled spirits, foreign-grown gin didn't stand a chance." Calhoun grinned.

Everyone in the room turned to face the PPP CEO, Jeremiah Calhoun, who had now moved behind the desk to grab the papers Evans had signed. "Gentlemen, if you will, follow me to the conference room. You'll see how this little history lesson matters, for what we're doing to help SRD recapture the market. Grab some coffee, and I'll meet you in the conference room in about fifteen minutes."

As the others departed, Calhoun had a private call to make. He pulled the burner phone from his previously locked desk drawer and pushed a single number. The rest of the digits lit up, though they were a combination of symbols and dashes.

"Hello, Jeremiah," a voice answered on the other line. "Is this connection secure?"

"As always, Mr. Parjeet."

"Great to hear from you. Thanks for helping me get this position at the FDA."

"High friends in high places." In particular, he was thinking of White House Deputy Chief-of-Staff Nick Bradley pulling strings for him yet again.

"So how can I help you out at the FDA?" Parjeet asked. "You wouldn't have used this line unless you were in the market for something."

"NR-120."

"It's 2-2, Jeremiah. And I'm the last vote. Which way do you want it to go?"

"For approval. And for the same price, Mr. Parjeet."

"I don't know, Jeremiah. SRD could go bankrupt without my vote. I think this is worth double my price. You can afford it, since they're probably paying you a pretty penny to get it passed."

"You know, Mr. Parjeet, I remember after you were confirmed to the FDA, how we celebrated down in Belize."

"Yes...."

"You know, I don't think the police in Belize have solved that particular crime."

He could almost hear the sweat pouring down Parjeet's head at the other end of the connection.

"It was an accident."

"That's not what the warrant said. I hear *they* doubled the reward."

He must be stroking his beard again, which is what Ajai Parjeet did when he was nervous, Jeremiah thought.

"It will be approved, Mr. Calhoun, for the usual price. But I want that warrant to disappear."

"Agreed," Calhoun responded quickly. "After the FDA approves SRD's drug, watch the online capital news. A local will be arrested for the crime. And you'll find the usual amount in the usual account at the bank in the Turks and Caicos."

An audible sigh of relief followed. What Ajai didn't know was that Calhoun still had enough evidence to have the FDA appointee go to jail as an accessory. And for murder, there was no statute of limitations, even in Belize, accident or not.

"We'll speak again."

"After the vote."

The line went dead. Calhoun replaced it in the drawer and sealed it with an electronic lock, along with the physical key. Only a good Russian hacker would have a chance at cracking the encryption, and law enforcement was rarely smart enough to solicit their services.

———

PPP CEO Calhoun waited until the room was sealed to begin. "I've spoken to my source, and NR-120 is to be approved by the end of this week." There were generally cheers and clapping, while Wallace Bragg slapped Howard Evans on the back.

"But Kipenium's Pasithea pills already grabbed a significant portion of your market share, and there's no reason to think that they'll give up the sleeping pill market anytime soon."

Some of the early enthusiasm over SRD's good news disappeared as quickly as the heat in their lattes.

Chip considered this. "So we do the product placement thing all over the media, right? Get newscasters to cover the FDA vote…"

"I'm afraid not, Mr. McLane. There's no time to get that kind of publicity out to really make a difference. That's why I called this group here. SRD is going to be the first in a series of clients who will receive…a *different* kind of service."

Seconds ticked by as several looked at each other.

"You've each heard me talk about those framed engravings in my office?"

He provided a short recap of Beer Street and Gin Lane and how Hogarth's artwork nearly destroyed gin drinking in Great Britain. "That's what we propose to do now."

"Get…some…bad publicity toward Kipenium?" SRD's CEO asked.

"Exactly, Mr. Evans."

Darcie rolled her eyes. "So now we have to wait until Kipenium gets some bad news? What are the chances of that?"

"Not wait, but *create*, Ms. Matthews."

CHAPTER 7:
Tuesday, January 21

Ex-Sgt. Paul Herrera took the elevator down to the game room, where he and Nat normally shot pool at the table, but his class would be all business tonight.

Sylvia Wright took notes on a legal pad from a book, as usual. But what was unusual was to see Trey right next to her, on the same couch, staring intently at a Xeroxed article. It wasn't every day that you saw the president of "Black Girls Matter Too" next to John Marshall Bradford III, the leader of the Campus Republicans.

"Where's Taira?" Paul asked, as if he already knew the answer.

Sylvia checked her watch. "Running late, as usual."

Trey looked up from his article. "I saw her an hour ago in the periodicals section. She had a stack of journals in her hands."

"You sure it was Taira with media research?" Nat laughed.

Sylvia lowered her reading glasses. "She hasn't stopped doing research on our class project since Dr. Pierce assigned it. She even turned down a date with a boy last night."

Paul shook his head. Before tonight, he wasn't even sure Taira even had a library card.

As if on cue, their Lebanese classmate bounded in and slammed down a stack of papers. "All newspaper and magazine articles on product placement in the press over the last twenty years."

The others clapped their approval. "And you, Trey?" Taira asked.

Her blond classmate, Trey, pointed to his own stack. "These are all scholarly articles related to our project topic. Just a little 'light reading' for us."

"What'd you bring, Sarge?" Nat inquired.

Sgt. Paul Herrera unzipped his duffel bag, and several DVDs poured out.

"Man, I thought the last Blockbuster store closed down already," Sylvia cackled. "Guess not."

Paul waved his hands. "You misunderstand. These are recorded DVDs with news broadcasts."

"Where's A.I.?" Nat wondered aloud.

"Saw her in the Dining Hall," Sylvia jumped in. "Girl ran through, talkin' a mile a minute about some computer project she's been working on."

"Well, she should be working on *our* project!" Taira complained. "I've been standing all day in the Alexandria Library, researching the media. My heels are killing me!" As if to emphasize the point, she tossed off her shoes and began rubbing the soles of her feet.

"And she skipped out on this meeting," Trey noted.

Paul hit a button on the old DVD player near the door. "Don't worry about A.I. If she's working on our project, we'll be in good shape." Before anyone could reply, "Wayne's World" cued up, and the jokes began from their product placement segment.

Hours later, all five were huddled around a picnic bench under the canvas tent that represented the porch for Montezuma's Mexican Restaurant off campus.

"It's weird," Nat said. "I should be 100% focused on the NFL Draft and all, but I can't stop thinking about this assignment. I was watching a flick about a high school coach in Texas, and all I could see were the Sprite cans and Fed-Ex trucks driving by in the background. The other guys on the team didn't even see 'em, but Marcus went out and bought a Sprite from the vending machine. He doesn't even drink anything that's not a Coke."

Sylvia nodded. "I caught the evening news out of Atlanta last night. Damn if the newscasters didn't have Pyramid Coffee on their mugs at their desks. I kept thinking 'Now how long has that been going on?' Mama didn't even seem to notice, but next thing you know, she's pouring herself a cup for dinner. And Mama don't drink anything with caffeine at night."

All five continued to munch on their late-night Tex-Mex snacks.

"You know," Paul began. "This reminds me of the time I went swimming at Clearwater Beach. Took my younger cousin Danilo, he's about five, into the water, up to my neck. We were enjoying ourselves until my brother Bobby yelled. Papi screamed at me to come in with Danny. Suddenly, I saw jellyfish everywhere. It was mostly clear, but you could see their outlines floating around. I put Danilo on my shoulders, so at least he wouldn't be stung, and I waded back slowly. It was like that '80s video game Frogger. But I kept moving, weaving, left, then right. It took like fifteen minutes, but I got out without a single sting!"

Sylvia yawned. "And your point was, Sarge…?"

Herrera stood up and grabbed the picnic table. "The point is, 'Always Wright,' that this stuff is everywhere. We just don't see it until we look for it. When I took Danilo out into the water, I wasn't looking for no jellyfish. We were just trying to find a spot to throw the Frisbee."

Sylvia glared at Paul, but the others nodded in agreement.

"My dad's been doing corporate work all of his life, and I never seemed to notice products in the media," agreed Trey.

Paul ignored his comment, glaring at Sylvia. "Why do you always have to be that way?"

"What way?" she snapped back angrily.

"Everything's gotta' have a point right away. Everything has to be the perfect argument, and not just a good story."

Sylvia looked away. "You wouldn't understand."

Sgt. Herrera wasn't going to let it end. "What…is it a girl thing? An ethnic thing? A racial thing? A valedictorian thing?"

Sylvia slammed down her glass so hard the others were surprised it didn't shatter. "Is that *all* I am to you? When I came here to Peach State

College, I took 'Always Wright' as a compliment. Didn't realize until later how folks really thought about me. You know why I gotta be "Always Wright?" Let me tell you a story.

=====

"Court of Appeals turned us down again yesterday," Sylvia remembered the past event as if it were yesterday. Preacher Braxton Quincy minced no words to the Gethsemane African Methodist Episcopal Church when he delivered the bad news to the congregation. "Our shyster lawyer dropped us as well."

The mood of the attendees was split between shock and outrage. How could they lose? Even in Central Georgia, those judges had to see that the town of Clifton wasn't getting a fair shake. Redlined into poverty, gerrymandered into powerlessness, bigoted into unemployment… and cowed into fear by the local State Senator, whose brother was the only law around.

"The spirit is willing, but the cash is weak," Rev. Quincy always knew how to turn a phrase. "We can save up, but it'll take years, maybe a *decade*, before we can afford a new attorney."

The shouts of anger turned quickly to cries of despair. It was back to square one.

"I met with the Elders before today's meeting," Rev. Quincy persisted. "We're gonna start a new plan, and a new collection. We need to get a new lawyer."

"But that'll take…"

"I know, Brother Maynard. It will take years. It could take at least six of them to raise enough for…"

"No lawyer 'round here will take our money, even if we could pay them!"

Rev. Quincy wiped his eyes, fighting off his desire to be overcome with emotions with the events from the last few days. "Sister Herron, I understand your concern."

The A.M.E. Pastor gazed out over his flock, even craning his neck, to see if he could spot the answer to his community's problems. As usual, they were keeping a low profile. But no more.

"Sister Sylvia, step forward."

The crowd murmured, as if they hadn't heard it right. What would the preacher want with the eldest Wright kid?

The heavyset, bespectacled teenager trembled as she exited the pew, as surprised as everyone else in the chapel that she had been summoned to the altar.

"You have the highest GPA in Douglass High School," the preacher began. As he continued to tout her academic achievements, confidence outdid her fears about being in the spotlight. When she set her mind to something, she never gave up. Whether it was making sure someone was at home to watch her younger siblings while her mom pulled a double-shift, or picking up the slack with the yardwork while her dad had to work overtime, she didn't know how to quit. She didn't even bat an eye when her mail slot on campus was empty before Senior Prom. There wasn't time for that.

Deacon Putnam quietly tiptoed forward across the aisle to hand her an envelope.

"We have passed the hat and raised enough to make up the difference for what a scholarship would pay to Peach State College."

Sylvia's eyes widened. "I-ah-don't know…how…th-thank…" her voice trailed off.

"Sister Sylvia, Douglass High School's Headmaster tells me you are rarely at a loss for words, child." The pastor smiled.

But she couldn't stop sobbing. "I'll never buh-be able to p-p-pay you back." Others in the church joined her tears.

Rev. Quincy came forward to comfort her. "Yes, you will, my child. You see, the money here has a price and a purpose. It is for your college education, so you can get into law school. Sister Herron is right. No one will take our case around here. But when the old apple barrel is spoiled, it's time to open up a new one." As the preacher launched into a recital of

Psalm 46 and the congregation rose to cheer his words of hope, all Sylvia could do was stare down at the floor, desperately trying to comprehend the awesome task before her.

———

"I…I…had no idea," Sgt. Paul Herrera stammered as Sylvia finished her story. "I…I'm sorry," he managed as she struggled to keep the tears from flowing.

Trey shocked himself as he found his arms around her, hugging her. 'Always Wright' of all people! Few would have expected that, given their numerous campus debates about everything. Eventually, she got herself under control, gave Trey a whispered "thank you," and waved off Paul's apology. "You didn't know" was all she could say.

"Some day, you'll hear my story about what I had to do in the military in the Middle East to come to Peach State College," Paul replied.

"Hey," Nat called out. "Isn't that A.I.?"

Everyone turned toward Archetype Coffee House across the street, where a figure wearing a coat, laptop slung under one arm, disappeared into the growing fog.

"Couldn't tell," Taira admitted.

Everyone was thinking the same thing. Why had their geeky friend ditched their study group? They all got Trey's email. And even if they hadn't seen her, she must have seen them out by the picnic table. Was she ducking them for a reason?

CHAPTER 8:

Thursday, January 23

"Classic Georgian," Wallace Bragg, the Chief Operating Officer of PPP, observed the white house gleaming in the moonlight in front of them in the ritzy Alpharetta neighborhood.

Hap Dixon, the security chief, laughed. "Well, we're in an Atlanta suburb, so what do you expect?"

"He means the style, Mr. Dixon," PPP's business leader, Jeremiah Calhoun, sneered. "It's associated with the reign of English kings named George."

Benefits of a well-rounded education, Jeremiah thought as he considered the house, owned by a man he despised. At least for a few more minutes.

"So, who's the target?" Hap couldn't resist.

Calhoun surveyed the place. "Reginald Wald. Attorney for many liberal causes. He's on the short list to be the new Environmental Protection Agency director."

Dixon shrugged. "Got the gear for the burglary, guns just in case, and pills, ready to go." He and Oeznik Turosz exited their Land Rover and slipped away into the shadows. Jeremiah knew the plan, of course, but he accompanied the two on this mission to Wald's mansion because he wanted to see it done right.

"If you don't mind me asking, why target Wald?" Bragg ended the silence after half of the vehicle's occupants departed. "Is it his liberal policies? Or money?"

Calhoun shook his head. "Neither, Mr. Bragg. It's personal."

Years ago, Calhoun had decided to play another game, pitting one group against another. Instead of abortion clinics and pro-lifers, he developed a new con. This time, it was environmentalists and gas stations. The members of

Green Justice, or GJ, were drawn to his money as much as his smooth talk. Calhoun gave them lots of clout as their leader and top lobbyist.

Little did they know that Marquis, a leading corporate chain of self-serve gas stations and stores, was paying him on the side to make the Greens fall just short of their goals. Calhoun was also able to siphon off some from GJ's own fundraising, just as he paid himself a tidy sum for his services. And he'd whip up Green Justice into a formidable membership with clout, enough to make the HQ of those gas station chains up the ante.

Meanwhile, Marquis always managed to wriggle off the hook, thanks to a legislator making a last-minute controversial about-face vote, or a surprise state court ruling. Knowledge of the secret lives of politicians was a plus in both scenarios.

Everything was going so well, until that hot-shot activist from Georgetown Law joined Green Justice. Calhoun didn't initially see him as a threat, as Reginald Wald kept a low profile. But the new lawyer slowly began to network and gather evidence on the GJ leader…almost the way he would have, Jeremiah had to admit. Suddenly, there was a snap election, and allegations from challenger Wald, which caught Calhoun off guard. When the dust settled, Wald had prevailed in a nasty, bitter electoral contest. Jeremiah had never expected a black man to beat him at the ballot box.

Immediately after the election, Calhoun had hard drives smashed with hammers. He then made sure more durable information devices had a date with a magnet. Papers were shredded. Accounts changed numbers and names. Wald would have his suspicions, even his allegations, but never any proof. And Calhoun would have his motive for revenge.

Wald was alone, as his wife and the kids had tickets to the Atlanta Center for the Puppetry Arts. But the environmental lawyer had opted not to join them. He had too much work on his hands, preparing for the possible cabinet confirmation hearings.

He was so engrossed in listening to Senator Morton's Alabama drawl on the recording that he never heard the two who had slipped through the basement window after taping and punching the glass. Confident in his alarm system, Wald would have been stunned to learn how easily Oeznik disengaged it. But it was too late. Within seconds, Wald had passed out, slumped in the arms of Hap Dixon.

The silent killer grabbed a handful of the Pasithea pills from the bag, but Hap held up his hand. "Change of plans. Calhoun's coming in."

Oeznik paused, betraying no sign of surprise. The two waited until Calhoun and Bragg entered the house from the rear.

"He's starting to wake up," Hap explained. "We don't have much time, Mr. Calhoun."

His boss grinned. "I'm counting on it, Mr. Dixon. I've waited too long for this moment."

He nodded to his associate. "Mr. Turosz, give me Kipenium's pills, if you please."

Bragg shuffled his feet uncomfortably. Making this personal went against every safety protocol.

Wald's eyes fluttered, then he looked wide-eyed at his old nemesis, who growled. "I swore I'd get even, Reginald. And you'll never be EPA Director!"

With that, Calhoun rammed the handful of Kipenium's pills into Wald's mouth. After flailing about and attempting to regurgitate the pills, Reginald Wald began shaking, then slumped down, as Oeznik held his nose closed and mouth shut.

"Mr. Bragg, the second jar, if you will."

His second-in-command produced the container of Kipenium's top sleeping pill, Pasithea.

Hap Dixon brushed his hair back from his eyes. "I don't see what's so important about that."

Jeremiah, savoring his triumph, was far less condescending than usual. "You see, Mr. Dixon, the second jar will show only a few pills of Pasithea missing, far less than what we administered to the late Mr. Wald here. If we left a jar almost half-full, the police would conclude that the lawyer took his own life. We need to show an accident, to discredit Kipenium and their Pasithea pills. People and regulators will think the company's product is deadly, an accident waiting to happen, even if they only take a few."

Bragg nodded. "That'll put SRD on top again in the pharmaceutical industry as well for their sleeping pills. Time to get to work on the angle."

———

USBC's top co-anchor, Paige Glass, had long since drifted off to her "beauty sleep," having taped the last news broadcast hours ago. Nothing was to disturb her, unless it was the buzzing from a slender private phone tucked into the pocket of her purse, hanging off the bedframe.

"Jeremiah, it's two in the..."

"Reginald Wald is dead, Ms. Glass."

The cobwebs that had slowed her brain disintegrated immediately. "Wha-...how?"

"Sleeping pills," Calhoun responded. "Looks like an accident."

The veteran newscaster was not without her suspicions. "Why not suicide?"

"He was angling to be the next EPA Director."

"Stress...nerves..."

Calhoun waved off her concerns. "No suicide note, either. Barely any pills were gone. And he was about to make history."

Paige nodded. "We'll make the usual tributes..."

Jeremiah raised his voice. "Wald is not the story, Ms. Glass. Kipenium's Pasithea pills are to blame. Anyone taking this little supplement to get a better night's sleep is going to be in trouble. You know our arrangement."

Wish I could have a few sleep aids now, Glass concluded. But Jeremiah Calhoun sounded like he had a breaking story. She and Mick could broadcast the exclusive newscast the next morning.

"We'll get on it. Gotta make some calls, run some statistics..."

"That's my girl. Darcie's emailing you the details."

Paige resented the label. After all, she was a woman! But she tolerated his tactics. That boost in income from his firm for slanting the story just right would more than make up for his condescension.

Calhoun clicked off the cell as Wallace Bragg hung up on his conversation. "Mr. Ajai on board?"

His C.O.O. nodded. "Parjeet will announce the FDA investigation first thing in the morning, as agreed upon. Looks like we can close the book on the SRD case, and move on to Talladega Motors," Calhoun announced via Zoom to those not at his headquarters.

Chip McLane nodded. "Their board agreed to the price. The money hits our account tomorrow."

Kimber Elliot stifled a yawn. "I don't see why Talladega Motors needs our help. Their Gyrfalcon is one of the fastest sportscars you can buy!"

McLane sneered. "Yes, but who can afford it? With all those cost-overruns from the union strikes, the Gyrfalcon is not just the fastest car on the market, but *also* the most overpriced."

Bragg looked at the CEO. "What's the plan?"

"I've had Mr. Murray work with Mr. Gordy, spending the last few hours researching who owns one of these, who could also be considered a celebrity," Calhoun explained.

All eyes slowly turned to PPP's computer mainframe, where The Spider furiously typed away.

"Pierre Bujols owns a Gyrfalcon," the computer expert said.

It was Chip's turn to chime in. "You mean that hockey hooligan from the New Jersey Devils?"

"'Big Stick' Bujols leads the league in penalty minutes and DUIs," Murray explained.

"Well, after his next game, Mr. Bujols will be perhaps the most well-known name in the National Hockey League," Calhoun explained. "And more importantly, his car will be even more famous than he will be, according to the newscasters who will be live that evening."

CHAPTER 9:

Friday, January 24

Long before the Pierce family had their breakfast, Jackson's aged Chrysler was cutting through the fog, on its way to the southside for Alexandria's city jogging path, the envy of Central Georgia.

Normally his colleague, Walter Diehl, was ahead of him, either working out with the outdoor machines or preparing for a three-mile run. But the biology professor was strangely absent that morning.

There was one figure out by the trail, going into an elaborate stretching routine, leaving nothing to chance. Peach State College Math Professor Mimi Grey was just as demanding of her undergraduates as she was of her own running regimen.

"Hi Mimi!"

Dr. Grey waved, but didn't speak, not wanting to break her concentration. Timing was precise in her routine. She had run track and cross country in college, and led a group of women who ran early in the morning to build up their distance. Rumor was that they would all try for the Marine Corps Marathon later that year.

Finishing her pre-run warm-up, Dr. Grey asked, "So how's the tenure track application going?"

"Jeez! Does *everyone* on campus know that?" Jackson groaned.

The Math professor then switched topics. "Where's your regular running buddy? Or do you need a new one?"

Jackson was about to reply when a cry made him stop. He spun around to see Diehl, sobbing.

"Walter…" Mimi began, but the biology professor cut her off.

"It's Reggie," he heaved between gasps. "He's…dead."

"Re-ginald….Wald?" Grey gasped.

Jackson remembered it clearly. Every year, Pyramid Coffee donated a generous grant to Peach State College to bring in a guest speaker. Diehl had won the coveted speaker grant, bringing in the famed environmental lawyer, a friend and colleague of the Biology Professor.

"Wha-what happened?" Pierce found himself fumbling for words.

"Sleeping pills…"

"But he seemed so… *happy.*"

"It w-wasn't suicide!" Diehl growled. "It was an *accident!*"

"I'm sorry he passed away," the math professor's voice attempted to soothe the grief-stricken professor. "That's why you're so upset."

"No!" he snapped. "It's not that. On the news this morning, they barely talked about his life's work… didn't even mention Green Justice!"

Jackson knew how hard it would be for Walter Diehl, a full-fledged member of Green Justice. Every spring, he and his toxicology class would take samples at Lake Satterwhite to see if there was any pollution in the water.

"All they focused on were those damn Kipenium sleeping pills! Couldn't even talk about how the guy was to environmental law, what John Lewis was to civil rights."

While Diehl complained about the unfair treatment Reginald Wald was getting in the news, Jackson thought about what he was saying. Normally, when a famous American like Wald passed away, they'd at least say more about the person who died. But then again, the media was just being care-ful, right? Nobody else should have a lethal overdose. It was just keeping the public safe. If there was a dangerous product, that was more important right now than lionizing a future EPA Director. Wasn't that the case?

But a nagging feeling in the back of Dr. Pierce's mind told him that something wasn't right.

"Wow," Mimi said a few minutes later as Diehl's vehicle disappeared from view. "And Wald was just at Peach State College."

The two ran in silence for a moment, thinking about the sudden turn of events that had shocked their colleague and themselves.

"Mimi… do you think there's anything odd about Wald's death?" All he could hear was the pounding of their feet on the concrete pavement for at least two minutes before she spoke.

"Walter said it was an accident. Why should it be anything else?"

"Diehl kept harping on how they covered the sleeping pills."

"C'mon, Jackson. They don't want anyone else to die from the same accident," Mimi pointed out. "The press is just keeping everyone safe."

Jackson shifted topics, telling her about his seniors in the Senior class, their research project, the contest, and how he hoped it would land him that tenure track spot. He also brought up his student, Alicia Ina Sheehy, and her mysterious absence from group project meetings.

"You've got A.I.?" Mimi's excitement was clear. "She's been my favorite student from the last few years. She's a bundle of nervous energy and talks a mile a minute, but she's got the brains to work for NASA! I know, because I helped train her."

"But is she antisocial…"

"Well, she's like an introverted extrovert, or maybe an extroverted introvert. I can never remember. At any rate, if she disappears, that means she's working on a huge project and doesn't want to stop until it's finished. She's okay with people, but loves numbers even more. I have the feeling she's had a rough life or a bad event before she came to Peach State College. Give her time, and you'll be glad she's on your group project. You might win that academic contest, and then you might get a tenure-track spot."

"Made it just in time!" Elena Pierce remarked as her husband bolted out of their house, computer bag in one hand and coffee mug in the other, as he jumped into the Ford Expedition with her and the kids. "But you didn't have time to snag a tie, I see."

He pointed to his coat pocket. "I'll put it on when I get to campus." He then glanced at his wife's hairstyle and scarf. "What's the occasion? Did I forget our anniversary?"

She laughed. "Not for a few months. Higher Education Dean Franklin Arbell wants to evaluate the English program top-to-bottom. I'm worried he'll come up with some dumb measuring standard, instead of focusing on what we do with the college students, which is let them express themselves verbally and on paper."

Jackson winced when he heard her say "measure," since he loved data, but knew what his wife meant. *You can't measure everything, hon,* she frequently said.

The kids seemed more engrossed in the radio. Of course, Wald's death even made the lead story on their programming.

"Did you know about it?" his wife asked. "I remember when he gave that speech on campus. He inspired the kids to go beyond words to working for reform and using their online social networking skills!"

"Yeah. I think half the kids joined Green Justice that night," Jackson admitted.

"Good!" his daughter Vivian began, who had been one of those kids. Then, she shifted focus.

"Hey Dad… did you notice that they mentioned the sleeping pills that killed him more than Wald himself? They keep saying Pasithea, and that Kipenium made it. They don't even talk about how he was out saving the planet, you know?"

"Just like your research project," Elena said. She turned into the modest parking lot for Alexandria Academy.

"Yeah Dad," Isaac laughed, gathering up his backpack and his Wilson US Open Tennis bag. "It sounds like… a *conspiracy,*" he said with fake dramatic inflection.

CHAPTER 10:
Monday, January 27

saac Pierce slumped in his chair in the weight room. With a singles spot on the line for Alexandria Academy's tennis team, he had blown his big chance losing to his doubles partner in a scrimmage. After an early lead, he found himself struggling to breathe.

"Isaac," Coach Gus said, sitting down next to him. His coach was friendly enough but made tough calls when he needed to. "I'm dropping you down to doubles on the team."

Normally, the youngest Pierce would have objected to the demotion. But all he could manage was, "I was lousy."

"It's not your technique," the one-time German Open winner explained. "In fact, you hit a lot of great shots. But physically, you looked like a fish stuck on a beach, desperate for air."

Isaac shrugged. He couldn't explain it either.

Gustav Erikson, or "Gus" to the kids, showed his tennis player an inhaler. "You may have exercise-induced asthma. See if you can get a doctor to check you out and prescribe one of these before your next match. If you get your stamina back and win this weekend, we'll see if you can rejoin the singles team."

Jackson's son nodded and offered a thank-you as Coach Gus departed the room. A TV was playing above the weights. ESPN was the preferred channel, and the subject was hockey.

"This week is Pierre Bujols' Last Stand," the sportscaster began. The guy went on to explain that if the New Jersey Devils hoped to make the NHL playoffs, they would need a win at home against the Toronto Maple Leafs.

Isaac's cell phone buzzed. Mom and Dad, and most likely Viv, were outside. He clicked off the program… hockey was not his thing. As for tennis, he didn't know which was worse, losing or learning that he needed an inhaler to play.

═══

Closer to New Jersey, several employees of PPP were watching the same ESPN special. They had received their orders from Jeremiah Calhoun and had been given their target. Now, all they needed to do was execute the plan, according to their supervisor, Wallace Bragg.

"Is his Gyrfalcon easy to spot?" Hap wanted to leave nothing to chance.

Ray Maillon, the hockey fan among the group, was the one with the answers. "It's got Jersey plates. Says 'Big Stick.' That's his nickname: 'Big Stick Bujols.'"

Darcie rolled her eyes and whispered something to Kimber, who giggled.

Oeznik had been scribbling on a notepad. He pushed it over to Hap, who said, "And we can be sure he'll hit one of the bars afterwards?"

Ray chuckled, then said. "The Devils' motto is 'Win, Lose, or Tie, Everyone Over To 'Ride Or Die.' It's the local tavern near the Devils' arena. Pierre's gonna be there to get loaded, *and* get a new gal."

Hap's eyes glittered. They zeroed in on the two ladies at the table.

Darcie saw where this was going. She stubbed out her cigarette and shook her head. "Oh no, Hap. I'm not gonna…."

Dixon held up his hand. "No worries, Darce. You just need to be the one to slip something into his drink to get things going. When you leave, make sure he follows your car. I'll be sure the police will be ready for you, with more riding on it than their usual bribe offers."

Kimber snickered. "For once, Bujols will be the one who gets a Mickey, from a gal no less."

"Mr. Dixon?"

Hap turned to consider the diminutive ex-mechanic. "What's your idea, Vinny?"

Vinny Moro spoke as much with his hands as his lips. "I was thinkin', maybe Pierre wants to stop… Then you'd never see how fast that car is."

Maillon yawned. "You got a better idea, Vinny?"

The former mechanic nodded. "I can play 'round with the brakes, so he can't stop. Let 'em lead the cops on a big chase."

Hap considered this. Their orders were to engineer an incident where a celebrity would use his car in a way that would get the country's attention. If the Gyrfalcon was as maneuverable as they said, then it would be a high-speed version of the O.J. Simpson Ford Bronco chase.

"Alright… go for it. I bet Jeremiah would like the excitement."

Kimber's smile turned to a frown. "But what if he gets arrested, or crashes early, or bills someone?"

Darcie read Oeznik Turosz's writing on the pad. "We get another test subject."

***

Mick Camden looked over the evening news notes that his staff had painstakingly put together. No matter. He'd improvise anyway, because few knew the broadcast news business better than he did.

When he was promoted to U.S. Broadcasting Corporation's lead evening anchor, he thought he had it made. But after several years on the job, he began to see the light. No matter how much hair coloring and skin crème one used, there was always some younger version out there, a reflection of yourself ten, maybe fifteen years ago.

It wasn't like the old days, when Walter Cronkite and Howard K. Smith dominated the airwaves. Now, even the *networks*, not just the anchors, didn't last long.

Then there was social media. It was no longer an add-on or gimmick for the established news organizations. Every BuzzFeed, DeadSpin, and Gawker site was slicing into the TV market share. Heck, anyone with a podcast or TikTok account could pry away more teen eyes than their best stuff. The deck was stacked against him. He could understand Howard Beale, the crazed anchor from the movie *Network*, who won an Oscar for playing Peter Finch with that iconic line *"I'm mad as hell…and I can't take it anymore!"*

And then, the big change occurred.

A few years ago, a woman approached him with an offer. A journalist of "pure heart" would have said no, maybe call the authorities, or at least report her to the FCC.

But he wasn't that kind of anchor.

He had grown cynical. "News" websites were ripping off his stuff. Podcasts were mocking him, stealing eyes and ears from his broadcasts. They were saying things that could get him nailed for slander if he repeated them on air. The execs were squeezing him on salary, benefits, and perks. His reporters, freelancers, and staff were demanding raises. And between property taxes, boarding school tuition, and alimony payments, something had to give.

And it did. All he had to do was focus a story on, well, a certain product. He had to make sure an image appeared on the broadcast. Get the cameraman to make a certain shot, and the reporter to interview her subject in front of a particular billboard. Money would appear in his account, a payout from "Internet Gambling" in Dominica for bets he never made.

Now, things were changing. Instead of small product plugs, he was getting *leads* for stories. Maybe it didn't take a Columbia journalism degree to figure out that the source was *too* good at predicting the future. It sounded like someone was making the news and wanted him to cover it. Fine… if the price was right. He'd have something to feather his nest a little more. So when the pink slip came down, he could simply smile and not have to plead or cry to stay on—a useless gesture anyway—and consider that book deal.

Speaking of pink slips, a vision approached him. Honey-brown hair, long legs, tall with the heels, and a strapless…

"Hot tip for ya, Mick."

Hot was right.

"Be on the lookout for a certain star from the New Jersey Devils, who may have a minor vehicular meltdown after the last game of the season."

The anchor straightened his tie. "I assume you mean Big Stick Bujols. I can send it down to the sports desk for you."

A flick of her finger told him that was the wrong answer. "This one will make front-page headlines. Better have the national team ready for this. Get a chopper on standby."

What an appealing second wife she would make, he thought. "And the angle is…?"

Darcie spun on her heel. "It's the car, Mick. Make sure your audience can see what it does, regardless of what happens to dear old Pierre."

CHAPTER 11:
Wednesday, January 29

Wham! An explosion of books and bags hit the oak table where Jackson was sitting in the English Department Lounge, trying to improve his tenure track application's "Statement of Teaching Philosophy."

He turned to see his wife, red-faced, eyes blazing, teeth grinding. "…and if I have to go through one more review with him…"

"Meeting with the new Higher Education Dean go well?" Jackson tried to elicit a smile from Elena.

"Don't joke hon, unless you want to see how comfy the outdoor tool shed is tonight."

The situation was bad if his attempts at humor didn't work. "Wow, what happened?"

"Not on campus," she hissed. "You can hear someone sneeze three classrooms away in this old building."

Ten minutes later, they were in a Chick Fil-A, eating their sandwiches. "Want to tell me…?"

"Okay, we all got to the review a few minutes early. Dean Franklin Arbell's waiting in the conference room at the end of the hall, glaring at us, checking his watch as we came in."

"Yeah. We met, remember?"

"Well, before we could even show him the powerpoint we made, Arbell cuts us off, tosses our flashdrive out of the projector, and puts in his own!"

Her hand smacking the table led several patrons sitting at the next table to glance over.

"He had a whole rubric of how every student paper is to be graded. Listen to what he said we have to evaluate: Paper length, the number of grammar errors, and number of spelling errors. Number of footnotes! We even have to measure paragraph length! Each one!!"

Jackson's mouth opened, but no sound came out. What the heck was going on? He liked numbers, but this was a major abuse of statistics in his opinion.

"Franklin f-ing Arbell can kiss my…"

"Did he even hear your presen–"

"No! We just got our marching orders. He didn't hear about what our current students are writing about, how Jasmine got her poem published in that literary magazine, or about how our undergrads put together *The Quill*. Nothing!"

Jackson tried to mollify her. "Elena. I'm sorry. If there's anything I can do…"

She frowned. "Actually, he did mention you today."

"Oh?"

Elena paused, taking a deep breath. "When I tried to politely steer the subject back to our accomplishments, he just glared at me and said 'Doctor…Pierce, is it? I understand your husband is going up for tenure. I hear that's not going well."

Jackson shook his head. "President Sullivan won't let him go around bullying the faculty."

Elena pulled a small notebook from her purse. "I wouldn't be so sure, Jackson. Dean Arbell's got a pretty powerful ally. That new board member, Louis Lederer, the hedge-fund manager, is paying Arbell's huge salary. They're looking for any excuse to oust Sullivan, and any faculty they don't like, tenured or not. And since you and President Sullivan are buddies, it would be one less ally for our leader."

His wife had a good point. Jackson had hoped to comfort Elena after a tough review, but now he realized both of them were in a bad position. "And I thought our biggest challenge was a light lit review, and A.I. going AWOL."

Now it was Elena's turn to hold Jackson's hands. "I know you're think-ing of your students, your colleagues, and PSC's President. But you've got to watch your back, for your family too! I know you like challenges and standing up for others, but you're not tenured! Keep your head down, say a lot of yes sirs, nod a lot, and for God's sake don't start arguing with him. We can't afford to both go on the job market in this environment!"

———

Dr. Franklin Arbell had watched the two professors walk away from the English Department. No doubt the female would complain to her male about the important reforms he had instituted for their program. Departments all across the country were too focused on what their stu-dents "felt" about what they had read. They thought it was their job to "inspire" others through their writing, as if anyone would ever read their drivel other than their professors.

"If you can measure it, you can manage it," Arbell had once heard. And that became his mantra ever since, as he earned his degree in Higher Education Administration from an exclusive, expensive, and prestigious private college. How could one judge an opinion? Whose was better? How could one show progress? Only measurables mattered, not just to show progress, but also to demonstrate control.

That Pierce woman had complained about his rubric. Perhaps the female could sense the trouble she and her colleagues were in. After all, if you make paper length and number of footnotes the standard, each subsequent paper would have to get longer and more detailed. Soon, pro-fessors would run out of time to grade and record everything, including paragraph length for increasingly extended papers.

The smart ones would catch on and flee somewhere else to teach. The slow ones would find themselves unable to fulfill their contract mandates and be terminated. Ousted tenured faculty would be replaced by tempo-rary instructors, saving schools a bundle. The improved financial picture would boost his career before anyone would evaluate school academic quality. By then, he would be at a better-known university, blazing a trail to the Ivy Leagues, and then, perhaps, be Secretary of Education? It was his dream job. Then he would have the power over academia he desired, to get back at those who annoyed him. Maybe.

Born into "The Golden Triangle of Greenwich, Connecticut," Arbell remembered his parents saying they gave him two last names so he could be a college president. Yet for all his academic brilliance, teachers didn't give him the top awards, clearly resenting his superior intelligence. He never won an election for class president. He then replaced social interactions with ambition. The inferior needed a superior to lead them.

His attendance at prestigious prep and boarding schools gave way to elite academies and colleges. He barely had to lift a finger to gain admittance to the best graduate institutions in the nation. A diploma led to one of the richest private colleges in Massachusetts...

And on the first day, he discovered a new lesson.

He hated teaching. And he hated research.

He couldn't stand the needy students, how they had to get help with their papers, their tests. Couldn't they figure it out themselves like he did growing up? He didn't know which he hated more, their questions during his well-polished lectures, or the few who tried engaging in some degree of critical thinking. As if they could match wits with his academic pedigree.

And there was research, where *he* would be expected to write, and gather data, in the world of publish or perish?

Arbell left his tenure-track position in the Midwest in favor of administration at this "Peach State College." The admin job was shunned by professors obsessed with foolish love for molding minds and studying mysteries. Nobody wanted to make the hard decisions, manage the accounts, or even carry out the unpopular decisions.

The Pierces, like other professors at Peach State College, would learn where real power in higher education lay. By the time they got wise, he would be well beyond this Central Georgia dump of a region, mingling with the greatest minds of the New England elite, while they picked up the pieces of whatever was left.

CHAPTER 12:

Friday, January 31

The regular evening medical drama was interrupted by the network's top anchors. "Good evening, I'm Paige Glass, and this is Mick Camden with USBC News." The brunette glanced over to her co-anchor.

"USBC has learned that hockey star Pierre Bujols is leading the New Jersey police on quite a chase."

Paige took over. "For more on this developing story, we go to Wayne Kitteridge in Newark, New Jersey."

The man in the trenchcoat spoke rapidly. "I'm outside the Prudential Center, where the New Jersey Devils lost to the Toronto Maple Leafs 3-1, to miss the playoffs. Witnesses spotted Team Captain and star Pierre Bujols leaving the bar "Ride or Die," getting into his Gyrfalcon sportscar, and weaving in and out of traffic. Two police cars tried to pull him over for a sobriety test, but Bujols evaded both vehicles and the chase was on."

Mick cut in. "Wayne, what do we know about the car that Bujols was driving?"

"Well, Mick, it's a brand-new Gyrfalcon, considered by some to be the premier modern sportscar. And it looks like the hockey star chose red for the color, one of three it can come in along with black and gun metal."

"It's a good thing it's cherry red!" Paige observed. "That way, 'Cody in the Chopper' can spot them from above in the darkness!"

The shaggy blonde throwback to the "Marlboro Man" days stubbed out his cigarette in the helicopter before yelling, "I can see 'Big Stick's' beautiful vehicle careening down the highway, with what looks four… no *five* police cars in pursuit! But that Gyrfalcon can go from 0 to 60 in less than four seconds."

"I'm sorry Cody," Mick interrupted. "But we have to cut away to Jed Morgan, the CEO of Talladega Motors, the maker of the Gyrfalcon, on the phone from his company headquarters in Birmingham, Alabama."

The boss of Talladega Motors drawled, "I sincerely think few cars on the market can outrun five smokies, but the Gyrfalcon can. I decided to build me a sportscar that can go just as fast as mah 'ol Number 17 went at Daytona!"

═══

As Jed Morgan continued to brag about the Gyrfalcon's engine, Pierre "Big Stick" Bujols was getting panicky behind the wheel. First, there was the Devils' loss to the Maple Leafs. Then, there was the blonde in the "Ride Or Die" bar, who bought him a pint. He didn't even need to slip something in her glass; she told him to follow her to a nearby condo. He felt woozy after slamming the beer as he staggered to his Gyrfalcon. He was so panicked by the flashing lights behind him that he must have missed her turning. He tried to pull over... a bribe of some bills with several zeroes in his wallet usually did the trick. But the brakes weren't working!

Now he had no choice, but to run.

At least he had a speedy sportscar, even if he couldn't stop. The dealer promised him it could top 200mph. With over 700 horsepower and 6000ccs, it had to outrun even the latest police models. Now, he could test that. He hated Jersey cops anyway, he thought, as he whipped around a curve and onto a turnpike. Three of his pursuers could follow, but one crashed and the other slammed on its brakes to help its fellow patrolman.

═══

The broadcast continued. "And the Gyrfalcon was a bird used by royalty in Europe and China for hunting..."

"I'm sorry, Professor Gates," Mick Camden interrupted the guest speaker from Princeton, "But I'm told one of our junior reporters is on the scene! She happened to be doing a ride-along patrol, and now she's joined the pursuit. Gabby, can you see the Gyrfalcon?"

"Not yet Mick, but we're driving at a high rate of speed!" she squealed. Her assignment, being "embedded" with the police car, was no accident.

"Gabriela," Camden's fellow anchor began. "Are you safe enough to be in this chase?"

The young USBC reporter spoke to the officer. "I'm sorry… yes! I will be safe, says Patrolman Tivey."

Paige Glass breathed an audible sigh of relief, for the sake of the audience. In reality, they needed some human drama.

Mick Camden pressed on, speaking into his throat mike. "And is the vehicle you are in fast enough to catch the Gyrfalcon?"

More conversation continued between the journalist and the police officer. "His police car is a Ford Interceptor. It can go almost 200mph. It may not be fast enough to catch the Gyrfalcon, but the officer will try."

The female anchor gasped in wonder. "Oh, those boys in blue. Such courage, keeping us safe by pursuing reckless drivers like Pierre Bujols, hockey star or not. They deserve all our gratitude."

Mick switched the subject. "Paige, if the Talladega Motors' Gyrfalcon is really the fastest car out there, as we can see from the chase, then why don't the police use this vehicle instead of the Ford Interceptor?"

As the two went on about the superior features of the car, Jeremiah Calhoun watched the spectacle unfold on his television in his condo. This was going better than he anticipated. The news channels, ESPN, Fox Sports, and even E-TV were running updates. While every broadcaster was racing to the Garden State, his USBC was already there and would have exclusive coverage as the chase continued down the New Jersey Turnpike.

And, of course, his newscasters would make sure the Gyrfalcon was the real story.

He checked his email from his phone. Yes, Jed Morgan was piling on the compliments, and his check cleared. Mick had hit on something…

Gyrfalcons as police cars? He began to scan the internet for police unions, so he could speak to their chief. Private sales would be good, but imagine if cops across the country would buy from his client. Better update the deal while Jed was in a good mood.

He pulled out his laptop and clicked a few keys. The Spider came through on this one; it was trending on Google, Yahoo, and Bing. *His* story was not only watched by nearly everyone at that hour, but it was sure to lead to plenty of Gyrfalcon sales in the coming days, netting PPP a big profit. The only question was what other company would benefit from his new method of creating the news to provide product placement?

———

A squeal of tires snapped Pierre Bujols back to his senses. He cut over to I-295 as he left the other police cars in the distance. But an eighth car joined in the chase just as he exited the interstate… this one looked local. He was far from the arena and bar, near some place called Burlington on his GPS. He decided to shift over to race along country roads.

Was that a news helicopter above him, or more cops? The hockey star was relieved to see "Live on 45" on its side, having joined the one from USBC now. But while Bujols didn't mind the extra attention, it would be hard to escape if their cameras kept him in their sights. *Time to lose everyone.* He slowed slightly until he reached a quiet street, cutting his car lights, and punched it left off Rancocas Road. That unexpected move might lose some of his pursuers, and maybe even the "eyes in the skies" above him. Sure enough, the pilots went the wrong way, and their searchlights continued straight on the road where he would have been instead of something called "Bridge Street," where he really was.

With the Gyrfalcon's lights off as well, total darkness seemed a good idea. But the driver failed to notice a critical sign, telling him the bridge was out.

Just as Bujols wondered what to do in his sportscar with the brakes gone, the vehicle smashed through the wooden barrier.

Officer Tivey, who guessed his prey had used the farm road, had followed behind on Bridge Street while the others raced down Rancocas Road. Even with his VIP passenger, Tivey gunned it, hoping for the most famous collar of his life. By leaving his lights on, he saw Bujols race past the "Bridge Out" warning, then proceeded to slam into the guardrail.

The Ford Interceptor hit the brakes, while the Gyrfalcon launched itself off the makeshift ramp, part of the reconstruction effort. The sports-car seemed to hang for a minute, with only Gabby's screams being heard. Then, the vehicle slammed straight into the Rancocas Creek and sank quickly, the whole spectacle perfectly illuminated by "Cody in the Chopper's" helicopter, which had magically returned to film the entire crash for a horrified American public.

CHAPTER 13:

Friday, January 31

All five students and their professor sat in stunned silence as they watched the conclusion of the biggest car chase caught on camera in decades, interrupting their review session.

Sgt. Paul Herrera let out an audible gasp. "That water must have been like concrete when his car landed."

"Could… could he survive, Dr. Pierce?" Sylvia Wright managed.

"Er… I'm not that kind of doctor, Sylvia," Jackson Pierce gave a nervous laugh.

They had gathered at Paragon, the nearby coffeehouse just off the PSC campus, for Pyramid Coffee. Paragon teemed with dorm furniture, donated board games, and frequent games of poker.

An argument broke out over Bujols' notorious past, broken up by an unlikely source. Trey rarely shouted, so that caused everyone in Paragon to stop and stare.

"Have you noticed something odd about the whole evening… how the story broke …how it was covered?"

"What do you mean?"

"Pierre Bujols is a celebrity, and he's breaking the law, yeah, but that wasn't really covered by the news. The focus was all about the car."

"The Gyrfalcon!" Jackson Pierce exclaimed. He could see where his student was going with this. "You're right. I never even heard of it before, but that seemed to be all what USBC was talking about, even more than the story itself."

All slowly nodded, as the sudden realization hit them.

"Is this like… we're starting to see these things just because we're studying them?" Paul asked.

"In Psych class, Dr. Branigan talked about something called 'Hawthorne Effect,'" Taira offered.

"Yeah," Nate added. "It's where something changes because you're studying it!"

Dr. Pierce shook his head. "That's reactivity. We're just observing it more because we're looking for it. Reminds me of a story about instability in Indonesia. The media reported that the violence doubled, even though our CIA experts reported that the situation remained unchanged over the previous years."

Sylvia frowned. "The CIA Agents were lying?"

Pierce smiled. "No. It's just that the *New York Times* sent a second reporter to Jakarta. There appeared to be more violence because there were more stories about the event, and more people were watching it. But there were just as many assassinations, armed attacks, and strikes as before. The violence appeared to go up because there were more watchers."

Trey remained skeptical. "Dr. Pierce, have you ever seen anything like this, where the product became the story?"

"Of course," Jackson remained patient. "Remember the examples we covered in class last week. Payola…"

"I don't mean to go all conspiracy theory here," Paul laughed. "But what if this whole story was one big product placement?"

Jackson frowned. "Ladies and gentlemen, let's stick with what we actually know. Remember, the Georgia conference is coming up soon, and we need a lot more material. How's the rest of the paper coming along?"

—————

The conversation shifted from car crashes involving sports stars to serious research. Early optimism over the strong literature review gave way to dread over the data.

"If we did every news story from every major network, that would be..." Nat shook his head. "...Bigger than my PSC football playbook!"

Taira's initial optimism faded. "It'll take all semester to gather."

"What'll we do?" Sylvia begged.

Jackson took a second. "Start with a week, for right now. We can code those mentioned verbally, those which are shown with an image, and the cases that have both."

The students nodded, but didn't look entirely convinced. "One day for each student?"

There was an awkward pause. Everyone was thinking it, but nobody wanted to be the first to say it.

"Okay, I don't know what's up with Ms. Sheehy. She's turning in her lit review assignments online. I'm sure if we assign her a day, she'll do her work. She may be absent, but when she gets into a project, she's..."

"Like a machine?"

"That's A. I. for you." Nat held out his hands, as if presenting a grand theory.

"Just give her a chance. I promise to grade her fairly."

Sylvia kept her frown. "Think we're gonna impress those judges up in Savannah if we only have a week's worth of data?"

"It's still innovative exploratory research. I'm sure they'll take that into account," Professor Pierce offered, as much to convince himself as his class. Sylvia was right, though. They needed more numbers. That big win for his tenure track application looked more like a long shot now. Where were they going to get more data with the Georgia conference looming before them?

———

Such thoughts were occupying Jackson's mind as he pulled into the carport a minute after eleven. Damn... he should have called. But she'd understand.

Maybe not.

Elena was slumped in her recliner, eyes bloodshot, glaring at him.

"Hon, I'm sorry. There was this wild car chase on the news that my students and I were watching… I should have called."

He saw the glass on her desk. It once was full of Moscato. That was bad. His wife let out a sob. "It's…"

"I swear I'm gonna talk to President Sullivan about Franklin Arbell…"

Now, she was mad. "*Listen* Jackson. It's about Viv!"

In a quiet whisper, he replied "What happened?"

"Vivian hasn't turned in a single assignment this semester at the academy."

Jackson's computer bag dropped, slamming to the wooden floor. "B-but she's been doing all that work!" he spluttered. "It's going to kill her college application if her grades plummet. And with our finances, she needs a full scholarship to go. Has she been pretending to…?" his words simply dissipated.

"Oh, she's doing the work. She just refuses to turn it in."

"Why?"

"Jackson Pierce, I've been screaming at her for the last two hours, and I'm no closer to figuring out why!"

Jackson eyed his wife. "There's more to this than you're telling me. It's about your high school experience as well, isn't it? This is about you not making valedictorian at that Catholic school in Nashville, right?"

"Don't you dare go there," Elena growled.

"You know, they're not going to give you back the top academic award you earned, or even apologize at this point, right?" Jackson pointed out. "Just because you would have been the first female graduation speaker…"

Almost immediately, he regretted bringing it up. His punishment was enduring a ten-minute harangue about how sexism cost her major academic honors, one he had heard all before, but was powerless to do anything about.

When she finally came up for air, a brief pause in her diatribe, Jackson settled on a peace offering.

"I'm sorry."

Elena's sore voice then rasped. "You know, Professor, you could *investigate* this phenomenon of your daughter's, just like you do with your research. You've been so focused on tenure. When was the last time you two went for a drive?"

Jackson paused. Had they even gone this semester? They were both so busy.

"I thought so!" Elena snapped. Then, she returned to a hoarse whisper. "Maybe you can repair some of the damage."

That could mean a lot of things. He could take a greater role in his daughter's life. He could once again play referee, smoothing over a difference between Elena and Vivian.

"Okay…" It was 11:15 pm, but his wife's gaze told him time was not the issue. He walked down the hall, lightly knocking with a single knuckle.

"Dad?"

"Go for a ride?"

Instead of defiance, she shocked him by enthusiastically agreeing to his plan.

As they pulled out of the driveway, narrowly missing a white-tailed deer, Vivian began the conversation. "I'm guessing the Alexandria Academy Headmaster called Mom, 'cause she went ballistic."

"Can you blame her?" Jackson replied. "You know her story about what happened at that Catholic high school she went to in Nashville. And now you haven't been doing any homework for the whole semester! And your college applications…"

"I'm doing the work!"

"But you're not turning it in then, for some reason!"

"Do you actually want to know my reasons? Or are you just going to yell at me, just like everyone else? I know Mom wants the awards for me that she was denied, but I'm doing something different."

Jackson paused. He could see that she had been fighting this fight nonstop. It was time for a temporary truce. "Okay kiddo… I mean, Viv. What's your story?"

The car continued down the highway toward the mall in silence. Finally, she began. "I'm doing the homework because I want to learn, and I like to learn. I didn't turn it in because… I'm… I'm *privileged.*"

"What?!"

"Dad, you promised to listen!"

"I agreed to listen!"

"Well, you know Naomi, my best friend from school?"

"Yes…" Jackson said, not sure where this was going.

"Well, her mom lost her job at the hardware store in Clifton. Her dad hasn't found work since the carpet factory moved to Mexico. Her mom's been hired to clean the Academy, while he's mowing the grounds outside the school."

"That's… well… better than being unemployed and broke, I guess."

"Dad, Naomi's one of the best students in the class. She's working really hard to get that Pyramid Scholarship that our Class Valedictorian gets, a full ride to any four-year college."

"That's great! I admire her for that."

"Dad, don't you get it? I'm standing in her way! I've got two college professors for parents, and her folks have to take odd jobs just to make ends meet. I've got an air-conditioned house with a fridge full of food. Remember how I spent the night at their place during the Christmas holidays? They don't have air conditioning at their house or even Wi-Fi in Clifton, so she can't do online research."

If only Vivian realized how bad our finances are, and how much we need her to get that scholarship, Jackson thought.

"But… you're not…"

"Dad, I can get into college, right? Without that scholarship, she can't. And you even once said 'Education is the Great Equalizer.' How can it be when I'm *privileged?*"

The two went back and forth. Vivian told Jackson about the "Privileged" group she had joined nationwide, where college students and high schoolers like herself would find ways to subvert the education system. They would give those less fortunate a real shot. Some were hacking the

SATs to distribute the answers, while others picketed colleges without DEI policies.

"And self-sabotage is your contribution?"

That led to another round of arguing while the car was parked at the Creek Mall. Jackson still had to admire her dedication to what she thought was right and wrong, even at personal cost. She'd rather give a fellow disadvantaged student a break, giving up personal honors and glory.

But she didn't realize her parents' precarious position, especially if he didn't get the tenure track position. They had kept it from the kids, not wanting them to stress. *But if I don't get that job, I may be as poor as Naomi's parents*, Jackson thought.

Finally, they hammered out a compromise. Vivian would turn in her overdue homework. She would also engage in after-school tutoring and lead study groups with her friends, giving up her spot in the Spring Play. And her parents wouldn't force her to leave the "Privileged" group.

"You can encourage the other students on there to think of positive solutions, instead of undermining the system," Jackson offered.

"If you two get off my back on this, I'll agree to it," Vivian finally smiled.

After a few minutes of silence, she hit the power button on the radio knob. The headline was Pierre Bujols and the car crash.

"Is that the Gyrfalcon story?" Vivian asked.

"Wha—"

"I was watching a YouTube video about it when you knocked. My friends on 'Privileged' were talking about it before then."

Jackson shook his head.

"You know, Dad, I was beginning to think you were being all conspiracy theory obsessed with that product placement topic you were doing with your students. But listening to the way they cared more about the car than the player, you may not be that far off base."

BRANDED PART II:

February

CHAPTER 14:

Monday, February 3

Officially, the company's name was Preston Powell Partnership, titled after the owner. But most knew it as Product Placement Partnership. And that new application of that old practice was about to pay off.

"Mr. McLane, the numbers." CEO Jeremiah Calhoun began.

"Yes, sir." Chip displayed a maze of online spreadsheets, showing Preston Powell how well the company was doing. The aged Brit, also the owner and namesake of the product placement firm, had a weather-beaten face that contrasted with the silver hair and dark suit. But the elderly man's wrinkles seemed to imply wisdom over weakness, with his eyes confirming it.

McLane's report showed PPP was now flush with cash, thanks to SRD's payments, leading to a measurable uptick in profits.

After everyone else filed out of the conference room, Wallace Bragg briefed Preston Powell on the Pierre Bujols crash. The Londoner nodded with understanding. "Has the hockey star's condition changed?"

Calhoun shrugged. "Still in a coma."

"Chance of recovery?" Preston asked.

The CEO looked down. "I'm not a doctor. But I believe his playing days are over."

Preston held up his hand. "Let us hope that, for your sake, he *does* survive. Two bodies, Jeremiah, would look quite suspicious. A third is even more likely to draw... unwanted attention. Let your next customer be one where there is no human death, so there is not a body trail that leads to us."

Calhoun spread out his hands. "Of course. Don't you trust me, Preston?"

Preston Powell was noticeably silent.

"We're being careful."

The old Brit replied. "It was one of your politicians, I believe one by the name of 'Barry Goldwater,' who said 'Trust, but verify.'"

<hr>

"Good afternoon, this is Bradley Bennett, with 'Before You Know It,' the weekly USBC show where we recap the events of the last seven days. Later, I'll introduce my special guest, Dr. E. E. Kirby, an Ivy League Professor specializing in media studies, who will comment on the shocking cases from the last month, while speculating on the economic fallout as well."

Calhoun could not resist a grin as USBC came through again, keeping the spotlight on their clients and opponents. And, of course, Professor Kirby's guest appearance was no accident, either.

"I am thoroughly impressed," Preston inclined his head toward the man who ran his company.

"The network serves us well," Wallace Bragg pulled the glasses from his face to clean them. "And according to Chip, they've displaced NBC and Fox in the ratings."

The commercial for Bradford Communications ended, and Bennett returned to the screen. "It's a rare occurrence when the field of sports takes center stage, but that was the case this week. No, it wasn't about the race for the Stanley Cup. It was a *different* kind of race."

The screen cut to a montage of news footage, the images all supplied by USBC, with commentary by Paige Glass and Mick Camden. Calhoun was pleased to see that they even had aerial reels from "Cody in the Chopper." They also had that Hispanic reporter, Gabby-somebody, in the police car ride-along, cutting to the dramatic images of Pierre Bujols' car diving into the Rancocas Creek in central New Jersey.

Preston Powell looked awestruck. He had scanned the article in the *Financial Times* but had not been privy to the graphic images.

"Divers recovered Bujols, who remains in critical condition at Pennsylvania Hospital," Bennett somberly reported. "He is still in a coma. Though his days on the ice are most certainly over, the question is whether he will ever regain consciousness."

USBC then had commentary from coaches, players, and the commissioner.

"But here's the best part," Jeremiah Calhoun pointed to the screen. As usual, his media liaison Darcie Matthews set it up.

Returning from the public service announcement, Bennett pointed toward his guest. "With me is Dr. E. E. Kirby, perhaps the foremost expert on media studies. He has been watching the events of this story with great interest. Why is that, professor?"

Kirby dramatically cleared his throat. "It seems there are two stories. One is the human tragedy, and, of course, our thoughts and prayers go out to the Bujols family and teammates. But there's another element to the story. Across the country, so much discussion has gone on about the vehicle Bujols drove, the Gyrfalcon. It's made by Talladega Motors in Birmingham, Alabama."

Bennett pressed. "And why is that, professor? Was the car faulty? Did that contribute to Bujols' accident?"

Dr. Kirby shook his head. "Quite the opposite. If anything, the world was able to see how well the Gyrfalcon performed. Bujols, in his inebriated state, evaded what looked like half of the New Jersey police force in that dynamic car."

The USBC broadcaster feigned a frown. "But professor, it *did* crash off the bridge into the river."

"It's clear to me," Dr. Kirby puffed up his chest, "that the Gyrfalcon crashed because of the intoxicated state of the driver in question, who ignored a warning sign that the bridge was out. Handled by a sober, experienced driver, Talladega's Gyrfalcon would never have been stopped. And, I must say, I would lecture law enforcement departments across the country to take notice. You are looking at proof that the Gyrfalcon is superior to even the Ford Interceptor."

Bennett feigned surprise, even though this interview had been carefully scripted and rehearsed all morning. "And what has been the result of this incident for Talladega Motors?"

"Well…" Dr. Kirby was now in full dramatic lecture mode. "Your own USBC market analysis has shown Talladega Motors stock in the top five among increases since the crash. Demand for the vehicle has skyrocketed. Orders are exceeding production. I hear rumors that Jed Morgan is set to announce the creation of a second auto manufacturing plant. We'll wait to see who will get the facility."

It was rare to hear Preston Powell utter the words "I am thoroughly impressed." But there it was.

"So, what do you have in mind for the next highly successful product placement, Jeremiah?" he added.

Calhoun smirked. "Wheels are already in motion on that one."

CHAPTER 15:
Tuesday, February 4

Professor Jackson Pierce was shocked to see the Dean of Higher Education sitting right next to the spot Alicia Ina usually occupied in his seminar, with her laptop and spreadsheets scattered haphazardly across the place. He made notes on some paper as Dr. Pierce entered the seminar room and then fixed him with a direct stare.

"I wasn't expecting an evaluation today," the communications professor began, appearing unruffled by the surprise intrusion. Inside his stomach, it was a different matter.

"Is there anything wrong with a superior seeing how his underlings perform under pressure?" Franklin Arbell offered with his usual condescending tone. "It will be useful to us for your final tenure decision."

The other students glanced around nervously. *Great*, Jackson told himself. Pierce had been planning to get the kids beyond the academic literature, theories, and hypotheses. He wanted them to explain their research design and how they might measure product placement in the news. He just had to play ball and be nice to the Dean, if he wanted to keep his job.

"Let's get Dr. Arbell up to speed…"

"It's Dean Arbell, Professor."

And so it went. As each student presented her or his work, Arbell was sharp with his criticism of their performance. Oh well, at least it would help them in that upcoming conference, Jackson realized, though their guest would make a particularly nasty judge. He wished it was going better; he needed a good evaluation for his tenure-track application.

As the students answered Arbell's critiques, Pierce began to see that they were a particularly extraordinary group. With no anticipation of an inquisition, they were holding their own. Wins at that state and regional conference seemed more within their grasp.

But their Higher Education Dean wasn't going to give them their due.

"*Why* is it interesting?"

Trey explained how much the field of product placement was worth in profits, showing charts he had developed.

Arbell yawned. "It still doesn't pass the 'so what' test."

Sylvia Wright countered that no one had done such research directly on product placement in the news in America. "This stuff's been going on in movies and television shows for years, but nobody's looked at the subject during the broadcast news."

"And how do you propose to research this… looking at all news shows across time?"

Of course they weren't, Jackson though to himself. *How were his undergraduates going to have the time to do that? It would take an army to gather all that data.*

Nat carefully explained how they were looking in depth at a specific week, for morning and evening network news shows, through each story, for product mentions and…

"A week?" Arbell snapped. "That's all you have to show for a semester?"

"That's a lot of stories!" Taira protested.

Arbell stood and pointed at the young Lebanese student. "If you and your classmates want precious funds to go to your little conference, young lady, you'll gather a lot more than 'just a week.'"

"C'mon, Dean Arbell. She's got a point!"

Jackson was pleased to see Sgt. Herrera stand up for a fellow student, but wished he didn't display it in front of Peach State College's number two administrator, someone who had a lot of say in whether he would be back next year.

Dr. Arbell's disdain was unmistakable. "Dr. Pierce, if you would, please dismiss your students so they can spend the rest of the time learning some manners when interacting with their superiors in a scholarly setting!"

The students filed out one by one, leaving the two academics alone to face each other.

Jackson thought of how Elena warned him about picking fights with Arbell.

"Perhaps we can gather some more cases," Jackson offered helpfully.

Arbell ignored him. "You need to show more evidence than your students have already done."

Jackson clicked on a few keys. "Here's evidence that shows that 93 percent of our graduates are currently employed, with more than half in some sort of graduate school or having a graduate degree." *Thanks, Elena for the hint,* Pierce thought.

Franklin Arbell viewed the slide with a mild amount of distaste, though the numbers would make any Board of Trustees or donor group smile.

"So, *Professor* Pierce," Arbell sneered, as if he discounted the title. "What about the other 50 percent who don't go on to graduate education? What about the seven percent unemployed?"

Brushing his hair in his hands, Pierce fought back exasperation. "Our employment numbers and graduate numbers are better than the national average for colleges and those with communications degrees."

"Really?" The Dean pushed back the glasses from his nose. "I did not realize the national unemployment rate was seven percent."

"We were at 100%," Pierce fought the urge to growl with these words. ",but the last recession…"

"So you're in decline from where your program was in prior years?"

Jackson remained quiet, trying to think of a response without offending his superior.

Arbell decided it was time to take the smug professor down a peg. "Perhaps it isn't *your* fault that you don't have a perfect employment record, or have every student going for a Master's or law degree. I noticed your class… *diversity* may be responsible…"

At that point, Paul Herrera didn't need the glass held to his ear to hear Professor Pierce's loud retort. The other students looked at each other in shock as they backed away from the door, where they had been listening, and "Sarge" had been feeding them details.

"We'd better get out of here!" hissed Trey, and the others scrambled away from the classroom. They made such a ruckus running away that would have normally alerted anyone in the room to their presence, but with the shouting match inside the class, their exit went undetected. When they were clear of their hall, they headed for the grill.

Even though Jackson was sitting under the awning of Alexandria Academy's tennis courts later in the day, his face looked flushed, as if he had been the one chasing a ball with a racket instead of his son. His prospects for coming back the next academic year were even worse than before.

Elena came over to join him, fresh from the Peach State College Tutoring Center.

"Oh good… Isaac's up this time," she noted, as the numbers on the scoreboard read 6-1, 5-3.

Jackson grimaced. "He's dropped two straight games this set and is fading fast."

Then it hit her.

"How did the meeting go with Dean Arbell?" Her voice fell to a whisper.

Pierce filled his wife in on the details, culminating with the fight at the end.

"*Jackson*," she hissed. "I told you not to mix it up with the Dean! You're not tenured. He could fire you *today*!"

But when he explained what the last fight was about, she nodded grimly. "I suppose I would have made the same choice. If you had to fight him on something, I'm glad you stood up for your students. *Diversity…*" she hissed. "So, he's a racist as well as a…" but her expression changed as the crowd on the other side of the awning erupted in cheers. Isaac had lost another game, and the score was 5-4.

The diminutive high schooler trudged back to the sidelines. All of the enthusiasm from the start of the match was gone. He fumbled through his bag for... for what, he didn't know...

Instead, he pulled out...

"An inhaler?" his opponent boomed from across the net. "You're asthmatic? No wonder you suck!"

That player from Stoney Creek uttered his remarks while everyone else was silent. No spectator missed it. Now all eyes were on Isaac.

Unsure of how to react, Jackson and Elena watched as their son took a puff. He stood up, tossed the inhaler back into his bag, and strode back to the baseline, ready for action.

Jackson looked at his wife in surprise.

"They think he's got Exercise-Induced Asthma," Elena explained, "Just like I do. So I got him one, with a prescription."

The effect on their son was electric. Soon, he was playing with an energy that had been lacking in the last several games, smashing hits, returning shots. It was his opponent's turn to falter as he failed to match Isaac's newfound confidence. Alexandria Academy's parents roared their approval as the youngest Pierce won the next game, the set, and match, which guaranteed a team victory and a shot at regionals.

Isaac bounded into the crowd for a brief hug with the parents before jogging back down to cheer on his remaining teammates.

"Wow... to think that inhaler seemed to make the difference," Jackson observed.

"I think it's his persistence and willpower," Elena observed. "Seems like you and your students could use something similar to get Arbell off your back, and break through at that Georgia conference."

"Damn!" Nat began. "I've never seen Prof. Pierce that mad. When they started fighting about..." Then it hit him what their argument was about. His voice trailed off.

"I didn't realize that's how he thought about us," Taira mumbled, still in shock. "And Dean Arbell… Isn't he the one who gave some long-winded lecture at Convocation?"

Sgt. Herrera nodded. "I almost went back to Iraq that night after hearing what he had to say."

"You fought in Iraq?" Taira gasped. Paul nodded.

"Wow," she replied. "I knew you were in the military and all, but I didn't know about…"

They each exchanged stories. Herrera elaborated on his fears about going on patrol at night, constantly worried about being ambushed. Taira responded with her anxieties about being deported to a place she barely knew.

Trey's jaw tightened as he heard these stories, and how Dean Arbell's words triggered that speech hated by his classmates.

"I know how we can get even with the Dean and help Professor Pierce."

Nat glanced up from his burger. "Prank?" The idea appealed to the notorious trickster.

Taira shook her head. "Win at the Georgia conference?"

"Win it all!" Paul grinned.

Sylvia Wright held up her finger. "No matter what happens, we stop fighting among ourselves. We stick together. We give Professor Pierce the best project any of his classes has ever done. We…"

She looked up in shock as an unexpected figure stood before their table.

"I think I can help," the girl said, managing not to stammer.

CHAPTER 16:
Wednesday, February 5

State Farm Arena was not one of John Marshall Bradford II's favorite locations. Its predecessor, the Omni, hosted the Democratic National Convention, and Bradford, like his father, was a Republican. At least the Democratic Party lost that race in 1988.

Tonight's event was about marketing. But this "talk" reminded him why he hated such events. The speaker, Dr. E.E. Kirby, was full of himself, something he hated about college professors. Kirby pretended to be an expert, though Bradford was sure the professor had never run a corporation in his life. Sure, Bradford had inherited the communication firm that bore his name, but he had taken the company from a regional business that his father started and built it into a national titan.

The President and CEO of Bradford Communications was initially skeptical of his son heading off to college. Would he be taught by leftists who disdained capitalism? But John Marshall Bradford III—Trey to his friends—loved basketball too much, even if he was only the backup guard for the Peach State College Sabers.

Bradford had traveled to Alexandria for a few games, proud of his son, but concerned about what he might learn in class. He had hoped to listen quietly near the door, but Professor Jackson Pierce brought him right in, making him a guest speaker on the spot. Not only did the CEO relish the chance to tell the students what it was like to run a leading communications firm, but he was also invited to be the school's Distinguished Fall Speaker in Trey's senior year. After the applause, he could finally see why people got into teaching. It was unlike any boardroom presentation or even CNN interview.

The memories of that college visit had caused him to miss some of Dr. Kirby's talk, but he had already made up his mind not to buy Kirby's book, ironically named "*Pay Attention.*" That product placement stuff seemed like a lot of effort for little reward, more rhetoric than results.

"Enjoy the speech?" The man asking Bradford the question looked like a carbon copy of himself, though the glasses were a different touch. Was it someone from his days in the legislature?

"I'm not sure any practical policies flow from his implications."

The man with glasses replied. "Wallace Bragg, PPP's COO."

Bradford took the card. "So, you're the one who invited me and funded the talk."

"I'd like to introduce our CEO, who can talk about the 'practical policies' that Dr. Kirby spoke about this evening," Wallace offered.

Unable to plot a quick exit strategy, Bradford stood face-to-face with his counterpart from Preston Powell Partnership, PPP. The balding, curly-haired man extended his hand and gave a courteous smile.

"Jeremiah Calhoun," the CEO introduced himself. "And you are John Marshall Bradford II of Bradford Communications. Care to learn how our firm might help Bradford Communications, especially with your Edict device?"

Edict was the company's latest creation for person-to-person communication. Unlike products laden with apps, Edicts were solely related to business functions: visual and audio communications, as well as internet access with detailed data on stocks, bonds, and money markets, so the user could track happenings in the financial world without getting lost in the profusion of products stuck on cellphones. Its simplicity revolutionized the corporate world.

"We really don't need product placement," Bradford explained. "Our device sells itself with user reviews and endorsements. I don't see how J-Lo or Leonardo DiCaprio holding it in a movie would move the needle much in sales."

Calhoun shook his head. "What I'm talking about is favorable publicity in the news."

Bradford pointed to a company report he had been carrying. "We've already received strong evaluations from the media. We've got enough positive publicity."

Calhoun bit his lip. He had a sale to make. "But what if your rival…"

"Miracle Communications?" Bradford laughed. "We're fortunate to be facing a company so poorly run. The joke is that if you reach anyone with their device, 'It's a miracle!'"

Calhoun surprised him by laughing. At least the man had a sense of humor.

"But what if… let's just say, hypothetically speaking, that they came into some good news, or you received some bad news. PPP could help reverse that. Remember how the Boy Scouts got sick after eating unhealthy freeze-dried powdered meals?"

Bradford shrugged. "With all due respect, we're not CampCorp."

"Or how their rival, Akela Association, stepped in to fill the void, and now leads with the new Scout contract, as well as survivalists? Think that was an accident?"

Bradford gave him a serious look. "What are you saying?"

Now, Calhoun had his attention. "I'm just saying that the business world is an uncertain place. Good or bad news can fall upon you quickly. You should be prepared for such emergencies, and we can help with that. Other companies enlist us for assistance. Will you do the same?"

There was something about the two men that unsettled Trey's father, a lack of authenticity, perhaps. That lesson his son told him about in class… implicit awareness-something …but it had to do with his subliminal feelings. And right now, they were warning him.

"Perhaps, another time," Bradford promised, with all of the sincerity they seemed to be showing him.

This was an opportunity that could generate a huge windfall, he knew. But Bradford inherited the company on a promise to his father, who started it, that he wouldn't engage in policies that would embarrass the family name. He owed the same to his son, the one he eventually wanted to run the company with the same integrity. And manipulating the news to squeeze out a few more sales *wasn't* what he had in mind.

Had Bradford kept his eyes on Calhoun, he would have seen him mouth "*Plan B*" to Bragg.

———

For Esther Ruth Harding, the words of Doctor E. E. Kirby were like church music to her ears. He had been preaching the gospel of product placement that evening, just what she wanted to hear. It was her desire… God's will, to be more exact, to have Miracle Communications use this very plan to get more people to accept "The Miracle" into their lives, to turn around the company's misfortunes.

It was as if the devil himself were working against her. Old Scratch must have taken her beloved husband, the preacher, from this mortal world. She certainly didn't believe those nasty reports that he perished in the arms of another woman. It was just those secular reporters who hated all televangelists and planted those evil tales. She was certain her husband, Preacher Gideon, suffered a heart attack while fervently praying with that harlot to save her soul.

There was no shortage of donations from Harding Enterprises to start up Miracle Communications. She had listened to Gideon's younger brother, Luke, now the company's Chief Operating Officer, to start that business. But Miracle Communications was getting to be a money pit. Their communication device kept conking out. She fired their tech guy who claimed it was the sheer volume of religious apps that came with the object, refusing to admit it was demons that needed to be exorcised.

That's why she had come from Chattanooga to Atlanta to hear Dr. Kirby answer her prayers and find ways to get more believers to use the Miracle. She had even memorized the faces of PPP's CEO Jeremiah Calhoun and his right-hand man, Wallace Bragg, so she could meet them to pay whatever they asked to save her company.

And there they were, talking with her bitter rival, Bradford Communications, and that horrible John Marshall Bradford II, whose wife, a federal judge, ruled against her education plan that would have required a Biblical exam given to every senior before they could graduate in her school district. Beelzebub Communications indeed!

She reached her hands to Heaven, beseeching Him for a miracle, just like her own.

"Esther Ruth Harding?"

She turned to gape at the professor. "Oh, Dr. Kirby! Your talk was heavenly. It's exactly what I believe would help Miracle Communications."

Dr. Kirby's presence was no accident. A quick text from Jeremiah Calhoun revealed that the big fish, Bradford Communications, had wriggled off the hook, and it was time to woo their competitor.

"Yes, Miss Harding. I came to offer my condolences in person for the loss of your husband, Gideon. His departure was a tragedy for the true believers."

"Professor, I did not know you were of the faith!"

Dr. Kirby smiled. He didn't believe any of the hokum that the couple had been selling. An unseen deity was no more than an imaginary friend. Social Darwinism was more to his liking. And it was time for the fittest to survive with the next transaction.

"His… *passion* was admirable, as is yours. So, let us talk about Miracle Communications, and how my friends at PPP can help Miracle make the news… and earn enough money to save countless souls in the process."

CHAPTER 17:
Friday, February 7

As Dr. Jackson Pierce entered the classroom early, all five students were looking at him, grinning, like they knew something was up.

"Okay… why all the smiles?" he wondered aloud.

"Professor Pierce… we have a confession to make," Nat began.

"We overheard that fight you had with 'The Mallet.'" Sylvia Wright interrupted.

"Who the hell is 'The Mallet?'" their professor wondered aloud.

"That's what the students call Dean Arbell." John Marshall Bradford III explained.

"And we want to get even with him… for you!" Sgt. Paul Herrera announced.

Jackson Pierce smiled. "If you want to really get Dr. Franklin Arbell mad, win at the Georgia Communications Conference and at regionals. Make it to nationals."

"Now *that* would be better than trashing his sportscar, Professor Pierce," Nat proclaimed. That earned him some well-deserved laughs.

Jackson Pierce held up his hand. "The problem is that unless we come up with a lot of data, we're never going to make it to Savannah."

"It's time for our surprise now, Dr. Pierce," Sylvia beamed and opened the door. Nothing happened, so she stepped into the hallway to drag in…

"A.I.?" the communications professor gasped, forgetting to say Alicia Ina. She was holding stacks of paper. On top of them was an external hard drive. The undergrad tried to speak, but she couldn't quite get the words out.

"What's this?"

Paul stepped forward. "*This*… is our ticket to Savannah!"

"It's data on the last four years of broadcasts" the excitable undergraduate's outburst was barely understandable. Trey translated for her.

"It's… a lot of numbers," Taira mused, looking at the reams of data on the papers. "Think we can make sense of it… by conference time?"

"We'll have to," Pierce noted. "Is anyone's schedule free for the next few hours?"

═══

After laboring in the computer lab, Pierce and his students headed to Archetype, another favorite coffeehouse among the collegians. Their favorite hangout even had a few beanbag chairs and hammocks inside.

After a quick call to his wife to tell her not to wait for dinner, Pierce joined his students, poring over laptops, hoping that numbers would lead to patterns, and patterns would lead to findings, and those could lead to an award, and possibly the next level. That might get him that tenure-track spot.

The communications professor was similar to his nemesis, Dean Arbell. He loved numbers. Did it come from perusing the statistics on baseball cards or his obsession with political polls every election? Maybe it was that class in graduate school where Dr. Fryman showed him how he could predict the future for some things, with a reasonable certainty.

But numbers were a curse, sometimes. They let you think you proved something. He had seen that. In a study for a local newspaper, he worked out an optimal efficiency standard for hours and billing, as part of a research project during his doctoral studies. He was paid well for his service, but every employee below that "standard" was fired within a week. They were hard workers, too, but they just hadn't fit in that cold, calculating model.

Maybe that's where he was different from Arbell.

He vowed that day never to run a statistical model for the sake of doing so, without considering the human element, and the cost. That image of middle-aged reporters clearing their desks because of him would stick around forever to remind him that numbers were great, but not the whole story.

He made sure the students knew that lesson too, even though they bought into his excitement over statistics.

"Anything to eat… Dad?"

He put on his glasses again and looked up in shock. "Viv?"

Archetype's waitresses didn't have a formal uniform, but they wore a royal blue shirt and a "Hello My Name Is" name tag. Viv handed him a menu.

"When did you start here as a server?"

His daughter laughed. "Dad, I'm cooking here. You know how I like experimenting with new foods. Now I get to try breakfast dishes. That's why the menu is new."

Professor Pierce scanned the revised list. "Blueberry pancakes for dinner, I suppose."

With a wave, she headed back to the double doors and her latest trial-and-error phase. He went back to work with his students. After another hour, Taira's computer, with a portable printer in another bag, started spitting out summaries.

"Any patterns?" Trey inquired.

"Not unless you like quilting," Sylvia laughed.

Nat pointed at the graph. "The number of product placements was cruising at a slow and steady pace, then spiked just over the last few months."

"Isthat… good… enough…?" A.I. worked to slow her delivery.

"It's a start," admitted Jackson. "So, we know product placements are increasing. Anything else?"

Nat held up his hand. "Does it matter if one network has more than any others?"

"It could." Now Jackson abandoned his laptop to look over the football player's shoulder. "Which one?"

"Look at USBC. Isn't that higher than CBS, NBC and ABC?"

"Yes, but we need to see if it is *significantly* more."

"Dr. Pierce… It… is!" Alicia stammered. She held up the printout from Taira's computer, showing the evidence.

"Figures," Taira offered. "They always focus on entertainment and gossip."

"But in the news, Taira?" Paul countered.

"And they're behind the recent spike in product placement broadcasts," Nat insisted.

"That would be something to report," Professor Pierce stated.

Trey stared intently at his laptop. "A.I., can your data put products in a correlation matrix like we did in research methods last year?"

"Of… course… Trey," she said slowly, to be better understood. "Why?"

"Because I want to see if some products are hyped more than others."

No one spoke for several minutes, though the clack of keys was still audible.

Trey broke the silence. "I want to get a list of those that are significant."

"Sure, but why?"

"I don't know… maybe there's a connection between them. I can ask my dad."

"Good idea," Professor Pierce announced. He had wanted to enlist John Marshall Bradford II's input at some point, for travel funds, in case they got anywhere in the conference circuit.

"It's weird," A.I. offered, after a spell.

"What is?"

"Not all of these involve positive publicity. Some products are taking a beating."

"That is strange, Alicia," the communications professor observed.

———

A few minutes later, they broke from analyzing data to gather around an oddly placed wagon-wheel table to plan the presentation.

"Any ideas on how to present our work effectively, Professor Pierce?" Sylvia sounded apprehensive. Others hoped to get special insight from their professor.

"Well…" Jackson sounded uncertain. "For a good presentation, you've got to know your material well, practice a number of times so you get used to it…"

"And?" Sgt. Herrera asked.

"Well, what else do you need to know?" Dr. Pierce replied. "It's about communicating our key findings to the audience. Our research will sell the audience, not how we say it."

His students looked at their professor, and then at each other. He couldn't understand the reason for their confused looks. His speech had convinced them that the presentation mattered, but did he have to explain how to give a better one?

=

As Professor Pierce got up to leave, he peeked into the kitchen, but his daughter wasn't there. The bald chef jerked his thumb at the rear door.

Outside, Vivian was sitting on the stoop with a boy from her class. It looked like they were discussing a book. After listening for a few minutes to their conversation, he realized his daughter was being a tutor.

After a few minutes, the boy stood up, stuffed the books in his backpack, and reached for his bike. Then, he set the bike back down and gave Viv a hug before disappearing into the night.

Vivian closed her eyes.

"So, who was that?"

"Tarriq Walker, if you must know." His daughter seemed to resent his spying, though she still appeared pleased with how her study session ended.

"Tutoring session?"

"On one subject. We're lab partners in Anatomy. He cuts, and I spot the organs." After a pause, she added, "He wants to be a surgeon."

"What was the book?"

"*Great Gatsby*," Viv responded. "I had already read it over the summer. Tarriq hates it, and I did too, at least the first time. It has lots of fakes and *privileged* characters behaving in such a *shallow* manner."

Jackson winced when she said *privileged*, and his daughter did not fail to notice.

"Dad, it's not like that anymore. Yeah, I'm tutoring classmates, but it's really helping me! Check with Mom on my grades… they've bounced back! And I'm doing something about being privileged, taking a stand."

After a moment, she added something. "You know what I discovered, Dad? When you teach someone, you understand it better yourself. For example, I'm doing a paper on 'Point of View.' My paper imagines how the story would have been different if Jay Gatsby had written the story… so superficial."

Jackson considered that. "I hadn't given the P.O.V. in a story that much thought. But I was thinking about *Moby Dick*. Imagine if Captain Ahab had written it instead of some guy named Ishmael."

"Dad, he couldn't have written it. He died at the end."

"Didn't Jay Gatsby as well?"

Vivian frowned. "Yeah…"

Their cell phones buzzed simultaneously. The two looked at each other, and without checking first, each said "*Mom.*"

"Guess we are out a little late," Vivian admitted. "I'll call her back."

"And I'll check on my students, if they're still here."

He went back inside Archetype. To his surprise, every student was still there, typing away, with a small audience of fellow collegians and local residents. *Take it easy, Jackson*, he thought, even as he imagined his students winning the "Best Presentation Award" in Washington, D.C., at the same time he was promoted from contract to tenure-track. *Focus on the Georgia Communications Conference in Savannah*, he thought, as he headed for his car.

CHAPTER 18:

Sunday, February 9

"**G**ood morning, USBC viewers, I'm Mick Camden, and this is the Sunday Morning Special Report. It's a tale of two Southern politicians, two scandals, and two technological devices at the heart of each accusation of corruption. The outcome of both affairs may settle more than two political fortunes. It may also determine the battle for supremacy between two leading communications firms. More after this commercial break."

Jeremiah Calhoun snorted with laughter. It wasn't much of a competition, at least until now. Bradford Communications' "Edict" could run virtual circles around "The Miracle." Today would be different, though.

"What's so funny, Jeremiah?"

Britt Adams knew Calhoun hated to be called by his first name. But it made him chuckle. The reporter's response was a frown.

"I don't see why you're upset. You got the promotion at *Forbes*."

"Yeah… only 'cause I'm here… in bed with you." She pulled the bedsheet up further over her chest, a flimsy shield at best. She was beginning to despise this arrangement.

On the TV screen, Paige Glass replaced the ad for Talladega Motors' Gyrfalcon.

"Our story begins in South Carolina, where Governor Ogden Stewart was in Columbia, calling a press conference to denounce the corruption charges against him. The darling of the South Carolina social conservatives was accused of purging the Palmetto State of allies to the former Governor."

Ms. Glass went on to explain how "Honest Ogden" had been working with his Chief of Staff, who was already facing indictment over using spyware to monitor emails and social media posts made by government employees.

"The debate is more than just about Governor Ogden Stewart's political career. It's also about whether authorities can access data from his communication device, 'The Miracle.'" When reached for comment, Miracle Founder and CEO Esther Ruth Harding had this to say at her USBC exclusive interview yesterday."

The screen cut to an interview near the altar of a Chattanooga Megachurch.

"Good morning, Miss Harding," Mick Camden began. "Governor Ogden Stewart is accused by Federal authorities of firing state employees for being less than supportive of his agenda, or even not as 'pro-Christian' in general. Will you agree to let law enforcement unlock 'The Miracle' to investigate these charges?"

Esther Ruth Harding rose to her feet to give her sermon. "Absolutely not, Mr. Camden! The forces of evil and wickedness are conspiring against the most pious of politicians. He has led the fight against abortion, gay marriage…"

"But Miss Harding, these charges of hiring and firing employees with contracts…"

"You focus on human law," the former televangelist's wife interrupted the broadcaster. "True believers like Governor Ogden Stewart and I believe in a higher law."

Mick Camden resisted the urge to roll his eyes at her remarks.

"'The Miracle' can't be unlocked by anyone, except on my command," Esther Ruth Harding explained. "In the case of a terrorist, especially one of those Muslims, then we would have no problem helping out law enforcement, but not when there's a Christian about to be crucified for his beliefs."

Jeremiah watched from the comfort of his suite. Esther Ruth Harding had paid quite a bit for this publicity. She was getting her money's worth.

It would be a different story for the company that spurned him.

"Governor Ogden Stewart is hardly the only politician in hot water these days, accused of carrying out misdeeds with a communications device," Paige Glass explained, helping lead the transition to the new story.

"Louisiana Senator Louis Boudreaux, the third member of the Boudreaux clan to serve as that state's senator, may see his legacy end if he's found guilty of the accusations. Charges have been made that Senator Boudreaux and his staff had been using campaign funds to cover up affairs with Shiraz, a New Orleans stripper."

Britt Adams frowned at the image of Shiraz on television, as Camden continued.

"It seems that both conversations with the Senator and his staff, as well as financial payments made… *allegedly* made…on the Edict, a rival communications device to 'The Miracle.' It's made by Bradford Communications. Like Miracle Communications, law enforcement wants Bradford to open up their Edict. And like Miracle, they've refused."

The screen cut to a pool of reporters swarming John Marshall Bradford II, who made a vow similar to the one that Esther Ruth Harding from Miracle made. The phone would not be unlocked unless there was clear and convincing evidence of the device actively being used to harm someone.

Following the Bradford media ambush, Camden and Glass cut to a professor from Freedom University, who specialized in free speech rights. He praised The Miracle for protecting its clients' privacy.

Britt yawned. "Why are you so interested in this news program? It's practically an infomercial for some products."

Jeremiah snapped his fingers. "So, you're catching on. News isn't all about politics, or macro-economic issues. It's always about selling something."

"Let's see… that Cheshire cat smirk tells me that whoever has the good news is your client, and it's bad news for whoever opposes you," Britt observed, as she fumbled for her skirt and top by the side of the bed, while vainly trying to find her other stocking.

"It's not the politicians," she guessed. "So it comes down to one of these companies."

The PPP CEO said nothing. He got up and searched for his robe.

Britt frowned. Ever since Jeremiah made such demands on her person, in exchange for the exclusive interview her *Forbes* editor required, she was searching for a way out of her predicament. Well, maybe being close to him could be a way to expose the real monster he was, getting her revenge. *C'mon girl*, she had told herself. *You're a reporter! Do some investigative work, along with your "leg work".*

The Mount Holyoke College graduate had idly been playing with her scarf in her hands. Suddenly, with a flash, they were wrapped around her wrists.

"What the heck are you doing?"

Jeremiah was grinning, having her pinned.

She tugged ineffectively, like a helpless damsel-in-distress, but that was the plan. Suddenly, she yanked her scarf in the opposite direction. Having impressive reaction speed, he managed not to fly face-first into the bed, having let go of the scarf. With a quick move, she retrieved her fabric. "Lay off my echarpe!"

But if she thought he would react in anger, she miscalculated. "Feisty… I like that in a woman, you know!" he laughed.

That was the last straw. She stormed out of the only bedroom on the highest part of the skyscraper.

"She'll be back," he told his reflection in the mirror. Britt had to come back. He had the financial options and a lot of friends.

He considered the television again. Neither Miracle Communications nor their rivals at Bradford Communications intended to make their data available. But he had a solution for that. It was time to activate The Spider, his prize recruit from the hacker community. The Spider would help the hapless Harding have a strong firewall.

At the same time, he'd hire The Spider to break into Bradford's Edict device, making sure that access to their devices fell into the hands of the USBC broadcast journalist team, to publicize the politician's secrets from the scandal, a setback for Miracle's enemy. They'd suffer the consequences for the brushoff they gave PPP at the most recent lecture.

CHAPTER 19:

Friday, February 14

Presidents' Day Weekend was the first extended break of the spring semester. While the Pierces' celebrated Valentine's Day, Jackson's students would no doubt return home. He hoped they would take with them the enthusiasm of their project.

———

Sylvia Wright caught a forty-five minute ride with her brother to Clifton, which might as well be a world away. After a Saturday of romping with younger siblings and post-church Sunday brunch, she was joined by Gethsemane AME Pastor Braxton Quincy.

"So, child, how is your semester going?"

"In class, we're working on a research project that we're hoping to get accepted into a conference in Savannah!"

Her family cheered as if she had been nominated for an Oscar. But Rev. Quincy eyed her skeptically.

"Is it about the law?" He asked, expecting affirmation.

Sylvia paused. "No, not exactly."

"Is it about helping other people?"

She described the project and what they were working on.

"Product… placement?" he asked. "How is that going to help you get into law school?"

She explained how presenting at a conference, if they were accepted, could help her get into a law program.

The Rev. Quincy considered this. "How could it build a better world?"

Sylvia now frowned. "Well, it's interesting work. But to be honest, Reverend. I am not sure how it helps people right now."

The pastor stroked his graying whiskers. "That's the problem with academia. They ask questions they find interesting. They should use all of that knowledge to serve those less fortunate, as we hope you would do in law school."

Her enthusiasm dissipated.

"You and your classmates and that professor need to think about how to make that project help someone, and not just fascinate them," Rev. Quincy insisted.

—————

Sgt. Paul Herrera stepped away from the rental car and towards the sensibly unadorned brick house, its lawn perfectly manicured lawn, and saw the Major calmly walking down the sidewalk to greet him. There wasn't a single wrinkle on his well-ironed uniform.

"Good to see you for the February break, Paul. I left early to make it back in time."

For his dad, that meant he left MacDill Air Force Base at 3pm, not noon. His mom had just arrived from the Tampa Elementary School, where she instilled the proud values of America in her 5th-grade social studies classes.

"So, with your senior semester almost done, how far along are you with your applications to the Officer Candidate School, to be commissioned as a Lieutenant?"

Paul hesitated. "Actually, I was rethinking some of my plans..."

"*Our* plan, Sgt. Herrera, was for you to return to the military... to serve your country."

Carmen put her hand on her husband's, the one not pointing at her son. "George, let Paul finish."

"You see, this semester, we're doing a major academic project… it's going to be accepted at a conference in Savannah, I bet. And I was thinking about a graduate degree."

His father flushed with anger. "It's that hippie-looking professor we met on Parents' Day who is behind all this, isn't it?"

"George!"

"Carmen, we agreed that Paul could *temporarily* leave the army to go to college. Now, he's breaking that promise to return to the military!"

"It's his life!"

He whirled on his son. "This country has given so much to our family. It's your patriotic duty! And you could learn a lot in the armed forces as a higher-ranked officer."

"Dad, we're doing a lot of statistics work in Dr. Pierce's class. And I was talking with a graduate from Ft. George Thomas. What we're learning in class could help me… help our country, looking for patterns, tracking down terrorists, protecting our troops."

The elder Herrera was about to fire back a reply, but his wife stopped him. "Hon," she whispered. "It's his choice, not yours. Be glad he served and still wants to help out our military after college."

George Herrera bit his lip. *Perhaps Carmen was right this time. At least Paul wasn't thinking of being one of those communist-loving professors… so far.*

Taira had the shortest distance to go, as her parents came to Alexandria more than thirty years ago, part of a refugee resettlement for several survivors of the Lebanese Civil War. Before then, her father worked in her grandfather's Parisian-style café in Beirut as a waiter. Sectarian strife between the Sunnis, Shiites, and the Christian population turned the country and its capital city into a scene resembling WWII. Israel's invasion and attacks by Hezbollah only exacerbated the destruction in Lebanon.

Her father told her the story many times. The young Lebanese President was assassinated. The American Embassy was bombed. Hundreds of U.S. Marines were killed by a massive truck bomb. Then came the awful day when a large blast destroyed their little café, once frequented by diplomats and tourists. Grandfather and grandmother were vaporized, along with two other relatives.

Little mention was made of an uncle, whose family had sympathies with the dreaded Hezbollah. She had never forgotten the bitter words her cousin had flung at her for how she dressed, how she acted, and how she had pride in her newfound country, America.

When Taira joined her family at their hotel and restaurant on the square in Georgia, she delighted them with tales of her research project, with promises that it would have a good chance of being presented in Savannah.

"Are you the lead presenter?" her mother began.

Taira shook her head. "That's Sylvia. She's going to be a great attorney. But I'm in charge of doing the PowerPoint and giving some of the talk."

"I thought, Taira, that you would take these classes to learn how to be a television anchor," her father explained. "This sounds like… being a researcher."

His wife glared at her husband. "I'm fine with her not being on TV, you know."

Taira ignored her mother and spoke to her father. "You'd be proud of me. I've learned so much about data collection and analysis, even statistics…."

"But… that pays only a fraction of what one of those USBC broadcasters makes," her father pointed out.

Taira held her head in her hands. For once, she had been valued in school for her mind. Couldn't they see she had a new dream?

———

Nat Hinton dropped to one knee, as if in prayer. *This one's for you Dad,* he thought, imagining his father cheering him on from his hospital bed. As the gun went off, he ran for his life. Along the sidelines, his legs churned until he cleared the 40-yard dash line. He looked up at the clock, almost in disbelief. 4.46? It wasn't bad, but he had run faster. To his horror, he saw the scout with the Broncos logo leave his workout at the NFL tryouts in Indianapolis.

Two players bumped into him. One was the hulking Justin Woods Jr., from Ohio State.

The other was Dionta Sims from Clemson, projected to be a top-five pick.

"Hey guys," Nat began, showing a wide smile. "Great battle for the National Championship…"

Dionta interrupted. "J.W… you ever play this guy?"

The tallest receiver in the draft shook his mullet. "Nah… This guy's from some Div II school."

"If you're Div II, you better run faster if you wanna be drafted," Dionta laughed, dreads flying.

This was not at all how Nat had expected the day to start. Not only was his time a little slow, but he was being mocked by two potential first-round picks.

"I'll step it up," he managed. "How'd you two do?"

"Better than you, Div II!"

Justin shook his head. "When you're 6'7" and as strong as me, you don't need to run fast." He flexed his bicep, showing barbed wire on his muscle.

"Don't worry, Div. II… maybe the CFL has an opening up in 'Sasquatchewan.'" Dionta laughed out loud at his insult, as he and Justin headed for the reporters.

"Hey, it's 'Sports Center!'"

Nat braced for more ribbing, but was surprised to see Rashard Bailey, another Heisman finalist. "Honored to meet you!"

The star defensive back from the Naval Academy stuck out his hand. "Glad I didn't have to cover you. Saw your catch and run against Tennessee that made the highlight videos." Then he indicated a player standing next to him. "This is Hank Polk, a guard from Delaware."

The stout Polk extended the biggest hand Nat had ever seen. "Don't let those other cocky rookies throw you off," Polk offered. "Maybe they're jealous of your ESPN video."

Polk agreed to be Nat's spotter for the weightlifting event. Several times, Nat wanted to quit, his arms on fire. But the Delaware lineman shouted repeated encouragement. "Think of those jerks from those other schools laughing at you!"

Nat survived, and no more scouts left his workout. One of the Buffalo Bills scouts even came up to them… to talk with Hank.

Then it was time for his pass-catching drills. To his dismay, he saw that he was paired with Shotgun Jimmy Thompson from USC. The guy had a cannon arm, but his throws could fly off in all directions, sometimes well off the mark.

As he charged down the field for the Fly Pattern, he could already see the ball whistling well over his head. He ran fast enough to beat his earlier time, then launched himself forward, into the air. The ground hit him like a hammer, and his knee screamed in pain, but the ball he had snared with his fingers was now safely in his arms. The Lucas Oil Dome in Indianapolis was now buzzing with excitement. Nat even saw a Jaguars scout clapping. *Wow.*

The second was underthrown, as if the USC QB was trying to compensate for overthrowing it earlier. Nat tracked it down and caught it just before it struck the turf.

Another errant throw from Shotgun Jimmy flew out of bounds, but Nat made a reasonably good effort to get it. He caught other routes as well.

Then came the post pattern in the end zone. Just as he made his cut to the middle, he saw to his horror that Shotgun Jimmy had thrown it behind him. With a Herculean effort, Nat threw on the brakes and launched himself backwards. The ball flew into his arms. He cradled it like a treasured icon.

Rashard ran up and playfully put a belated tackle on Nat. "That's what I'm talkin' 'bout!" he screamed. "I may be defending you yet in the NFL!"

Hank ran up and pointed at the steps to the stands. Several scouts had come down from the seats with clipboards, waiting to talk to him. Jacksonville's head scout was there, but so were the Packers, Ravens… and the Falcons too. He ignored the glowering looks from Dionta and Justin, as his draft stock had just gone up a notch or two.

Nat knew it was a longshot. A few Peach State College players made practice squads, and played up North, over in Europe, or other semipro leagues. None had ever been drafted. Who knew? He might even get a rookie contract big enough to cover his dad's medical expenses.

CHAPTER 20:
Friday, February 14-Saturday, February 15

On Presidents' Day weekend, most college students drove home or hosted parents on campus, but Alicia Ina Sheehy's trip would be a little different. She recognized no one else at Alexandria's bus terminal.

Her ticket took her to Lake City, Florida, with a transfer to Tallahassee. Her parents would be within walking distance of her final destination.

She passed two more houses, as well as an administration building on the other side, and then headed past the tall black gates with sharp golden tips to prevent entrance after hours.

Here, her parents shared a spot with many others. However, their conversation wouldn't disturb anyone else.

They were in a graveyard.

She arrived at the two headstones with the same final date.

It was to be the happiest evening of her life. She had been asked to Homecoming, even getting a corsage from the head of the Math Club. He didn't even have a car, but her parents offered to drive them and then have a date night across town while the kids enjoyed their dance. As the night wore on, and most of the couples had cleared out of the gymnasium, there was no sign of her parents.

That's when the police car showed up. An officer spoke briefly to the teachers serving as chaperones. Both rushed to console her as the math kid looked at her helplessly. Her parents' killer was a drunk driver.

At their markers, Alicia told them everything, as she always had. Both parents had been college professors at Florida State University, so she knew they'd be proud of her research, happy that she had finally made a few friends, that she was learning to slow her speech so others could understand her, something that began that fateful evening and never seemed to quit.

"I couldn't help but overhear the last part," a voice behind her began. "I know Lee and Theresa would be proud of all you've done."

"Aunt Helen," Alicia began. "I... I... Imissthemsomuch. I-I'm about tograduate and..." she began sobbing, "All alone... don't know whattodonext."

Her mother's sister, a lobbyist for public education, embraced her. "I know."

═══════

Trey pulled the Mustang up the driveway, but his dad wasn't there to greet him at their Alpharetta mansion. The doorbell brought the maid, who pointed upstairs. Her expression, normally a cheery one, indicated concern. His mother met him at the landing, exchanged a quick hug, and then led him upstairs to the study. John Marshall Bradford II was hunched over three computers. Two faces on the screens were men in suits and the third was a woman in business formal. Each seemed to be talking all at once. The Bradford Communications CEO gave a perfunctory fist bump, whispered, *"Hey sport"* and then resumed the frantic dialogue. Tech, finance, and marketing were all represented in the room.

His mom, a federal judge, ushered him from the room. "Bradford Communications is in a bit of a tight spot since that scandal with the Louisiana senator broke earlier this week."

Trey nodded. "I saw the story on USBC. But Dad's not going to give them access to Edict, is he?"

Her shocked expression spoke volumes. "Haven't you listened to the news today? Somebody hacked State Senator Boudreaux's Edict and posted all the dialogue and payments on CleanGov this morning!"

Trey gasped in shock.

"And that's not all," his mom added. "Whoever cracked the code posted how to break into an Edict this afternoon. Now every user is scrambling, trying to protect their data and messages. It's a disaster!"

Their only son swore out loud. For once, his mom didn't chastise him.

———

"I don't see how they did it," John Marshall Bradford II began at the dinner table, as a nervous servant brought in their food. "They didn't just penetrate our firewall. They shredded it."

"How's our stock looking?"

"Don't look on Yahoo Finance," his dad admitted.

Trey's mom's eyes narrowed. "And, by some 'Miracle,' those same hackers haven't gone after Esther Ruth Harding's company, even though I bet it is child's play to unlock that device. She probably doesn't even know what a firewall is!"

Trey knew their worry. It wasn't just money they were losing. Their employees, investors, and even the family name were taking a beating. Maybe becoming the future CEO wasn't such a good idea after all. The USBC Channel on their big screen kept harping on the Edict story, until they switched over to cover the Miracle and how the government was unable to pursue the South Carolina governor due to its privacy settings.

"Hey, Dad, my classmates and I are working on a project with Dr. Pierce where we're looking at product placement... like what USBC is doing with our Edict and the Miracle right now."

"This is like an infomercial for Miracle and a hatchet job on us," his mom spat out with unusual venom.

Bradford broke his silence. "You know, Trey, the oddest thing happened to me two weeks ago. At a lecture, I was approached by a guy from some firm wanting to sell me on product placement for the Edict. I turned him down... sales were good, and deliberately forcing ourselves into the news artificially isn't our style."

Lyndsey whirled on her husband. "Well, was *she* there?" His wife pointed to the screen where Ms. Harding was being interviewed. Esther wore the biggest cross on a necklace that could be fitted without snapping the chain. Hands were clasped in prayer, eyes rolling artificially to heaven.

John Marshall Bradford II considered his wife's question. "Come to think of it, I remember seeing the two of them in the reception area."

"So, she talked with those sketchy people at the State Farm Arena that you turned down," the judge remarked. "Then, by some weird coincidence, you start getting a lot of bad luck and Miracle gets a ton of free publicity..."

Trey interrupted his mom. "Dad, do you remember the name of that firm?"

"I had the guy's card, but I misplaced it. It won't solve our immediate problem," John Marshall Bradford II admitted. "But it would be nice to see if they're working together, and if they've engaged in any sort of illegal activity."

"We've got a classmate who is so good at computers that she got us tons of data from all broadcast news coverage of products," Trey offered.

"Maybe the company could use some help from that girl," Lyndsey, his mom, pointed out. "Trey, can you contact her?"

═══

PPP meetings had grown noticeably brighter since the company switched from product placement in shows, to the news. The coffee tasted better. The donuts tasted better. *Darcie looked even hotter,* Jeremiah thought.

Chip's report included the huge check Harding had written to PPP, but Jeremiah only half listened. The majority of his focus was on one person.

The Spider.

Evan Gordy was, as usual, fiddling around on multiple devices; his laptop, tablet, cell phone, and a pair of devices, which the CEO assumed were the Miracle and the Edict.

As if sensing Calhoun's stare, the kid with the spiked hair and round glasses met his gaze, then nodded. They would meet alone afterwards.

"Edict remains fully penetrated," The Spider answered Jeremiah later. "They've issued a patch for their clients, but it's only temporary. I hacked a user and have the code. I can hit it any time you want."

Jeremiah considered this. "Let me talk to Mick and Paige about what time frame in the news cycle might provide maximum exposure. Maybe there's a target on Wall Street or in Hollywood who might fit the bill."

The Spider nodded in agreement.

CHAPTER 21:
Friday, February 21

The normally chatty Senior Communications Class students were unusually silent in the classroom. A cryptic email from their professor told them that big news was on the way.

As Jackson entered the room, they could hardly breathe. He stepped forward, he flipped open his laptop, clicked on the remote for the projector, and logged into the PSC account.

All six seniors stared at the rectangle on the whiteboard. Dr. Pierce then enlarged the font.

"We… WE GOT ACCEPTED!" Nat yelled. He stood up and pumped his fist, then gave Trey a high-five. Paul mimicked making a toast with Sylvia, who received a hug from Taira.

Only A. I. looked confused. "Doesthat mean we're… g-g-going to Savannah?"

There was a knock on the door. Without awaiting a reply, Dean Franklin Arbell walked in.

"I hope I'm not interrupting anything special," the bald man with the glasses said in his most insincere apology. "Dr. Pierce, report to the Academic Funding Committee for your undergraduate research and travel proposal's evaluation. Don't be late."

Jackson looked disappointed. "Yes, Dean Arbell. I'll see you at 4pm."

The Higher Education Dean smiled and shut the door.

The students looked as if all oxygen had vanished from the room.

"That sounds like a no, professor," whispered Paul.

"We'll deal with that later," Professor Pierce seemed to shake off the news. "Now, let's figure out what we've discovered from A.I.'s dataset, and your analyses."

The students forgot about the impending Academic Funding Committee meeting. They wrote on the whiteboard, dissected the numbers, developed graphs, and reworded hypotheses; fine-tuning them until all could agree on the phrases. They seemed to be having so much fun, focusing on the research instead of academic politics.

"Dr. Pierce," Trey raised his hand. "I'd like permission to run an additional test."

Jackson shrugged. "What do you have in mind?"

The senior hesitated. "My dad's the head of Bradford Communications, and our company's taking a beating in the press over Edict and that sex scandal in Louisiana."

Trey continued to explain what had happened, from the confidential payments from a politician to a paramour, to the data on Edict, to the hacking of the Bradford Communications device. He contrasted it with what happened in South Carolina with The Miracle.

"Sounds personal," Sylvia observed.

The heir to Bradford Communications flushed. "I didn't mean to make it that way. But the head of some marketing company offered my dad a chance for Edict to make news. When he turned them down, this scandal hit."

"That sounds like more than a coincidence." Taira pointed out.

Trey paused. "My dad saw the head of The Miracle at the same lecture where the company made the product placement offer. Now, they're the heroes for protecting that supposedly pious South Carolina governor, while we get hacked and hung out to dry in the media. Our stock's tanking!"

A.I. whirled around. "Hacked?" Trey nodded. "Could… could I h-help?" she offered.

Jackson held up his hand. "I've got that meeting to go to."

None of his students made a move. "Hey… let's meet at that coffee shop you all love afterwards… Archetype. Sound good?" he added.

They nodded, remembering what was at stake.

———

"The Academic Funding Committee will come to order," began Dr. Barbara Strayhorn, a professor of German. She'd led the AFC for more than a decade and had earned tenure long ago. She could resist the pressures of Dean Franklin Arbell at PSC. He found that out the hard way when he tried to oust all committee chairs so he could appoint new faculty members to these posts. Dr. Strayhorn and others prevailed in The Scholars Court.

That was one vote in Jackson's favor.

As Professor Strayhorn reviewed last month's minutes, Dr. Pierce glanced around the room at the voting members. The wide grin of Ime Udo, the Nigerian biology professor, greeted him. The two frequently teamed up to hit Traveler's and sample the "beers of the world" downtown. He was another ally serving on the AFC.

After that, it got a little murkier.

Few on campus were more nattily dressed than Chad Warner, Dean of the Accounting Department. Warner was all about the bottom line. You either had the numbers or you didn't. Jackson barely knew him and had no clue how he would vote.

Rudy Caraway gave him a nervous glance. The young, newly hired sociologist didn't have tenure yet, something they shared in common. Rudy's anguished expression told him that Dean Arbell had let him know how to vote if he were to remain at Peach State College.

Then, there was Dean Arbell, who named himself an "interim" replacement at the start of the Fall Semester after pressuring a graphic arts professor to resign from the committee.

Proposal after proposal was defeated. Then, it was Jackson's turn.

"We've reviewed your request for your students to travel and present at the Georgia Communications Conference in Savannah," Dr. Strayhorn began. "This experience will really help the students. I am in favor of the proposal."

Dean Arbell started to raise his hand to speak, but Professor Udo pretended not to notice. "I love it, man. The product placement... I now look for it everywhere on T.V. I agree..."

The impatient administrator cut him off. "I would like to highlight my memo that outlines my opposition to the funding of this... 'school trip.' It's a lot of money to be spent, to present a research project that's frankly quite thin on data... only a week or so of analysis. Perhaps those of you who voted for this project may wish to re-read it and reconsider your vote."

"It's not a week of analysis."

All turned to look at Chad Warner, who was staring intently at his laptop.

"It's months of data."

"What?" The Higher Education Dean was stunned.

"Chad's right," Ime, the biologist, added. "His students came up with a computer program to analyze a lot of news programs."

Dr. Strayhorn looked at Dean Arbell. "Didn't you get the addendum?"

"The... what? *When?*"

Arbell looked at his computer again, blood rising to his temple. "We... simply need more time to analyze this 'addendum,'" He insisted.

Strayhorn and Udo shook their heads. "Such a delay would amount to a vote to reject, and the by-laws say that Professor Pierce provided enough time to respond to your 'memo,'" the chair replied carefully, as if translating from German to English. "Let the vote continue."

Chad continued to stare at the laptop. "I vote yes, as well."

Jackson caught Rudy exhaling.

"This is... irregular!" Dean Arbell snarled.

"Speaking of irregular, Franklin, you are really overdue for stepping down from the committee," Barbara lectured. "Interim appointments can only be voting members for a semester, and your term ended in December." She looked at the other professors. "We'll reconsider these rejected requests at the next meeting, when the new committee member is fairly elected at the faculty session this Friday."

Arbell's eyes narrowed as he glared at Dr. Pierce. *This isn't over*, he thought. Pierce and his wife, Elena, as well as Strayhorn, Udo, and Warner, would all pay for their insolence. *Enjoy your excursion to Savannah. It's likely to be your last funded trip, and don't count on getting a tenure-track slot.*

⸻

Students and faculty at Archetype burst into cheers when Jackson announced the good news to the gathering. "And there's more!" Jackson beamed. "I sent your write-up of the preliminary research findings to a publication called VLM. They've agreed to publish the article we've done."

"VLM?" Paul asked.

"It stands for *Veritas Lux Mea*, Latin for 'Truth is my light.' It's a magazine that specializes in academic work by professors," Jackson explained. "Their stuff goes out to newspapers all over the country!"

After a long round of celebrations and a selfie, Jackson stopped them.

"Now that you're in the conference's competition, we've got a lot of work to do. The PowerPoint needs editing, and you all need to practice what you're going to show and say. A trip to Savannah is fun, but let's add an award and a trip to regionals!"

He knew they'd probably head over to Traveler's soon. *Fine*, he thought. Let them have their fun, because he'd make sure they were ready to be the best Peach State presenters ever. And while Dean Arbell was pissed at him now, an award might boost his chances at tenure.

He noticed Ime Udo telling the story of the committee meeting to Elena. He joined them at their table.

"I would have given up my faculty award to see Arbell go down in flames." His wife beamed. "How'd you get a response to the Dean that he didn't read?"

Jackson tapped his skull. "I uploaded it to the online committee files. I noticed Dean Arbell does all his business by email and never bothers with the folder. He seemed pretty smug this afternoon, so I could tell he had no idea that I had responded to the memo he emailed."

"He'll want revenge," Elena warned. "You had better steer clear of him if you want to be a future tenured professor."

CHAPTER 22:

Tuesday, February 25

Dr. E. E. Kirby came in late, as usual, to the weekly Preston Powell Partnership meeting. The scholar's usual confidence was replaced with worry. He showed a newspaper to Jeremiah Calhoun.

"What?" the CEO gasped.

It was an article about product placement in the news that day. Somebody named Jackson Pierce was tracking mentions of business in media broadcasts. The bar chart in the middle showed USBC leading the other networks for touting corporations in their reporting.

Several of their clients were in the article, with the sleeping pill company SRD or "Sleep Rest, Dream," Talladega Motors, and the Miracle occupying three of the top five spots on the second graphic.

Calhoun swore out loud, something he rarely did in public, which got the attention of others. Kirby loaded a printout of the article on the document camera.

"What does it mean?" Ray Maillon asked.

"Gentlemen… and ladies," he growled. "It's time we dealt with this new *threat*, Professor Jackson Pierce."

Wallace Bragg looked skeptical. "The article doesn't mention us."

"Mr. Bragg," Calhoun snapped. "They clearly mention our clients and our chosen network partner. It's only a matter of time before they get around to exposing *us*. We need to end it before it begins."

He glanced over at his staff. "I want everything we can find on Jackson Pierce. He's at a university named…" Calhoun looked closer at the article. "Peach State College."

The Spider typed a few keys, and the Georgian college website sprang into view.

"He's in the communications program," Larry Murray observed.

"It said that in the story," Hap Dixon snapped.

The Spider flipped through several webpages. "He doesn't appear to have tenure."

"Good!" Calhoun snapped. *The professor would be easy to fire*, he thought.

A few more clicks from The Spider. "He has a wife who works at the college too, as a professor in the English Department. She is tenured."

Calhoun smiled. "Perhaps we can work a nepotism angle and force him to back off."

Wallace Bragg stood suddenly. "You're not going to directly confront him, are you?!"

"And you would have him killed?" Calhoun laughed.

"No!" the COO stopped suddenly. "It could generate a trail that would lead to us."

"Mr. Turosz does clean work, I assure you," the CEO replied.

"More deaths may get back to us, no matter who is sent on the hit," rasped a voice behind him.

Jeremiah whirled around. The unmistakable clipped tone from the British Isles belonged to Preston Powell, the company's founder and name-sake. "But discrediting this 'Jackson Pierce' would be easier, and cheaper."

Professor Kirby smiled. "It's far easier to kill a professor's academic career and reputation than it is to do away with a professor's life. And he is untenured."

Preston Powell walked over to their "scholar-in-residence" and asked, "So... do you have any contacts at Peach State College?"

Kirby frowned. "Most of mine are in the Ivy Leagues and the North-east, certainly not some *southern college*, but I could scan their administration or faculty list... see if they actually have any *distinguished* scholars or graduates of elite universities."

Bragg rolled his eyes. Kirby was getting on his nerves.

Preston Powell scanned the article carefully. "It looks as though there are several co-authors for this article."

Professor Kirby looked flabbergasted. "He actually shared credit with his undergraduate students?"

"We can go after them, too." Calhoun pointed out.

"But Jeremiah, they're just *kids*." Darcie protested

The CEO's eyes narrowed. "Their research is targeting the success of our commercial enterprise. That makes them legitimate targets."

Calhoun paused at the shocked expressions. "Don't look at me like that. We won't hurt them… just convince them to drop their little research project. Everyone has a pressure point, you know."

═══════

"Franklin, someone's on line one for you."

"Take a message, Jennifer." Dean Arbell moved the rook across the board to take the bishop.

"I think you'll want to answer this one."

"Fine!" He punched the button on his phone. "This is Dean Arbell. Please keep your business short. I am in the middle of an important matter…"

"Dean Arbell, this is Professor E. E. Kirby of the…"

Arbell dropped his jaw several inches. He couldn't make out the rest because he was trying not to stammer. It wasn't every day that one of the best-known academics in America was calling. He could barely follow what the caller was saying.

Arbell began. "I went to Atlanta to hear your lecture at the State Farm Arena."

Kirby smiled. "Yes, it was an effective speech that night. I was glad you were in attendance. If you'd like an autographed copy of my latest book, I can have my secretary provide you with one." And she'd sign it, with the machine that mimicked his signature.

"Thank you!" Arbell beamed. "It will find a prominent place in our college library."

Kirby paused, as though considering his next words carefully. "I have a matter to discuss with you about Jackson Pierce."

The Higher Education Dean reddened with anger. "Yes, he teaches at Peach State College," Arbell responded through clenched teeth, jealous that this esteemed scholar wanted to talk about that untenured professor on his hit list.

"Your professor has written an article that has made some high-placed associates of mine very upset."

It was like a dream to Dean Arbell. Was Dr. Kirby really looking to target his nemesis? The Peach State College administrator's glee was almost too hard to contain. "I am sorry this communications professor is the source of your trouble."

Kirby's next words shifted from concern to praise. "It seems that I have found the right person to work with at Peach State College. I was worried that your school would go overboard to protect one of your own."

"No, we would not even think of doing that to those you work with!" Arbell insisted.

"Do not worry, Dean Arbell. My associates and I have no intention of pursuing a case against Peach State College at this time. However, holding one of your own accountable would go a long way toward mollifying my colleagues."

"I shall initiate punitive procedures against him immediately."

Impressive, E. E. Kirby thought. *He hadn't even mentioned which article or what it was about, and this college leader couldn't wait to run Jackson Pierce off campus.*

There was an awkward pause. "What... is the nature of this injustice?"

Dr. Kirby filled in the administrator with the details from Pierce's recent article, and how it targeted businesses in a consortium that Kirby had ties to.

"Pierce ran his numbers, and then assumed the networks and the businesses had done something illicit," Kirby concluded.

"There will be a fair hearing, and then we'll see to it that Jackson Pierce is terminated, and that the record will be so damning that he'll never get another job in academia."

The distinguished professor smiled. Arbell sounded ruthless enough to be recruited for PPP.

CHAPTER 23:
Thursday, February 27-Friday, February 28

Funds from PSC allowed the Pierces' and six undergraduate co-authors to stay at the Quality Inn across from both the DoubleTree and Hilton Garden Inn, where the Georgia Communications Conference would be held.

"I've called Kat and we're on for dinner," Jackson's wife informed him of her sister's plans. "She said R.J. and the kids can join us."

"I'm good with that." The four adults were friends from their undergraduate days at Tulane. Only a few hours apart now, the families had visited so frequently that Isaac and Vivian thought of their cousins Mia and Hugh as siblings.

Elena added, "Kat ran your product placement article from VLM in her newspaper. She really liked it."

"Thanks!"

Before the students left, Dr. Pierce had them go through a conference rehearsal. Nothing worked right. Sylvia kept tripping up on her lines. There was a statistical error in Nat's data. Taira had to rewrite two slides. Paul forgot to add a pair of sources. And A.I. had a panic attack, leading Trey to miss the Q&A while he chased her down the hallway.

"I don't expect you to be perfect the first time," Jackson began after the disastrous rehearsal. "But I do expect you to keep practicing until you get better. Sound fair?"

They did it again, reserving a study room from the Alexandria Library, repeating their presentation until they felt satisfied. They even used their lunch break the next day, practicing it on campus before several of Nat's football teammates, to applause and even some good questions, which gave Trey the practice he needed in handling queries from their college crowd.

When they learned of their competition as the schedule was emailed out, the students' optimism seemed to vanish. They would face Emory, Georgia Tech, and the University of Georgia.

"Hey, this is about you doing your best and getting good opportunities after Peach State College. Ignore what the other schools do. Pay attention to *your* presentation. Let the judges focus on the balloting."

Even A.I. seemed slightly less nervous.

———

"Matt Donovan, how are you?!" Jackson waved at his friend in the lunchtime reception at the Hilton Garden Inn in Savannah. "I didn't expect you to come down from Atlanta to the conference."

The editor of *Veritas Lux Mea* gestured for him to come over. "Loved your article on product placement. More than 100 newspapers have said they will run it."

"101. Kat over at the *Savannah Herald-Post* said she'll run it, too."

"I want you to do a follow-up."

The communications professor set down his blueberry muffin on the plastic plate. "I saw you hinted at it already in VLM, Matt. Why would you do that, when we don't have a second article?"

"I had to tell them something… so many wanted one!" Editor Donovan explained. "Besides, you can squeeze several articles out of a single subject. I've seen you do it before."

"Okay," Pierce continued. "If I get a few weeks to work on it."

Matt glanced around. "Don't you have a gaggle of undergraduates at these shindigs?"

"They took their breakfast to the ballroom… getting another practice in. They're terrified of the competition."

Matt shrugged. "At some point, they have to get used to pressure."

After a morning panel comparing the impact of bloggers versus columnists, followed by a roundtable on the media, censorship, and propaganda, Jackson left Doubletree's Amber Room, heading toward the Grand Salon. He was surprised to see Sylvia outside in the hallway. He was even more shocked to watch her hyperventilate.

She looked embarrassed to see her professor as she fought to control her emotions. "I don't think I can do the conclusion," she admitted weakly, a shadow of her normal, confident self. "Can Taira do it? She's more of a natural than me... wants to be an anchorwoman."

"I'm one of the few people who knows what your goal is, Ms. Wright," the communications professor whispered as a graduate student headed down the hallway past them.

"That's why I'm struggling, Professor Pierce. I feel like the weight of the town of Clifton is on my shoulders."

"You're presenting an academic paper at a conference," Jackson explained. "You're not in court. You're not fighting racism to help your town, at least not today. Today, you're taking an important step... excellent practice for the real deal."

She considered his words.

Paul Herrera popped out of the Grand Salon. "Sylvia, are you ready?"

There was a pause. "Yeah, yeah, Sarge. Just going over a little last-minute strategy with Doc Pierce." She smiled. "You got the tech set up?

"Yeah... yeah..."

The two disappeared inside, and Jackson's attention turned to the women heading toward their room.

"Elena? Kat?"

"The kids are at the City Market," his wife said, referring to the shops and booths in the street between Ellis and Franklin Squares. "I gave Viv a few bucks so they can take an Old Town Trolley Tour."

"I wanted to see the students you've been bragging about in action," Kat explained. "I may do my next story about them for the *Savannah Herald-Post*, and not just your research."

Jackson smiled, then lowered his voice. "Don't say you're with the press or start interviewing them until you're done. They're nervous enough as it is!"

———

Glancing at the program, a visitor might look at the prestigious Georgia colleges, and then wonder how Peach State College students made the list of the best undergraduate papers that year. Packed into the Grand Salon, which seemed to fill to the promised capacity of 120, that year's undergraduate research competition was to be the pre-lunch highlight.

Georgia Tech's team started their presentation with their Cox Proportional-Hazards Model, a statistical regression comparing the survival time of newspapers during a recession. *Damn,* Pierce thought. Their data and methods were first-rate. His students would be hard-pressed to top their work. He looked around and saw several confused faces. Jackson realized that while he understood their research methods and results, not everyone else did. The Peach State College team still had a chance.

The University of Georgia went second. Their presentation on violence in videogames began well, with some excellent visual images and even a few videos. But halfway through, Pierce noticed they had only gone through seven slides, and the counter showed they had another 23 to finish. As the timekeeper gave them the one-minute sign, the UGA students panicked. The smart thing to do would have been to find a natural stopping point and hope the judges didn't have access to their PowerPoint. But their captain elected not to do that, rushing through the rest. Finally, the head judge had to cut them off at 17. The Bulldogs would likely not advance to the regionals.

Emory followed. It was clear that they were the most experienced team in the room. Their presentation on fictional podcasts was interesting, though most of the adults didn't seem to recognize the cases the team mentioned. Once they got into their theory, about how such radio-style events would supplant books, Emory's conference paper returned to familiar footing. The hypothesis test of sales versus downloads and sub-scribers seemed a little contrived. It was still a good presentation, which would give Team Georgia Tech a run for their money.

Then it was his PSC kids' turn.

Clearly, his pep talk had helped the students. Taira began with a confident voice, introducing their topic, commanding everyone's attention. Those examples of product placement in the media got lots of nods. Trey took his turn to provide the connection to the networks. A.I. managed to introduce her model slowly and carefully, without rushing it… too much. Paul gave his part, then called upon Nat to cover the statistics, and the football player broke it down like he was explaining sports stats to an ESPN audience. When Elena flashed him a smile, he knew they had done well.

Sylvia stepped forward for the closing argument.

Then, disaster struck.

Sylvia froze.

So did the rest of the PSC team.

Pierce began to panic. What had happened?

Trey rose from his chair. He whispered something to her.

Without missing a beat, Sylvia cleared her throat. "And John Marshall Bradford will give the conclusion."

Trey smiled at the audience. "Sorry… thought we were going to a commercial break there." A few in the audience laughed. "But as you can see from our presentation, such advertising has seeped into the news coverage as well." He proceeded to outline the key lessons learned about the increase in the practice of product placement, and how frequently A.I.'s model showed that it was occurring in the broadcast media, especially USBC.

When he finished, he sat down confidently, and Sylvia squeezed his hand. Trey thought he saw her whisper thanks. Some applause broke out in the Grand Salon. It was a serious breach of decorum, but others joined in. Jackson saw Kat among the clappers. It was nearly impossible to resist the urge to join in. Whatever the results, he was proud of his undergraduates. They had gone toe-to-toe with students from the best colleges in Georgia. And they would make it difficult for the judges that afternoon.

But as he took his eyes off his smiling, relieved students sitting near the front, he was surprised to see a familiar figure get up from the front to depart along a side door. Jackson tried to place him, but couldn't quite do so, until the man turned for one last look, staring straight into his eyes.

It was someone most academics knew by sight: Professor Edward Edmund Kirby.

CHAPTER 24:

Friday, February 28

Dr. E. E. Kirby occupied a more discrete section of the lobby, tucked around the corner by the fireplace, which offered more privacy. He normally craved public adulation, but he had to keep a low profile under orders.

It would be bad luck if that glorified community college won against the likes of superior schools. Jeremiah wouldn't be pleased.

"Anything to report, *Mr.* Dixon?" he snapped as he answered the call.

Hap ignored Kirby's anger. "The professor and the kids went to Vinnie Van Go-Go's across the street. It's a hole-in-the-wall, but the pizza smells great."

It was a typical lowbrow establishment for a state school teacher. "Just them?"

"Two ladies joined them. I think one is his wife."

"And the other?"

"I'll email the pic to New York," Hap offered. "We'll have The Spider run the images."

———

Just as Jackson, his wife, sister-in-law, and students had squeezed into a table, Trey looked up to spot a figure entering the small pizza establishment. "Dad!"

John Marshall Bradford II extended his hand. "Great presentation, Trey! I hid in the audience so I wouldn't throw you off." He produced a fedora that looked almost comical in its appearance when it adorned his head.

The Founder and CEO of the Bradford Communications firm glanced at the others. "You all gave a strong performance. Pizzas are on me. We're not bankrupt yet!"

As the others talked among themselves, Jackson fretted over Bradford's last comment. "What did you mean by that? Is your company in trouble?"

Bradford proceeded to get the academic up to speed on Louisiana Senator Louis Boudreaux, his use of campaign funds to pay off a stripper trying to blackmail the politician, and how someone hacked Edict to get that data.

"Meanwhile, that phony pastor Esther Ruth Harding and her "Miracle" communications device is getting all the positive press." He went on to explain who South Carolina Governor Ogden Stewart was, and what he had *allegedly* done. He ended with how the same hacker or hackers who had made his life as CEO miserable were ignoring the "Miracle."

"We could probably penetrate it," John Marshall Bradford II said. "But that would be illegal."

Jackson had been sitting quietly, a pen cap just touching his lips, thinking intently. "Wait… what did you say earlier about Miracle? Something about 'positive press?'"

"Yeah," the CEO remarked, almost squinting. "Every time you turn on the news networks, they're covering us in a bad light, especially USBC. And because Harding won't budge on cooperating with law enforcement on the Stewart scandal, she's like some sort of 'Joan of Arc,' of the electronic privacy movement."

The white pizza with pesto arrived. When most of the slices were gone, Trey looked at his father. "Tell him about that conversation."

The elder Bradford shook his head. "I don't know… there's not much…"

"It could explain what's going on."

The businessman relented. "Well, I went to a lecture at the State Farm Arena in Atlanta. Some guy promised to help Edict do well in the media.

We were doing well in sales, so I felt confident in turning him down. Besides, it sounded fishy."

"And that was when all the trouble started?" Jackson pressed.

"Well, Senator Boudreaux's problems predated that. But let me check my schedule to see if there's some sort of cause-and-effect."

Bradford whipped out a handheld device. "Our hack occurred after the Atlanta event," he said, as if he already knew the answer.

"Who was the guy you met in Atlanta?"

The CEO nodded. "I originally misplaced his business card, but found it after the card went through the cleaners. What's left says "-ston Powell Partn-"

Trey did some typing on their laptop. "It's Preston Powell Partnership, or PPP."

"And they're the ones who met with Miracle afterwards, I'm sure."

To his right, Jackson heard Taira say, "Maybe for our second part in the series, we should look into whether there's a connection between this PPP and some of the companies getting favorable publicity."

Nat joined in. "Maybe there's a fix going on."

The *Savannah Herald-Post* editor smiled. "When you get more details, give me a call. Someone in my newsroom would love to do a story on that."

———

Jackson met up with his students at the poster session in the lobby of the Hilton Garden Inn. They told him about the social media panel they had attended. As they maneuvered over to the easels and displays, Paul nudged his professor. "Dr. Lois Levy with Georgia State University tried to recruit me for her graduate program."

"Really," Professor Pierce exclaimed with delight. "Why did she seek you out?"

Sgt. Herrera smiled confidently. "She attended the undergraduate research panel. She wants us all there, as a team."

Pierce nodded. It was an unlikely occurrence, but a great idea. It made him wish PSC had a graduate program, especially this year. "Did you interview her about GSU?"

His star undergraduate hesitated. "I asked about the money. They'll do a tuition waiver for me because I've gone to a Georgia college, even though I'm originally from Florida."

The professor persisted. "And the stipend, Sarge?"

Paul shrugged. "It's competitive."

"And did you ask about the course load, the opportunity to be a research or teaching assistant, how many students were in the program?"

The senior blushed. "She gave me her card. I can do a follow-up call."

Jackson nodded. "That's a good idea."

═══

The Georgia Communications Conference board meeting set all attendance records. Attendees hoped to hear the winner from among the four strong presentations at the undergraduate research panel. Many came from their home schools to cheer on their classmates and students.

Everyone seemed to know what award would happen next. Jackson had fingers crossed from both hands. He glanced over to see Sylvia with her head bowed, rubbing a crucifix from her necklace with her right hand. Taira was whispering "please please please" quietly to herself, while Trey had his hands pressed together in prayer. Nat was kneeling on the floor next to his seat at the end of the row, while A.I.'s eyes were completely shut.

Anthony Williams of Oglethorpe stepped to the podium with an envelope in his right hand. "And the winner of the Georgia Communications Conference's undergraduate research paper and presentation is the entry from Peach State College, featuring John Marshall Bradford, Paul Herrera, Nat Hinton, Taira Malek, Alicia Ina Sheehy, and Sylvia Wright!"

Cheers, shouts, and high-fives followed. Elena and Kat pulled Jackson over to his celebrating students, and reactions from other schools ranged from polite congratulations to looks of shock and dismay at the success of the upstart PSC school.

In the commotion, no one noticed Professor E. E. Kirby departing from the ceremony, using an Edict to send Jeremiah Calhoun a message, confirming the outcome.

CHAPTER 25:

Friday, February 28

Jeremiah strode into the PPP boardroom wearing a gray Nehru jacket. His employees were too nervous to comment on the tight-fitting clothing. As he marched from the door to the podium, he could almost smell the fear in the room.

Good.

"Let's have the NR-120 report."

Chip almost stammered through his presentation. "Sales are down nearly 50 percent at SRD-d-d-d. And Georgia's B-bbbbureau of Investigation is… asking about… Reginald Wald-d-d…"

The financial wizard never finished his sentence. With a push of the button, his seat began to glow red. Screams followed as his flesh began to melt, before he mercifully burst into flames, his life snuffed out before everyone's eyes.

His piercing gaze swung toward the others. Kimber Elliot was next on the firing line, so to speak. Her topic was Talladega Motors. The PPP employee tried to put on a braver face than Chip, but she was unsuccessful. The makers of the Gyrfalcon dropped their contract with PPP. Those were her last words, as a push of a button on the newly installed podium tipped her chair downward, so she slid toward the floor. A trapdoor opened, the source of her screams as they faded down the tunnel she traveled.

"Anyone else want to slide on out of here?" he taunted his employees. The sharks on the floor below would be well-fed.

Larry Murray was next. He was supposed to talk about The Miracle, but given that they'd filed for bankruptcy, and seeing what happened to his colleagues, he made a run for it.

"Mr. Turosz?" Calhoun pointed with a finger, closing the others around an invisible handgun grip. PPP's sinister security man whipped out his pistol and made sure Murray didn't make it to the door.

Calhoun decided he'd had enough. He yanked the Mac-10 from the box at the base of the podium, and fired into the conference boardroom. The bullets continued to find their mark, until the floor and table were littered with bodies.

"The meeting is now officially adjourned," Calhoun laughed.

"You're... you're a monster," wailed Darcie, one of the few survivors, looking at the destruction. "These were your employees... friends. They worked hard for you! They trusted you. And you killed them all!"

Her boss smiled. "Everyone here has failed me. And it's all because of that article..."

═══

With a start, Calhoun woke up from his dream, where he resembled a nefarious James Bond villain, from where he napped on his couch. Parts of it were fun, a stress relief for him; it was an outlet to release his anger. The dream was a harbinger for the CEO, telling him that he should focus on that *damned* product placement article.

Oh, how he wanted to quash that story! Part Two could be blocked. Part One could be "walked back" by those who published it, but too many eyeballs had seen what the professor and his undergraduate students had written. So, in addition to taking it out of circulation, he had to discredit those who wrote it.

Calhoun looked over the files brought in by Mr. Dixon and Mr. Turosz. Academic professors lived on their reputation, and reputations could be destroyed. He noted that one of the students, Nat Hinton, was a football player and a long-shot for the NFL Draft. They'd make sure he never played in the pros. Paul Herrera's dad was in the military, while his mom was a schoolteacher. Something undermining their character could permanently jeopardize their careers.

He pushed aside these earlier dossiers to look at the new ones generated by his security team. Sylvia Wright was from Clifton, Georgia, one of the poorest towns in the Peach State. Folks without much money were also often without many options, providing additional pressure points. As he guessed, Taira Malek was the child of immigrants. Even if her papers were perfectly in order, and she was a U.S. citizen, she was perhaps not quite home free in today's political climate. It wouldn't take much to deport somebody, for the right price.

The irony was evident when he saw John Marshall Bradford III's name on the list. His father was CEO of the very Bradford Communications corporation that was being targeted. Jeremiah promised to up the pressure on Miracle's rival company. The biggest surprise came not from what the briefing papers contained, but what they didn't have.

"Sorry, Mr. Calhoun, but we haven't been able to locate anything on Alicia Ina Sheehy," Hap Dixon had written in a note attached to Taira's file. "Kids on campus say she's got a stutter, and a possible learning disability like dyslexia or something like it. Personally, given that she's nervous and excitable, I doubt we need to do much to intimidate her into quitting the project or going against Professor Pierce."

Jeremiah smiled at that assertion, though he didn't like to leave loose ends.

After a lunch with Harry Engles, the billionaire Financier of Science and his *Veritas Lux Mea* publisher in their downtown Atlanta Headquarters, editor Matt Donovan waved at Emily Coolidge, his hardworking lead editor. Her usually cheery smile was replaced by a worried expression. She pointed toward his office, where his administrative assistant was gesturing like a windmill in a hurricane to hurry. What was all of this about?

The large man in the matching gray suit had a definite East Coast accent. "Mr. Donovan, I'd prefer that you... shut the door, so our conversation may be more private."

Donovan complied, not liking the theatrics. Then, he caught sight of the slender dark- suited man with black circles where glasses might be. VLM's CEO didn't like this one bit.

"Who are you, and what's this all about?" he began.

"My name is Dewey Symington. I'm an attorney."

"And who do you represent?" Donovan demanded, barely allowing the gray-suited man to finish his sentence.

The lawyer paused, as if slowing the pace in order to calm the head of VLM. "I represent… certain business interests, which will remain anonymous for now."

"What do you want?" Donovan's patience was running out.

"You are to neither run the second half of the Jackson Pierce column, nor are you to forward it to any of your associated newspapers."

Damn. He really liked that one. Donovan had convinced Pierce to run a sequel, with details. It was one of the reasons he attended the Savannah conference in person, instead of sending Emily or Lacey.

But Donovan relished a fight.

"Feedom of the press," Donovan leaned in, his voice clipped. "It's in the Constitution. The First Amendment, in fact. Maybe you've heard of it?"

Symington frowned. "This is no joke, Mr. Donovan. The interests I represent are very powerful and have deep pockets."

"And we…"

"I am aware of Mr. Engles' net worth. However, it may not last very long. An associate of ours has a friend on the Securities and Exchange Commission. Mr. Engles made a lucky trade, dumping stock in a home-builder company, which was found later to be utilizing defective materials, and is facing many lawsuits. This friend might feel he could have leaked such confidential information."

Donovan opened his mouth to respond, but nothing came out.

"He could face frozen assets, leaving you less able to defend yourself against our considerable finances," Symington intoned, as if he regretted breaking the bad news. "Of course, such a lawsuit need not take place…"

Donovan gasped. "Lawsuit?! Okay, we won't run the second part."

"And you'll retract the first article."

The legal blows were raining down on him now. Unable to speak, he simply nodded, hating himself for it. *Sorry, Jackson.*

"Anything else?" he said through clenched teeth.

"Write a letter to all newspapers who ran the VLM article, telling them to retract the story as well," Symington added in an even tone.

"Sheesh! That'll take…"

"The lawsuit then goes away."

Donovan nodded, unable to bring himself to say the words. VLM had never done this before. He hated to throw Dr. Pierce under the bus, especially while he was going after a tenure-track position and needed the publication. But if he didn't, that would result in an expensive lawsuit and be the end of his newspaper, his career, and his wealthy benefactor.

"Harry also doesn't face any SEC charges." It was the head editor's final play.

"Agreed." Symington smiled, as if he planned it all along.

He'd have to explain it to the others. It wasn't like they had a choice.

A loud crack ensued, and Donovan looked over. His laptop was broken in half, each part in a different hand of whoever Symington's partner was. That man flung both to the floor, cracking the screen in the process. Dewey Symington pretended not to notice. Donovan opened his mouth to speak, but one glare from the lawyer's tough-looking companion made him stay quiet and rethink calling the cops.

The VLM leader wasn't sure who Pierce had angered with his research. But he said a silent prayer for the communications professor. He'd need it now more than ever.

CHAPTER 26:
Friday, February 28

That evening, the Peach State College team celebrated at The Pirate House, a legendary restaurant on Broad Street in Savannah.

While the students looked at their cell phones for activities to do next month at regionals in New Orleans, Elena and Kat planned what to do in Savannah for the weekend. John Marshall Bradford II swapped seats with Nat so he could sit next to Jackson, and indicated he wanted to chat.

"Consider tonight's dinner on me," the CEO promised. "This was my favorite competition since Trey's basketball days."

Jackson sighed with relief. "Thanks. I am not sure we would otherwise have the funds to cover this *and* the ghost tour the kids want to do later."

"I'll take care of that too, if I can tag along," Bradford laughed. "Trey and I went on one in New Orleans with my wife when he was a kid."

After the appetizers arrived, Jackson's hand went to his chin contemplatively. "Speaking of New Orleans, that's where regionals will be held."

"Do they have a chance?" Bradford asked.

"Maybe," Jackson replied. "I read in a brochure that Georgia has one of the most competitive state contests in the region, if not the most. But the quality of their work isn't the issue."

"What is the problem?"

Jackson sighed. "It's Peach State College."

"I thought President Sullivan was a good guy," Bradford interrupted.

"It's not him," Jackson explained. "Our biggest obstacle is going to be Franklin Arbell. Our 'Higher Education Dean' has made it hard to be a faculty member, and harder still to get any money for scholarly purposes."

Jackson added his tale of the ordeal just to get funds for the Georgia Communications Conference trip in Savannah. "We lucked out… caught him when he wasn't ready. We expanded our dataset past where he thought we were, and he didn't have a response to the committee on that one."

"What happens next?"

"We have to go back to the Academic Funding Committee to try to get some money. There's no guarantee that we'll win a second time. Arbell might intimidate some faculty into voting against us, so we'll probably forfeit at the Southeast Communications Conference."

And it would be hard to tout the state victory with such a humiliating forfeit, Jackson sadly mused. *Goodbye tenure, if that's the case. Arbell will get his revenge.*

Bradford shook his head. "I am on the Pyramid Foundation in Alexandria." He went on to talk about the local businesses that contribute to their fund. "Make a good pitch, and I bet the board will vote to fund your trip."

Jackson sighed in relief. Ever since their win, he had been dreading how to pay for the regional competition, even offering to dip into the Pierce family savings, though Elena insisted that option should be a last resort. "We have the kids' college to consider," she reminded him.

He imagined the look on Arbell's face if he could outflank his superior again.

———

The PSC students dropped their discussion of New Orleans outings, turning their attention to their professor and Trey's father. "Okay, so we've figured out the shopping, which sites to hit, and the ghost tour," Taira announced.

"But what happens in New Orleans?" Nat asked.

Jackson held up his hands. "It's a full day's drive out and a full day back. So, there goes Tuesday and Friday. I doubt the admin would let us have those days."

"But Professor Pierce, isn't that Spring Break week?" Sylvia wondered aloud.

Their communications professor scratched his chin. "Come to think of it… it is! That's one thing we won't have to worry about." He pointed at his team. "You have to practice Monday before we leave, and Tuesday in the car. Stick around campus, if you can."

The food arrived, but no one even touched it at first. All of them were focusing on what Professor Pierce had to say.

"All undergraduates present on Thursday, even though the conference begins in New Orleans on Wednesday. The brochure says that there will be 12 states, four panels, and three presentations each. There'll be state winners from Georgia, Florida, and the Carolinas, plus Virginia, Tennessee, Alabama, Mississippi, Louisiana, as well as Texas, Arkansas, and Kentucky.

Piece continued, "We'll see who you draw on your panel. It's nice that here, they give first, second, and third-place trophies, but only the first-place team goes on to nationals to compete, though other finalists go to present. Nationals are held in D.C. every year during Easter Break, but it's worth it if we make it that far."

Paul slammed his palm on the table. "I don't know about you all, but I'm booking a trip to the Capitol for Easter Week Break!"

Howls of approval from the others broke out, even among the normally shy A.I.

"Ifwewin…"

"*When* we win," Sylvia corrected her.

"What… next?"

Jackson showed them the National Communications Conference brochure.

"At nationals, there are four regions: West, Midwest, South, and Northeast. The best of each of the four regions battle each other on Friday at the final panel of the day, and we learn about the winners on Saturday."

That night, an additional patron at The Pirate House sent a text to Dr. E. E. Kirby, which included who was at the PSC table. Hap Dixon added a few snippets of conversation, which would be relayed to the PPP headquarters.

<hr>

After the conference ended, Elena and Vivian went to look at the Savannah College of Art and Design, while Jackson and his son went off to nearby Pooler, Georgia, for the "Mighty 8th" Air Force Museum. Isaac had a paper and presentation to do for National History Day and he wanted all the evidence he could get.

"Check out the diorama, Isaac," Dr. Pierce began, but Isaac shook his head. He whipped out a cell phone camera and proceeded to slow-pan shots of the B-24 "Liberators" attacking the oil fields of Ploesti in Romania, helping grind down the Axis War Machine. He'd said earlier that his paper would be about how the Allies won the war with their bombing of oil supplies, not manufacturing plants in urban areas.

Jackson could hardly believe his eyes. Movies! His history assignments as a kid would be closer to the diorama.

The two headed back through the last section before the exit, where the special exhibits were. This time, there was a new display featuring the German products manufactured by factories that the Allies tried to bomb to undermine the war effort.

Isaac picked up a heavy iron explosive, thankfully a dud. "Dolintz Iron Works," he read out loud. "Dad… don't they make the pots and pans we use on our campouts?"

The kid didn't miss a trick. He noticed everything. "Yeah, I think so," Jackson stated.

"Why did we buy those from Dolintz if they helped the Nazis?"

The professor fumbled for an applicable lecture. "Well… they don't make bombs *now*. So, I guess they're okay."

His son was unconvinced. "But they helped our enemies back then, right? They have the same name."

Jackson studied the pamphlet nearby for more details. "It's a different leader in charge of the company now."

"But, it's the same family," Isaac continued.

Dr. Pierce nodded. "Yes, but they support good causes now. The Dolintz family donates to the Holocaust Museum, and…"

"Did they help Hitler come to power?"

His dad held up his hand, searching for an online history site. "It looks like they did back then."

"Why did they do that? Didn't they know better?"

Jackson stuffed his cellphone back into his pocket. "Hitler promised a lot of things to a lot of people. The economy was broken, and people were desperate for jobs and profits. They must have felt it was worth it, if only a few people needed to suffer. Maybe that's all the company leaders cared about. It's a good lesson for today, because history shows how terrible it can be when you follow someone like Hitler."

Isaac deleted a few items on his camera. "I'm changing my National History Day project, Dad. I now want to do it about the German companies who helped Hitler come to power, and why they did it."

BRANDED PART III:

March

CHAPTER 27:
Friday, March 7

The dorm phone rang at 4:00 p.m. in the common room. Nat Hinton's roommate and teammate, "Moose," made a wisecrack and fumbled an apology, stammering, "It's Guh-Green Bay!"

"Nat, this is Dodd West, Special Assistant to the G.M." Rather than talk football, the Packers executive asked more questions about Nat's academic activities.

"No offense, Dodd, but I thought we'd talk about football, the NFL, my college career, that kind of stuff."

The Packer draft specialist laughed. "We've seen the highlight reel of you from the Gator Bowl enough times. We know you can play ball. But, we need guys who can follow our playbook. Nowadays, you need a grad degree to follow these complex plays and decipher your opponents' schemes. We need someone who can do the kind of research you've done in your class."

Hinton was stunned. He hadn't considered that angle. Maybe he could make the NFL and earn enough to get his dad the treatment he needed. He couldn't wait to call his parents.

"That's not all," Moose said after Nat finished his call with the Packers. "On the voice mail, the New York Jets said they want you to fly up for a private workout."

The senior students all shared their stories for PSC's Public Relations Department about the Savannah conference, and their good news since.

Taira got an interview with "The Big Ten," Channel 10, the Fox affiliate from Atlanta. Sylvia had a Skype session with the Nashville School of Law. Paul held up an acceptance letter from the University of Southern California's graduate school in Communications.

Deb Hardiman with the P.R. Department looked over at Trey and A.I., the remaining team members. "And have you had any good news, Mr. Bradford and Ms. Sheehy?"

The two looked at each other. Their big news wasn't anything they could share with the Public Relations Department of the college. Yet..

======

"I appreciate you coming up, Trey," the CEO of Bradford Communications began a few days earlier. "And I'm glad you brought Miss Alicia. But I'm not sure you or she could do anything that we haven't already tried, or considered, before."

"Dad, Alicia Ina knows... well... a *lot* of cutting-edge stuff."

After firing off a string of rapid-fire words few non-techies could understand, she seated herself between the Korean computer whiz with tattoos all over her arms and the guy with the Cambridge T-shirt.

"So..." his mom wondered aloud, and Trey had a good idea of where this was going.

"No, Mom, it's not like that. Don't '*judge*' me."

She laughed.

Trey explained. "We call her A.I., because she likes to machine-program just for fun. We could have never gathered all of the data for our paper from all of those broadcasts without her."

Hours later, the head of IT came forward. "Not sure how we did it, but we got a patch. Edict 2.0 should be relatively hacker-proof, until we can figure out a new firewall."

"That's amazing," John Marshall Bradford II gawked as he looked at the printout, full of the data confirming the success of the patch.

Trey couldn't resist. "Did Alicia Ina help out?"

The IT department head paused. "Well, we had already made a lot of progress, but she was thinking next gen."

Trey's mom looked at her husband. "Hire her when she graduates… before someone else gets to her first."

———

A.I. held up her hand nervously. "Wha-what do we needtodo… now?"

The communications professor clicked a remote and the image of their paper showed up. Or, more accurately, what used to resemble their paper. Instead, it was covered with red markings and blue underlined paragraphs.

"You may not realize it, but this competition is as much written communication as it is oral communication. And your paper needs a lot of work. A sharp presentation alone won't win at regionals. And James LeBlanc's research team is waiting for us.

"Who's he?" Nat asked.

"LSU's Department of Communications Chair. His undergraduates have taken more regional awards than anyone else," Dr. Pierce explained.

"Damn," Sylvia muttered.

"They name the national award for best professor for undergraduate research after him."

Taira sighed out loud. "Well, at least we get a trip to New Orleans out of it."

Sgt. Paul shook his head. "I was looking forward to seeing Washington D.C. for the first time."

"Hey, hey!" Jackson surprised even himself with his loud tone. "Why are you quitting on yourselves? Where's all that swagger you had at Savannah? LeBlanc and his students are good, but they don't walk on water. You gotta get back in the trenches, fix the paper, tweak the presentation, and practice, practice, practice!"

All nodded.

"Hey guys," Paul began. "Let's divide up the responsibilities. I'll make a sign-up sheet for the sections to edit in Google Docs."

Each of them picked a section as Jackson smiled. He had hoped they would step up and own their research project and not rely on him to hold their hands throughout the process.

The way Dean Arbell was treating him, he wondered if his students needed to win it all at regionals.

Suzanne LeFleur, one of the secretaries in the administration building, opened the door and hissed loud enough for everyone in the room to hear, "Dean Franklin Arbell wants to see you in his office."

"Ooooohhhh…" several of his students intoned.

"Busted," Nat added, to laughs from others.

"Do you think he wants to congratulate you?" Taira asked.

"Hardly!" Sylvia snorted.

Jackson shrugged. "You all have this. I'll go see what he wants. Thanks, Suzanne." He gathered his laptop into his bag as the students returned to their editing. He smiled as Paul was pulling up a Google Calendar to set up presentation practice times.

As he reached the top floor of Callaway Administration Building, he heard a familiar voice.

"Jackson! Congratulations on the win. Did Elena and Vivian have a successful visit to Savannah colleges, or can we expect your daughter to remain here with us in Alexandria?"

"Well, you know how it is, President Sullivan," Jackson admitted. "Your own kids went to William & Mary."

"It is hard to convince the kids to stay where Mom and Dad teach," Alexander Sullivan admitted.

An audible cough interrupted their conversation.

"President Sullivan, if you wouldn't mind, I have need of a conversation with Professor Pierce," Franklin Arbell's tone was as unmistakable as his contempt for Peach State College's president.

"Of course," Sullivan's response was quick. "And how are the efficiency evaluations coming along?"

Dean Arbell's face froze, but only for a minute, as he recovered from the surprise reminder. "They will be ready in time for the Board meeting, President Sullivan."

He turned, flushed with anger at having been reminded. He couldn't wait to replace PSC's president, or to move on to a better college.

Alex gave a mischievous wink at Jackson when he saw his college's Higher Education Dean go back inside his office. The president's feelings for his subordinate were mutual.

"Guess he's not producing those reports as *efficiently* as he claimed," President Sullivan whispered. Jackson couldn't resist a smirk in response as he went in to see the Higher Education Dean.

Once inside his office, Arbell dismissed Ms. LaFleur with a well-practiced flick-of-the-wrist.

"Thanks, Suzanne, for bringing me over," Jackson added, earning a weak smile. The secretary just realized that she'd have to put in a lot of overtime because her boss was behind on those efficiency reports, and hoped the on-campus Pyramid Coffee Shop was still open.

Franklin frowned, then resumed his false smile. "I'm sorry, Professor Pierce. But with the Peach State College Sabers women's basketball team making the NCAA Tournament, I'm afraid there is no money left for your students to attend that regional conference in... New Orleans, is it? I hear those hotels can be quite expensive."

What Dean Arbell wasn't saying was that he'd used up the extra funds for that International Higher Education Consortium in Tokyo he'd booked for himself. Karen in Education had let that news slip at the last happy hour.

"I understand, Dean Arbell," Jackson smiled. "College funds are limited, and we do have to balance the budget."

Dean Arbell seemed confused about what to do next.

"Well, then... anything else?"

"No, I suppose not," Arbell managed.

Jackson stood up and headed out the door.

The Higher Education Dean paused, puzzled. Professor Pierce had just been told his team wouldn't be competing in regionals, and he actually took it rather well after fighting him on the funds for Savannah. Why wasn't he mad? Why did he seem so upbeat? What was his game? Was he trying to act nice so that he could get that tenure-track slot? If so, it was hopeless while he was at Peach State College.

CHAPTER 28:
Wednesday, March 12-Thursday, March 13

Shinnecock Hills on Long Island had hosted five U.S. Open golf tournaments. Today, Jeremiah Calhoun and his distinguished guests, Summit Movie Studio President Irv Tannen and director Hans Schoeffer, were playing.

"Nice four-iron," Tannen remarked to Wallace Bragg as the PPP's second-in-command hit his second shot onto the green.

Jeremiah Calhoun scowled. Nobody knew all of golf's tricks of the trade like he did.

"So... how's your latest film?" the CEO of PPP blurted as Tannen was making his swing. The question rattled the movie mogul just enough to have the iron shot land in a lake.

"Not so great," Irv admitted. "It's called 'Strong and Free,' a Canadian romance flick set in the modern-day wilds of the Alberta province."

Giving in to Calhoun's interest, Tannen pressed on. "It's the old 'rich-girl daughter of a ranch owner resists, then falls for 'tough-guy cowboy' who can't be tamed'. With all of the rewrites of the script, the whole premise is now a cliché. I guess I liked the Canadian angle too much to be thinking straight, or the chance to cast Giselle Robideaux."

Calhoun smiled. Working with the French-Canadian beauty would indeed be a dream, except for reports of her aloof and demanding behavior.

"And she's hardly the only problem," Hans growled in a thick accent.

"Dale Travis has the looks, but little else," Tannen moaned, now missing a short putt. "He lacks polish in his acting skills, is arrogant when dealing with everyone, and won't leave poor Giselle alone."

Wallace Bragg came over as the Summit Studios pair moved to the next hole. "I'm not so sure we can do anything for this company," he whispered to his boss.

"Patience, Mr. Bragg," Jeremiah counseled. Few knew how to work a "miracle" like Jeremiah Calhoun.

Calhoun glanced back at their caddies. Juan Fernandina was busy playing with his cell phone. Darcie Matthews was reading a spicy romance novel while lounging in the driver's seat of the golf cart. The cover of her book gave Calhoun a hint.

"How can we help you with product placement in your movie?" Calhoun asked.

"I'd like help," the portly producer replied. "Getting a product in theaters isn't the problem. It's getting cinemagoers to even *watch* it."

Jeremiah waved off his comment. "You worry about getting your film finished. I'll take care of the product placement." And, with a whisper to Bragg, he promised, "And my plan's 'bound' to succeed."

<hr>

While Juan Fernandina took the Summit Movie producers to the next hole, Jeremiah turned to Darcie Matthews in the golf cart. "What do you know about Dale Travis and Giselle Robideaux?"

She gave an exasperated sigh. "Dale's a 'Me Tarzan, You Jane' kind of guy, with looks and a boorish behavior."

"And the lady?"

Darcie shrugged. "She's good-looking, but she's also stuck-up and high-maintenance. They deserve each other."

Jeremiah mulled her words. "Think she'd ever fall for him?" Jeremiah offered.

"Only if he slipped something into her drink," she smiled, reminding herself how she did something similar for that hockey star who later crashed his car, part of a successful mission for PPP. "And even then, that would only work for a one-night stand."

"Maybe there's another way…" Jeremiah mused, glancing at her wild romance novel cover, featuring a pirate capturing a maiden.

=====

The golfers arrived at the next tee when Jeremiah asked, "So, Irv, how are you financing the film?"

Summit Movie's producer looked a little embarrassed. "Between Giselle's contract and demands, and continuously bailing Dale out of trouble, we're hemorrhaging money. I agreed to this golf round to see if you could help us bounce back."

After each hit their first shot, the four discussed every possible product from Giselle's wardrobe to Dale's truck. Some items, like the saddles, were dismissed as too small a market to make much money. The boots and hats worn by the actors and actresses held more promise. They started talking about Texas Paydirt, the company that produced both items.

During the discussion, Jeremiah flipped a quick hand signal to Fernandina, his caddie, who proceeded to put his golf bag over the CEO's ball, mired in a bad patch on the rough. In a practiced maneuver, Juan walked over to the fairway and casually dropped an identical model Titleist from his pocket into a perfect lie on the ground. As Wallace continued to engage their guests, Jeremiah struck the ball perfectly. Irv and Hans marveled at the flight of the ball.

Jeremiah grinned.

=====

"Is there anything… signature that either of your film leads uses or wears?" Wallace asked as they walked off the 17th hole. "Does Dale Travis have some sort of… gun? Cigarette? Bandana?"

Hans smirked. "He has a lady's scarf."

"What?" Jeremiah was stunned. "Why does he do that? Is it a 70s throwback?"

Irv shifted uncomfortably.

"It's like guys who put notches in their guns, or people who put them on their bedposts," Darcie said from the golf cart. "He has a different scarf from every actress he's bedded. He'll wear it until he takes another. It's his signal."

Wallace squinted. "Why a scarf?"

"You can see it clearly around his neck," Darcie sighed. "So can the other ladies. So can the tabloids. So can his exes. It's always a specific type of scarf, from a brand called Knotty Scarves," she said, then laughed. "See, I've got one." She unwound it from her neck and passed it to the men.

"Looks like any other," Wallace observed.

"The silk is soft," Darcie pointed out. "It has the KS logo, too."

"And deceptively strong," Hans admitted. "You could not rip this one so easily."

"Gentlemen… and lady," Jeremiah began. "We need a shocking pre-film scandal, to make the publicity for the movie incredible. People won't want to miss the show. That's when we make our move to ensure they not only buy tickets, but the products in the cinematic feature, as well. It's how we do business."

———

On the bleak set of the film, set an hour from Edmonton, Giselle shivered in her coat outside, which was created more for the style than to keep her warm in the Alberta climate. She stood next to the movie trailer at the edge of the ranch compound, cigarette in hand, not allowed to smoke inside.

"*Fascists!*" she audibly groaned.

Even the most optimistic of the film crew knew this was going to be a bomb, a bad mark on everyone's record, and no slick acting or last-minute cameo was going to change that. For Giselle, it went from bad to worse.

"Notice anything different about me?" the cowboy approaching her began. He wore a Stetson, boots, Levi's, and something that resembled a buckskin jacket.

"Everything looks the same," the actress remarked. "Unless you're showing me that you finally did your laundry."

Dale Travis resisted the urge to smack her.

The actress who played Giselle's sister in the movie whispered into the female lead's ear.

She nodded at the actress and replied, "It looks as though you are keeping that crude tradition of wearing that certain scarf, when all it does is reveal your insecurity."

"They all want it," Travis snapped.

"Do you have one with my name on it?"

"Giselle, one day I'm gonna make you mine!"

By now, a small crowd was growing, even with the blizzard on its way. The shouting match was too intriguing.

"You couldn't force me to!" The actress' blazing eyes matched her tone.

Travis scratched his stubble where a beard was trying to make up its mind whether to go full length or be shaved off.

"Maybe one day, I might try!" He spun on his boot heel and stalked off in the opposite direction.

CHAPTER 29

Friday, March 14

The professor and his students headed from Alexandria's library in the heart of Peach State College to Pyramid Coffee's iconic production facility ten kilometers to the south, passing the town's multipurpose exercise path; good for walkers, cyclists, and joggers.

Today wasn't about running a race, but a race for funds. After his narrow escape from the committee with enough dollars for Savannah, Professor Jackson Pierce knew he couldn't trust that the school's money would be there again. Dean Franklin Arbell engineered the election of a toady of his to serve on the Academic Funding Committee in his place. Elena had told him that last detail, which prompted the trip to the Pyramid Foundation. He had to worry that it could be his job, not just funds, that would be at stake.

"I feel nervous asking these corporate types for money," Jackson admitted.

"And you think it's easier getting college funds from Scrooge McFranklin?" Elena shot back. "You'll do fine. I picked your outfit, didn't I?"

As the giant pyramid that served as a production facility and headquarters to one of the fastest-growing coffee companies in the world loomed ahead of them, Sgt. Paul Herrera asked from the back of the van "So, what's the story behind the geometric shape?"

For years, the southside of Alexandria had been neglected, with abandoned textile mills, shotgun houses falling into disrepair, and boarded-up schools south of the East-West railroad tracks. But that all changed in the 1940s, when Amos Beauchamp came to town. The heir to the Pyramid Company had signed up to fight during World War II and was assigned to Ft. George Thomas. After earning a Silver Star at Anzio in Italy, he returned determined to build a new headquarters for the company in Alexandria. He raised eyebrows everywhere by hiring African-American workers long before the Supreme Court ruled on *Brown v. Board of Education of Topeka, Kansas.*

Some old-timers complained, but they remained few in number after Beauchamp spread the wealth around town. His sister Dottie oversaw the 100th anniversary of the Alexandria Library, committing money and input with her art degree to make it the highlight of the Peach State College campus.

As they arrived at the gates of the Pyramid, a cheery guard waved them through. With his other hand, he held the signature mug with the red triangle on it, with black lettering reminding viewers who produced the drink.

———

Once inside, they were met by a white-haired gentleman in a formal gray suit and black tie.

"Ted Beauchamp," he introduced himself. "Let me give you the five-cent tour while we wait for the others."

He showed them the grinders, roasters, and all types of other machines inside the facility.

"We call this one the Ferrari," he spoke softly, though he was clearly animated by the experience.

"Why?" Taira asked. "Is it because it's bright red, like a Ferrari?"

"No, dearie," chirped an elderly lady with a British accent. "It's because it costs as much as a Ferrari!"

She introduced herself as Anne Beauchamp, Ted's wife. "British ex-pat from the African continent."

"So where do they grow the beans?" Sylvia asked. "They're not from Georgia, are they?"

"We get ours from Puerto Rico," Ted noted. "Kick-starting that operation really helped their economy after the last hurricane. But demand is outstripping supply, so we've started buying from Costa Rica, Tanzania, and soon, Rwanda."

Anne pointed dramatically at a map. "That's where I come in. I was working at a plantation outside Arusha in East Africa. Ted had come to Tanzania to buy the Ferrari. He got me in the bargain too, though he certainly didn't *purchase* me." She patted his hand.

———

A secretary popped her head into the door. "The other Pyramid Foundation members are starting to arrive."

The Beauchamps led the professors and students into a conference room that would be the envy of any corporation. Seated around the room were several well-dressed individuals.

"Alfonso Hargraves!" Trey gasped, then reddened in embarrassment at gaping over the famed jazz trumpet player, who normally spent most of his time in Atlanta. His Hargraves Amphitheater on the east side of Alexandra provided a venue for nighttime concerts of local bands, with the occasional free performance by Hargraves on Labor Day.

Around the room, they met Danny Yarborough, CEO of the last remaining textile mill that was still open. But Yarborough's operation survived due to environmentally-friendly production. Also on the Pyramid Foundation was Dustey Wheeler of the Wheeler Horse Stables on the Westside. Her family's thoroughbreds became famous after her "Prize Peach" became one of the few fillies to ever win the Belmont Stakes. Rounding out the Foundation's Executive Leadership Committee was Wen Lee Yim, the elderly CEO of Taipei Tires, with a base off the industrial park in the Southeast rim of town.

Sylvia moved toward the laptop Jackson had set down, clicking the button to fire up the device, but Yarborough held up his hand. "That won't be necessary today, ma'am," he said in a thick Southern twang.

She looked confused, halting her actions.

"Don't you want to see our presentation?" Paul asked.

"We already read your paper." Wheeler pointed to her copy of the essay.

"And we have seen a video of your presentation in Savannah," Yim added.

"So… what would you like us to do?" Paul asked, unsure where the conversation was going.

Hargraves leaned forward. "What we don't know from you," he began with his deep baritone voice. "Is who you are."

———

Each of the six undergraduates exchanged looks that conveyed surprise and worry. Jackson looked similarly unprepared.

Having received no direction, Sylvia elected to go first. "I'm Sylvia Wright. I'm from Clifton, Georgia, which some of you might not know about. I went to Frederick Douglass High School, and… our town's being run into the ground. Our neighborhood's been victimized by a local government which pretends the Civil Rights Act and Voting Rights Act never passed. So, when I was a high school senior, they passed the hat at the congregation, so to speak, and scraped up enough to send me to Peach State College so I can get a college degree, go to law school, and sue the hell out of those people who have kept us down our whole lives."

"I've heard of it."

Everyone looked at Hargraves in surprise. "I was born there, so I know a little about life in Clifton. I moved to Alexandria when I was ten. How's your law school search going?"

Sylvia froze. "M-my LSATs aren't too bad, and my grades are good. But there are so many applicants that the counselors are saying my file better be a little stronger. I'm in student government, but this kind of conference experience could make the difference."

"I'm also in student government," Trey picked up the baton. "My name's John Marshall Bradford, and you know my family name. You've got an idea of what I'm going to do after graduation. But companies like Bradford Communications could learn some of the research skills I'm developing in this project, and one day I'll have to stand before the board, explaining why we're doing something."

The Pyramid Foundation Board nodded in agreement.

"Nat Hinton," the next student began. "Some of y'all know I hope to make it in the NFL, if you've seen our games, or watched ESPN. But I'm a long shot for the pros. I've always been interested in communications. Now, I'm realizing there's so much more to it than this."

"What do you mean?" Wen Lee Yim queried.

"Thanks to this research project, I see a lot of Next-Gen statistics, how the whole game can change with math. Maybe there are ways we can apply the data to subjects beyond sports, too. I can see kids in my high school getting into math the way I have in my classes."

Danny Yarborough nodded enthusiastically. He worshiped the movie "Moneyball."

Nat then proceeded to tell the story of his dad, his injury from his trucking days, and the seemingly endless pile of medical bills. "I have to earn something to help with his care."

Taira Malek moved to her stage in front of the podium. She treated them to her story of coming over from Lebanon with her parents, dreams of being a broadcaster. "I still want to be one. But it's not just about being on camera… at least not anymore. Our findings have me thinking about how easily news anchors can manipulate the system, what we watch, and what we buy. Maybe, knowing what I know, I can change some of that."

There was a pause as the foundation members took in what Taira was saying. Paul stepped in to fill the void. "My name is Paul Herrera. Before I started at PSC, I was in Iraq, getting an education the hard way." He told them what a struggle it was to serve during a full-blown civil war.

"I'm now a senior in communications. My dad, who's an officer, wants me to go back into the military after I graduate, but frankly, I'm looking to get a master's degree, maybe even a PhD. This class has shown me that this is what I want to do for a career. There are so many more things we can study on this topic." He exchanged glances with Jackson, who looked totally unprepared for this revelation. "I'm applying this spring to a couple of colleges… I'll be needing your letter of recommendation, Dr. Pierce."

The scholar nodded, still taking in the news.

"And what about you, hon?'" Dustey asked Alicia.

A.I. could only look at her shoes. Paul sighed while Sylvia took her hands. "She's shy…"

"Ah, I can see that…"

"She shouldn't have to…"

"No… that's all right." Alicia Ina surprised her classmates. In a soft voice, she began to speak. "I-ah-I don't have a great plan like everyone else here. To be honest, I don't even have a family. They died…"

It got very quiet.

"You can do this, A.I." Trey whispered. He hoped the committee didn't hear him.

"I just wanted to help my classmates. That's all. I know a lot about c-c-computers, putting artificial intelligence to good use to collect a ton of data." She breathed slowly, then continued. "I l-l-like the findings, of course, and the manipulation and stuff. But for the first time since I… lostmyparents… I feel like I have a f-family with my five classmates."

Nobody said anything. The committee members exchanged knowing glances.

"Normally, we have to have a formal meeting to discuss the matter, make it official," Ted Beauchamp's voice broke the silence. "I see no reason to wait. You'll have our backing for the trip to regionals…"

The students and both Pierces' broke out in cheers.

"…and for nationals, if you win…"

CHAPTER 30:
Saturday, March 15

A clink on the glass doors leading to the balcony startled Giselle Robideaux. Probably just another acorn dropping from the tree onto the wooded lodge where she was staying near the set. But a minute later, there was a louder crack in the same location. Tiny shards of glass fell from the doors. A small stone accompanied them. *What the hell…*

She threw open the door, ready to scream at whoever the intruder was below, looked off the balcony, and instantly regretted it. Tugging at her lilac silk robe, she pulled it over herself, but not before the man she despised more than anyone else in the world got a good look at her black lingerie.

"You better have a damn good reason for doing that, Dale Travis," she yelled. *That's the last time he ever sees what I wear to bed*, she told herself.

"I love your French accent when you're mad!" he called out.

Dale's affable demeanor changed to surprise, as he had to dive to the right to avoid a flower pot that whizzed past him, shattering on the rock behind him.

"What was that about?"

"You broke my window… and interrupted my sleep!"

"Sorry about the rock, but the acorn didn't seem to wake you…"

"And I don't want to talk to you at this hour," she insisted. "I can barely speak to you in the daytime when we're on the set. I can't wait for this picture to end, so I never have to speak to you again!"

Dale gritted his teeth. This wasn't going according to plan at all.

===

An hour ago, when he was in the honkytonk, the blonde he shared a drink with had given him what he thought was good advice.

As he stared at the remains of his fourth beer, she had shown up with a cold one of his favorite brand, Shiner Bock, a drink they didn't serve in their little town near the ranch.

"Where did you get that?" he gasped as she held out one of the two bottles.

"Consider me a fan." Darcie grinned. "I saw you with one on your Instagram page."

"In Texas, I fell in love with this beer," Travis remarked. He pretended to glance at the bottle label but was actually checking out her legs.

Pig! Darcie thought.

"How'd you get it, Miss…?"

"Call me Daphne," Darcie cooed. *Dale was certainly hotter in person,* she thought. "I'm an exec with Summit Pictures, coming out to check on the film. I know a liquor store in Calgary that carries it, so I got a six-pack in case I ran into you."

A moment later, she saw why he had his reputation. Or rather, she felt it, as his hand gripped her thigh. It was hard enough to rip her hose. *Oh, great.*

Darcie politely, but firmly, guided his hand away. "As flattered as I am by this attention, I get the feeling you've got some other lady on your mind. Curly hair, reddish-brown color, nearly six-feet tall in heels, French accent?"

She saw he finally looked less than confident.

"Yeah… but it's not going so well," he admitted. *Maybe she could even give him some help,* he thought. "Every woman I meet can't resist me, but she's the first to say no. Why?"

The PPP employee could give him twenty reasons why she'd never go out on a first date with him. But that wasn't her mission. She'd have to build up his confidence tonight, so he'd make another play for Giselle.

"I'll help you get the girl," Darcie promised. "Summit Studios would love a romance between their best actor and actress."

"How?" the Texan inquired. "I've tried everything I know, but nothing works."

The blonde smiled. "Well, you probably tried everything *a man* knows, but maybe you need *a woman's* advice."

"Sure," Dale drawled. "At this point, I'll try anything!"

Darcie rolled her eyes. This mansplainer was going to get exactly what he deserved. She drew a breath dramatically, as if revealing a national secret.

"Women want a man who won't take 'no' for an answer when it comes to pursuing them and sweep her…"

Travis interrupted. "But she keeps giving me the cold shoulder!"

The blonde's eyes flashed mischievously. "That's because she's testing you, to see how committed you really are. She knows how much other women want you and can count the number of different scarves you wear in a week like any other gal. She won't say yes until you go for broke, and let her know she's the one for you and no one else will do!"

———

Dale said the words that Daphne, the blonde in the bar, told him. But when he insisted Giselle was the only one for him, and a "no" wouldn't do, the other flower pot on the balcony came whizzing down, missing him by inches.

He barked, "If I can't have you, nobody else will!" with a roar that seemed to wake up the rest of the house. Travis then realized how bad it sounded. *It was the beer… or beers… talking.* He scurried away, out of the floodlights. It was time to head to his favorite spot on the set, the rock that overlooked the valley, to consider his next move.

———

Giselle slammed the balcony doors so hard that the rest of the glass on the right side broke. She needed something strong to calm down her nerves, and the Rothschild she had spotted in the wine rack earlier that day would do. As she headed downstairs, she was still furious…

Suddenly, a rag clamped over her face! With a panic, she guessed what that sickening sweet smell was. Her right arm was useless, pulled back behind her body, the left arm pinned ineffectively behind the attacker's arm. No doubt, he was trying to render her unconscious, and after that, who knew.

"Ah told you that you'd be mine, and ah meant it!" the Texas accent hissed, leaving her wide-eyed with panic. As she lost consciousness, she wished she had been wearing her stilletos instead of the comfy pink slippers she was wearing as she kicked him.

Dale jumped into his truck, hatching his plan. He'd rush back to the bar and see if Daphne was still there. No more Giselle for him. Daphne's advice was good, but it didn't work on that stuck-up…

The blue lights flashing in his rearview mirror startled him. He had been drinking, and this wasn't Texas, where a smile and an autograph was what he needed to get his way out of a ticket or court.

What did Canada have anyway… cops? Troopers? Mounties?

The officer tapped on his window, indicating he should roll it down.

"Shore, oci-officer. What seems to be the problem?"

"Sir, have you been drinking this evening?"

"Don't you know who I am?" Dale Travis asked.

"Sir, if you were really that famous, you wouldn't have ask that question, eh?"

The cowboy groaned. There was at least one smart one. He hoped Summit Studios would pay the fine and bail him out, if necessary.

"We need to do a sobriety test," the cop insisted. Travis wedged his way out of the vehicle and lined up at the ready.

The second officer laughed. "This doesn't exactly look like your debut with this sort of thing."

Dale smiled and shrugged. He hoped he did well enough to fool them.

At that moment, all standing in front of the Tonneau Cover over the trunk bed could hear a tapping from inside the trunk bed, followed by some muffled sounds. Both the suspect and officers looked at each other; it was difficult to determine who was more surprised.

"Well, that sounds like probable cause," the first officer said to his partner. He reached in and yanked the keys from the ignition, tossing them to the second officer.

"Hey… *hey!*" Travis yelled. But the rhythmic banging from underneath the cover trunk bed was unmistakable. It was obvious the sounds from the depths of the vehicle were made by a person. The officer fumbled with the truck tailgate, but eventually worked it open to reveal under the truck cover…

Giselle Robideaux, wearing a purple robe and black lingerie, sporting a Knotty Scarf between her teeth, tied behind her hair. Reaching into the truck bed, the officers found an identical Knotty Scarf binding her wrists behind her back, while a third scarf secured her ankles.

Though she was wiggling around as much as she could, switching between muffled pleas for release and angry grunts of frustration, the officers seemed in no hurry to free her. One produced a small camera and took pictures of the damsel-in-distress, while the other trained his gun on a shocked Dale Travis, who could only gasp, "What'n the hell?!"

Once her legs and arms were freed, Giselle pulled the scarf from around her neck, and gasped, "It was Dale Travis who kidnapped me! I heard his voice as he abducted me."

═══

From the crest of a hill nearby, Ray, Darcie, and Larry watched the proceedings. The two men each had binoculars and relayed their observations to their co-worker.

"Did you make sure to use the Southern accent when you chloroformed her?"

"Of course, Darcie," Ray said.

"And you used the Knotty Scarves we found in his hotel room to tie and gag her?"

"We didn't forget, Darce."

"Case should be pretty strong against him," she mused.

"Best job with PPP ever," Ray admitted, savoring the experience of trussing up and silencing one of the best-known females on film.

They may have bound up poor Giselle, Darcie mused, but Dale Travis would find himself the real captive in hot water in the end.

CHAPTER 31:
Monday, March 17

A beep came from Kat Roemer's cell phone, a message for the editor of the *Savannah Herald-Post*. She groaned as she read the text. "Send him in."

Roemer's tone remained annoyed as the attorney strolled in confidently. "Ah, Dewey Symington. And here I thought I smelled a garbage scow sailing by."

Symington sniffed indignantly. "Charming comment, my dear... as crude as the ladies who walk the streets at night."

"I bet _you'd_ know how crude they are," Kat shot back, and Symington's anger flashed in his eyes. "So... 'Slymington,' who are you suing today?" she snapped.

"You, unless you pull that sequel to Jackson Pierce's story, and print a retraction, as I instructed in my phone message yesterday."

Kat's hands slammed onto her hips angrily. "I heard you twisted Matt's arm at VLM and scared a bunch of newspapers to walk back that story."

"My client feels like your tabloid-like trash impugns them," Symington bellowed.

"Wow, you used the word 'impugn,'" Kat mocked. "I'm impressed. Did you learn a new word in legal night school?"

Symington exhaled loudly, as if trying to dispel something from his mouth. "It sounds like you won't listen to our reasonable request. Instead, you prefer the potential for bankruptcy. Expect our filing later today, then."

Kat tapped her foot on the floor impatiently. "Just what's your interest in all of this... *Dewey*? Who's your real client?"

The gray-suited attorney opened the door so all her reporters, ad people, and secretaries could hear him. "The Blanchard and Gentry Syndicate will only be able to defend your reckless editorial policies for so long, Katherine Roemer. They got hit pretty hard during the Great Recession. A big loss to our firm in court will force them to file for bankruptcy!"

In response, the editor picked up a green Tulane mug from her desk and hurled it through the door. He screamed and held up his attaché case to deflect the incoming object. But the mug was made of foam, not a ceramic one. Roars and squeals of laughter emerged from the newsroom as Symington reddened. "You'll pay!"

"Well, I don't know about pain, but you are suffering… a *lot* of embarrassment," Andy Van Kamp, the Sunday columnist, roared to the delight of co-workers.

Symington paused, hurled a crumpled piece of paper into the trash, and then stalked off the floor, slamming the door behind him. Kat almost wished the glass had broken, so she could charge him for damages.

———

A slight cough from behind the door made Kat wince. Bob… She forgot to check, again. Her sly star reporter had once again hidden in her office for a confidential meeting, hoping to get a story assignment.

"So, what did you hear?"

"Nothing much, except demands for retractions, threats of lawsuits, and other newspapers being forced to say uncle," Bob Carlson said in a dramatic tone. "When can I start writing?"

Carlson was a pit bull; once he sank his teeth into a story, he never let go. Ten years ago, he got Pulitzer nominations while covering politics in Washington, D.C.. Then, he thought he had caught a Michigan Congressman from the House Ways and Means Committee red-handed in a bribery scandal for padded contracts. But his enemies set him up, feeding him false information.

That fall from grace a few years ago was spectacular. He went from a memorable byline, covered by many papers, to being dropped from every media outlet that once ran his material. A visit to a cousin in Savannah led him to Kat. Stunned at discovering the former legend sitting at a bus stop, she offered him a job on the spot. He accepted, more out of desperation than anything else. He rebuilt his career, slowly but surely, plotting his comeback. One good, national-breaking story should do it.

"I want in on this one."

Kat rolled her eyes in frustration. She knew once Bob found a lead, he wouldn't let go.

"Okay," she sighed.

"Tell me the details." Bob whipped out a small device, an Edict. He wasn't old school.

"A few weeks ago, *Veritas Lux Mea...*"

"VLM?"

"They're a publication that runs works by scholars, and then newspapers can pick stuff for their editorial page or columns. They're from Atlanta, and I know their editor, Matt Donovan."

Kat continued. "He ran an article written by my sister's husband, Jackson Pierce, and his students. Jackson's a communications professor at Peach State College in Alexandria. According to my sister, Elena, some people at his college are giving him a rough time."

"Can I talk to him?"

"Of course. Talk to his students, too. They were researching product placement in the news. One of his brainy kids created an algorithm, and the kid-scholars used stats from class to write a great paper. They won a college contest at a Savannah conference with that paper."

"And VLM did a story about it?"

"Yeah…. Jackson sent it to VLM and they published it. So did newspapers across the country, from California to Connecticut. VLM was going to do a follow-up story, but then Dewey Symington's mystery client kicked down the door. He got Matt to pull the story from VLM and issue a retraction and apology. Symington also forced most papers to pull the article, express regret for running it, and not run part two. But I'm not throwing my brother-in-law under the bus. I'll call Blanchard and Gentry at the HQ…"

"That's actually why I want to do this story."

Kat looked at Bob Carlson. She knew he wanted this story, but didn't know why.

"I'm tired of journalists playing defense. It's time we play offense, go after those jerks and expose them." *And I want to be the one to break the story and get back to covering our nation's capital,* he thought.

CHAPTER 32:

Tuesday, March 18

"**I**s this Franklin Arbell?" The smooth voice of Professor E. E. Kirby was unmistakable.

The Higher Education Dean began with praise, but Kirby cut it short. "Dean Arbell, while I appreciate your flattery, we still have a problem: Jackson Pierce."

That makes two of us, the administrator thought. "I thought you shut down his articles in the press."

"Yes," Kirby said. "But he's conducting that same research with his students… the type that was cut from papers and retracted. This cannot be allowed."

As Arbell contemplated a solution, Dr. Kirby thundered on. "He's taking them to a regional competition with their research. If they manage to win, however unlikely, it'll generate more publicity, especially if they go on to present at the nationals."

Peach State College's Higher Education Dean insisted, "You are right. We have to stop him from competing."

Kirby continued. "If you pull this off, I may be able to visit, perhaps as a graduation speaker or distinguished presenter, which will be good for your fundraising."

Arbell was positively beaming right now on the conference phone, coming in loud and clear over the speaker. "Yes, yes, of course."

"So, what is your plan?" Kirby inquired.

Arbell told him about attempts to block the communications professor in the Academic Funding Committee, and how many friends Jackson had on campus.

"May I suggest a 'Peer Review Committee'," Professor Kirby offered.

"Wha-what would that involve?" Arbell asked nervously.

"A Peer Review Committee would involve collegiate experts, preferably from outside your school. I can suggest some panelists who would ensure that Professor Jackson Pierce won't be able to publish any more research or get his students to do so."

Arbell smiled. *That would be a great start.* He wanted Pierce fired, but some sort of suspension, or any mark against the communications professor, would be a great start.

Kirby pressed his case. "May I suggest a few members of this committee? I assure you that they are all prestigious."

"Yes, I would like to hear who you have in mind."

Kirby grinned, then added. "The first name is Dr. Doris DeVaughn, who is currently the president of Southern Senators School. I assume you know her."

Peach State College's second-in-command swallowed. Dr. DeVaughn was almost as well known for her frequent newspaper columns, extolling the virtues of virtual classes. Rumor had it she was popping up on short lists for Secretary of Education.

"And there is Peter Sheldon," Kirby continued.

Franklin's jaw dropped. The powerful Atlanta developer was the former Chair of the Board of Regents for all public colleges, including PSC.

Arbell was now profusely sweating. "And the third?" he managed to add.

"Why, *me*, of course."

"You'd do that for us?"

"It is important that we take care of this Professor Pierce problem right away," Dr. Kirby explained. "And, as promised, I would be willing to help with a fundraising dinner for donors and impress your undergraduates with a special lecture."

The Dean was in heaven. "Yes… yes of course. When do you want the committee…"

"Next Tuesday."

"But that's not much time, Doctor…"

The professor's tone became sharper. "That is the week Professor Pierce and his students are scheduled to present at the regional conference. If you schedule this hearing for that time, he can't go. And without an official representative from the college, he and his team will be disqualified, unable to present."

"I can approve that."

"Moreover," Kirby went on. "We can focus on the termination of contract employee Jackson Pierce… at another time." He let those words hang in the air.

———

A few minutes later, the Higher Education Dean burst through his door, which had been ajar. Suzanne LaFleur, his secretary, gaped at him, not used to seeing this display of emotion. "Dean Arbell, can I help you with some–"

"I need you for several hours of emergency work," he snapped. "We have a special group of educators coming, and we need to prepare for their arrival immediately."

He did not tell her about the Peer Review Committee, which would need to remain a secret. He didn't want Jackson or Elena Pierce, or any of their allies among the faculty and staff, to hear about it.

An email from Kirby's account confirmed that the professor would contact the other two peer members. *He probably wants to ensure how they vote*, Arbell had concluded.

In his haste, he had failed to notice the thin college student who was standing behind the door. But Taira Malek had heard every word, silently listening to a most *illuminating* conversation. She was shocked. Dean Arbell was plotting with someone named Kirby on the other line on how to get rid of her professor, Jackson Pierce. Though her instructor was tough on papers and assigned way too much reading, she liked her go-getter teacher and believed their class project would help further her broadcasting career.

"Miss Malek, are you finished with your graduation petition?"

She spun around to answer Ms. LaFleur's question. "Yes, I'm finished here."

═══

"How was your day?" Elena asked, crashed out on her recliner as Jackson stumbled into the house.

"Want the truth, or do you want me to stretch it?" her husband sighed.

"She wants you to lie, Dad," Vivian joked, following behind him.

Elena smiled as she finished adding lettuce and tomatoes to the sandwiches. "I see you didn't forget my daughter from her work at Archetype this time. How was the coffeehouse shift, Viv?"

"Only one spill this time, but I did burn a full pot." She shook her head. "My academic pursuits have not prepared me for mundane tasks."

Isaac laughed. "Just don't tell the Pyramid Coffee Company you wasted a single drop. They might not let Dad go to New Orleans."

"Speaking of which," Jackson added as he sat down at the table. "We have to coordinate that."

Elena thumbed through her Google Calendar. "Indeed, we do. Somebody has to stay here with Isaac."

"What?!" Isaac almost spit out the bagel he was munching on. He looked at his mom in horror.

"Don't you want to be in the tennis competition?" Jackson asked.

"Well, yeah," his son laughed. "But I really want to go back to New Orleans. If I win in straight sets, could we rent a helicopter?"

"You must not know what college professors get paid." Elena shook her head. "The point is, only one of us can go."

"Mom?" Vivian piped up.

"You can take the other *adult's* place if you don't have work that weekend."

Vivian decided to forego her usual rant about not being considered an adult. "I'll see if I can switch with Stefon."

The sound of Star Wars music filled the room. Jackson grinned. "I had turned off my phone earlier, and it looks like I missed a text."

"Who's it from, hon?" his wife asked, as the kids focused on the turkey and cheese hoagies she had prepared for dinner.

Jackson stared at his phone.

"Jackson?"

"It's… it's from Taira Malek."

"Your student." Elena frowned, pretending to be jealous. "From the presentation. What does *she* want… at this time of night?"

Jackson's look showed it wasn't time to joke anymore.

CHAPTER 33:

Thursday, March 20

"Jackson Pierce? This is Gordon Henry."

The communications professor almost dropped his campus phone. What did the lead blogger from the website "Restless" want with him?

"Care to comment on how dozens of newspapers are pulling your column and printing retractions?" Jackson could almost hear the reporter puffing away on his trademark stogie.

Jackson paused for a moment, collecting his thoughts before responding. "I haven't heard why. They haven't emailed me an explanation yet."

But it always seemed to Jackson that Gordon was one step ahead of those he interrogated. He would have to be careful.

"Sources say your data is fabricated."

"It isn't," Dr. Pierce shot back.

"Then share your data with us via email."

"I'd be happy to meet with any authorities on that matter," Jackson said.

"And you may get that chance," Gordon happily replied, and then added. "Is it true that you've exploited your students to make money for this?"

Now it was the college professor's chance to get the upper hand. "I didn't make a dime from VLM, or from any other paper. Nor did my students."

Gordon sneered. "That's not what I will write."

"And that clicking sound comes from my recording of this conversation," Jackson beamed, glad he had that function installed on the college's phone.

The blogger's silence was worth it. "Perhaps the media would like to hear this recording," Jackson continued. For once, it was Gordon Henry who slammed down the phone in disgust. *Finally, a win for our side*, Jackson thought.

———

The students were meeting for the first time since Taira sent word about the shadowy "Peer Review Committee".

"Knowing Dean Arbell, he'll summon me for the conference the week of your presentation in New Orleans, if not just days before," Jackson groaned as the students asked him about it.

"Can he figure that out?" Sgt. Paul Herrera asked.

"Unfortunately, yes," their professor admitted. "The conference details are posted online. That's how we all know when you're going, the day, time, and who the discussant is."

Nat looked hopeful. "Can we get President Sullivan to help?"

Their professor shook his head. "He's got his hands full with an accreditation review. It's probably another reason why Dean Arbell is making his move against us now."

Trey popped his head up. "I've been looking at the website on my laptop. It says we need a faculty advisor to be present at the conference and at our talk. What're we going to do?"

Their professor held up his right hand. "I don't know. By the way, we're at the Hyatt Regency. Pyramid Coffee's Foundation paid for it already."

"So, have you figured out who's going to take us?"

"Working on that."

Trey jumped in. "Who's making our lives so difficult?"

"PPP," a female voice called out.

All looked at A.I., even though she was buried in her laptop.

"Preston Powell Partnership," she clarified.

"Yeah, but how do you know they're the ones making us miserable?"

Jackson moved over to look behind his students. "We already knew from your research that USBC is showing the biggest product spikes."

"Yes. I lookedatthe companies that were mentionedthe most... Five of the six, including theweekend updates."

"Wait... you are still running numbers?" Nat gasped.

"Yes... m-more data." Sheehy proceeded to explain, listing SRD, the sleeping pills, the Gyrfalcon car from Talladega Motors, the Miracle, Summit Studios, and Knotty Scarves. "And-and they're all wuh-with PPP."

"What's the one not on the PPP list?"

"Not sure about MyCycle. It must have been for that blood doping scandal," Trey responded.

Jackson jumped in. "Say A.I... I mean, Alicia. How did you know that these are all clients of PPP?"

A.I. grinned. "Of theten wealthiest ad firms, they were the hardest... t-to hack."

"Alicia Ina Sheehy! Did you break into their...?"

"Well, I wantedtoknow if therewas a connection!" she blurted out.

Nat gaped. "Isn't that... you know... illegal?"

"They won't catchme," she laughed. "If they l-l-learn thatthey were spoofed, they'll think it was some big beefy Serbian!"

Paul glanced at her write-up. "PPP's clients pay a lot more than market value for what they receive," he intoned. "And they're more likely to appear in the news."

The class hacker beamed triumphantly. "Case solved!"

"Yeah, but is this something we can prove in a court of law?" Professor Pierce added. "And could we even use this evidence you obtained by hacking?"

A.I. could only offer a sheepish grin.

"What did Arbell mean by you being a 'contract employee'?" Taira asked.

"They could fire you right now... like... *today*?" Paul asked.

He nodded.

"They can't!" Sylvia demanded. "That's so… unfair!"

Their professor shrugged. "My wife's got tenure. But yeah… this is kind of like, everything for me."

Nat clapped his teacher on the back. "We promise to do our best at the next competition to help you get it."

Pierce lowered his head. "Thank you so much. It means a lot to me."

———

Meanwhile, the parents of their students were getting a very different education.

"Major George Herrera?"

"Sir?"

"You're being deployed to Qatar."

The officer's jaw dropped. He relished getting back in the field, but this sounded like transporting his job to a different location halfway across the world. And it was right in the middle of the semester for his wife, and just before his son's college graduation.

The caller sensed his hesitation. "We need a communications officer a lot closer to the Middle East than back here at CENTCOM HQ. You specifically are the one we need."

"I understand. It's just that my wife is a teacher…"

"I'm sorry, but we have no available education position for her on the base."

"She's going to finish up her obligations…"

"Then you'll have to go alone," the voice interrupted. "She'll have to wait until her semester is done, and then, we still may not get clearance until late July."

"Will I be able to visit my son's college graduation?"

"I'm glad you brought up your son. He's engaging in some controversial research, isn't he?"

"Wha-wait! Where is this coming from?"

"Get him to drop his research, and you don't have to go to Qatar."

"Listen, you…"

Then the line went dead. Maj. George Herrera dreaded telling his wife they would be apart for a long time. But someone was targeting their son.

———

"John Marshall Bradford II?"

"Speaking."

"You are now facing an IRS Audit."

Bradford laughed. "We just came out of an audit. It's a case that's 'closed and shut'. They're not going to retry that."

The caller paused. "Well, there's a call for a re-audit, so to speak, to correct any errors in the original audit."

"That's a made-up…"

"Have your files ready by Monday of next week," the voice on the other end interrupted. "And one other thing."

Bradford wondered how it could be worse.

"You have a son studying at Peach State College. He's a senior, right? About to graduate?"

"Yes, that's true!" Bradford beamed.

"Unfortunately, he's doing some of that controversial research that was turned down by a lot of newspapers, who were forced to print retractions for the column."

"What does that have to do with…"

"Convince him to stop work on the research project," the caller offered. "Perhaps this re-audit goes away."

Before John Marshall Bradford could scream out an angry response, the line went dead.

———

Rev. Braxton Quincy had just returned to his office, exhausted by the ordeal of spending the evening by the bedside of Nattie Powell, who was not expected to make it through the night at Clifton's sorry excuse for a low-income medical clinic. His mind was not particularly ready for the call that reached him on his phone.

Nobody really enjoys hearing "This is the IRS." This time was no exception.

"Is this Rev. Quincy?" the caller asked.

"Yes," he replied, his good nature was slow to rebound. "What can I do to help you?"

"I'll get to the point. Your church, Epiphany A.M.E., is having its tax-exempt status reviewed."

"Why, may I ask?"

"You endorsed a candidate for the City Council of Clifton, Georgia, from the pulpit, no less."

The pastor felt the pain in his chest rising. "I see preachers of all denominations do that on national television!"

The speaker was unmoved. "The complaint has been specifically lodged against you, and the Internal Revenue Service will investigate."

Trying to contain the panic in his voice, Rev. Quincy paused before speaking. "What kind of punishment might we expect if the charges are warranted?"

"Your donations will be taxed, at a punitive rate, I'm afraid. By the way, do you know a Ms. Sylvia Wright?"

"I certainly do."

"You funded her scholarship," the IRS agent added.

"The whole community did…" Rev. Quincy explained, but he was cut off.

"Do you know that she's been involved in some controversial research?"

Rev. Quincy said nothing, his mind racing. *Would they go after one of his flock?*

"Get her to drop that line of work and write about something else," the voice went on. "If you get her to stop, perhaps we may not look into her scholarship, or your endorsement of a candidate as a preacher."

The A.M.E. pastor stared at the receiver in disbelief as the line went dead.

CHAPTER 34:
Friday, March 21

"Let's have a report on the financials first," Jeremiah began, starting the meeting of Preston Powell Partnership, or "Product Placement Partnership," as the company was informally known as these days. "How is the SRD account looking?"

Chip McLane rose to his feet, somewhat nervously. "Sales are great," he began, then faltered slightly. "But there's a good chance their competitor will make a comeback."

"I think it's time for a congressional investigation into Kipenium," Wallace Bragg said before drumming his fingers on the conference table. "Since Jeffrey Van Pelt is on the payroll, let's have that Michigan representative earn his campaign contribution by demanding answers about the deadly overdoses."

"Agreed." CEO Calhoun nodded. "We can then charge Howard Evans at SRD a little more. Next?"

Vinny Moro was in charge of the Gyrfalcon presentation. "Talladega Motors… their payments are good, and people are buying Gyrfalcon sports cars. But their head guy, Jed Morgan, wants us to do some bad publicity on his rival," Vinny elaborated.

"And who would that be, Mr. Moro?"

"Marshall Motors, sir," he explained in his thick Italian accent. "They make pickup trucks. Their Pioneer is beating the Talladega Jalisco almost 2:1 in sales."

"We'll think of something," COO Wallace Bragg said reassuringly. They had to plan that one carefully, without so many ears present. "Our rate for 'accidents' may go up."

"What about Miracle?"

Kimber trembled slightly at being put on the spot. "Paym-ments are good, but Bradford Communications fixed the hack on Edict. It's making a come… back." She cringed, anticipating Jeremiah Calhoun's wrath.

Her boss adopted a sour expression. "Tell Esther Ruth Harding that God's Grace will smile on her Miracle Company, in the form of an audit upon her foe. And perhaps tell her she'll need to increase her tithe to us once that goes through." Several laughed at his joke, which put him in a better mood.

"Then, there's Summit Studios," Hap Dixon began enthusiastically, without any respect for the speaking order or agenda.

It was Juan Fernandina's turn to report. "There is a lot of buzz about the film, but Giselle Robideaux doesn't want to continue with the final scenes."

"Why not?" Calhoun barked.

"Jeremiah, the poor girl's been kidnapped," Darcie said soothingly. "She's not excited about rushing back to reshoot some of those scenes."

The features of her boss darkened. "Well, we'll… *persuade* her to continue."

Kimber winced.

"And 'Knotty Scarves'?" Bragg changed the subject.

Darcie's presentation was as smooth as ever. "They've already released a commercial, with a few scenes of the kidnapping. And romance novelist Roxanne Bainbridge agreed to work the scarves into the title of her next book, *Knotty Situation,* about a kidnapped actress." She smiled; persuading Bainbridge to get on board with their scheme was a major coup.

"Good," Calhoun sneered. "Remind Roxanne that if she plays ball with us, then USBC *won't* do that exposé on her infidelity with her publicist to lead the evening news."

═══

With the coffee break over, the second part of the meeting could commence.

"Who do we have for new clients?" Calhoun spoke sharply. "We still need more revenue."

Larry Murray jumped in. "I was talking with a company exec from Richmond & Webb Firearms."

Vinny dropped his cell phone. "Are they the ones who make the 'Rebel Yell'?"

Oeznik snorted.

"Crappy firearm if you ask me," Hap Dixon pointed out. "Loudest gun on the market with that stupid whine it makes when it goes full auto. Everyone's going to hear that damn weapon from miles away."

"Unless your goal is to drive fear into your enemies," Murray said with a sinister tone that hushed the small talk. Even Oeznik turned to look at his co-worker in surprise.

"So, the Tally-ban Af-ghans might want 'em," Dixon shot back. "No wonder Richmond & Webb needs our help at PPP."

"Or a school shooter might want one."

Kimber looked wide-eyed at the prospect of Larry's words.

Wallace Bragg sought to steer the conversation back to business. "How can we help them?"

"Celebrity endorsement?" suggested The Spider. It was the first time the techie said anything that day, which drew some attention.

"Pit the Mack Attack against the Rebel Yell in a shooting contest." Now Ray was giving a suggestion.

Hap shook his head. "The Mack Attack would *literally* kill the Rebel Yell."

"Do you know what 'literally' even means, Hap?" Darcie laughed.

Calhoun shocked all. "We need an incident."

The argument ground to a halt as everyone looked at their CEO.

"But, Mr. Calhoun, won't that hurt business for Richmond & Webb?" Kimber asked.

"Funny thing, Miss Elliot, remember the Exxon Valdez?"

She shook her head, but most of the older members of PPP nodded.

"Exxon didn't go out of business," Calhoun pointed out.

"But wasn't there a boycott?" Chip inquired.

Calhoun sought to provide a lesson. "In one of his books, Donald Trump was quoted as saying 'All press is good press'. He didn't mind bad publicity, so long as his name was the one people paid attention to. Exxon was all anyone talked about back then, and how their tanker ran aground in Prince William Sound, Alaska. When the chips were down, they could accuse the captain of being drunk, deflecting blame. Sure, the tree huggers called for people to shun the oil company, but those who hated liberals were more than happy to gas up with Exxon."

"But Deepwater Horizon…"

Now the CEO sought to put his financial guy in his place. "That oil rig explosion and leak didn't hurt BP too badly. British Petroleum was able to escape a lot of blame, while President Obama caught hell for not being able to clean it up fast enough."

"Good news beats bad news," said COO Wallace Bragg. "But bad news is still better than being ignored."

"So, what kind of incident, gentlemen… and ladies?" Calhoun reopened the discussion.

"How about a shooting at a school?" Larry jumped in with the first idea. Kimber's mouth dropped in horror. Calhoun's eyebrows rose.

"Now that would make the news!"

———

After an hour of discussing the next client, Baikal Liquors of Russia, it was time for the last item on the agenda: the "PSC Project."

"What do we have?" Jeremiah opened, after a special catered dinner was concluded.

"Deputy Chief of Staff Nick Bradley, a colleague of mine, has great contacts in the DoD, IRS, and National Park Service," Wallace Bragg answered. "And as we speak, Dr. Kirby is working with Dean Franklin Arbell at Peach State College, pressuring the families of the students."

"As Machiavelli said, it is better to be feared than loved," Jeremiah explained. He glared at Ray Maillon. "Did you make it clear to Nick that they had to mention the students and their research?"

"L-loud and clear," the employee who made the most recent call stammered.

"Good." Calhoun smiled. "Let's see how many make their kids quit. Some might leave the school."

As a few laughs circulated around the room, all turned to note the entrance of Dr. Edward Edmund Kirby, fashionably late as usual.

"So, Dr. Kirby, what are we going to do about Professor Jackson Pierce?"

The academic's grin widened. "I convinced his college's Dean Arbell to have a special 'Peer Review Committee'."

"Why?"

"Professor Pierce is too chummy with his fellow faculty members," Dr. Kirby explained. "They wouldn't convict him of anything."

"Who did you get for this committee?" Juan Fernandina wondered aloud.

"A rich developer on the Georgia Board of Regents, and an online college president, who wants to work with us, by the way."

"And the third?" Bragg asked.

"Why…me, of course," Kirby beamed. "It practically guarantees a conviction."

"He doesn't have tenure," Chip said, frowning. "Why don't they just fire him?"

Kirby shook his head. "We have to discredit him first, so no one else thinks of doing that kind of research. We'll suspend him from further collegiate activities." Then his voice adopted a faux worrisome tone. "Oh, I'm afraid there will be no trip to New Orleans, and no more research articles for the professor and his students."

Hap laughed. "That was a good impersonation of the Evil Emperor from Star Wars."

Kirby smirked and added, "Later, when this all dies down, his college can fire him."

Calhoun chuckled. "Sounds like Professor Pierce is about to get schooled by us. I *love* it!"

CHAPTER 35:

Tuesday, March 25

"The meeting of the Peer Review Committee will now come to order. I am Dean Franklin Arbell, and I am convening this panel to investigate charges of wrongdoing by Professor Jackson Pierce."

"I understand," Pierce replied, sitting in a chair, facing the podium and table with three chairs occupied by academics.

The Higher Education Dean frowned for a moment, expecting an outburst from the defendant, but nothing happened. *Didn't he know what was at stake?*

"Let me introduce the panelists for the defendant," he began, as if it mattered to the professor in the hot seat. "First, there is President Doris DeVaughn from the Southern Senators School."

Online vulture, Jackson thought as Dean Arbell recited DeVaughn's accomplishments, but held his tongue.

"And there's Peter Sheldon," Arbell continued.

The communications professor didn't recognize the name. But the Dean droned on about how Sheldon was a former Georgia Board of Regents member and an Atlanta developer. *He sure did get a lot of heavy hitters in a very short period of time*, Jackson mused.

"And there's Professor Edward Edmund Kirby. His Ivy League degree from Cornell University is supplemented with many publications and speeches."

During this academic preening, Jackson became worried. Dr. E.E. Kirby was well known nationwide. He did not come cheap. *Who is funding this meeting?*

"And the defendant is Jackson Pierce, who has taught for a few years here at Peach State College," Arbell added in an off-handed manner to the three panelists.

"This is a hearing to determine whether this *teacher* in Communications should be suspended from external activities."

Wow, Jackson thought. Arbell is really making it sound like being a teacher was a bad thing. As much as he enjoyed researching, he was, indeed, a teacher. He still liked teaching, after all.

"I hope this time isn't *inconvenient* for you," Arbell said, knowing exactly what was really going on. In fact, the timing couldn't be worse, as the hearing had been deliberately scheduled for the week the students were supposed to be presenting their research at the Southeast Communications Conference.

Jackson responded with a shrug. "It's too important to miss," was all anyone could catch him saying back to Arbell.

Unsure of how to handle that odd remark, the PSC Dean began. "I will present the concerns of the college." Then he indicated Dr. Pierce. "You may then respond, and then the committee will be able to ask questions."

Dean Arbell then launched into an extra-long description of what had happened when he became aware of the problem. Then, he launched into how he learned that *Veritas Lux Mea* had to cancel a promised second column, and how all of the newspapers had to print retractions and apologies, a great embarrassment to Peach State College.

President Doris DeVaughn of Southern Senators School asked for details of how damaging the professor's research had been to PSC. Arbell explained that the professor's byline mentioned Peach State College.

"Plus, with the undergraduates being featured so prominently, it reflects adversely upon our teaching and research. It makes it look like we committed academic fraud," Arbell snapped after additional questions were raised.

"Suspension seems like a harsh punishment," Peter Sheldon, the Atlanta real estate mogul, observed. "How is it justified?"

"We're not suspending him from all activities involving the college," Arbell said as he rubbed at his glasses. "At least, not yet. This is just a suspension from external activities until a more formal committee can be convened to rule on his guilt in this matter, and if a full suspension or termination is necessary."

Wow, thought Jackson. *This was like a propaganda hearing.* He wondered how much of a Kangaroo Court this would become.

"Dean Arbell, I object to the langua-"

"Professor Pierce, you will have a chance to respond in due time," Arbell lectured. He looked at the committee members. "Please continue with your questions for me."

There was a short spell of silence before President DeVaughn asked, "So, you plan to pursue further disciplinary action that may result in termination?"

"Yes, Madame President."

"Good," she hissed, a reply which was audible to all present at the hearing. DeVaughn wasn't known for being faculty-friendly.

"*Now* you may respond." Franklin Arbell indicated to the accused.

"I am aware my columns were pulled, and retractions were made," Pierce began. "I was informed by at least one person in the media of intimida-"

"Is that person here?" Arbell interrupted.

"No, but we can call…"

"I'm sorry," Franklin replied, unapologetically. "But the Peer Review Committee requires witnesses to be here in person."

"So, what 'crime' have I committed?" Jackson asked Arbell.

"Perhaps there may not have been a *crime*,' Professor Pierce," Dr. E. E. Kirby said every word slowly, as if explaining a simple step-by-step procedure to a child. "But there *has* been a serious lack of judgment."

"And what would that serious lack of judgment be?" the accused replied.

Kirby looked through his notes. "You've made serious allegations in your article."

Now it was Pierce's turn to lecture. "We only reported on product placement, coverage of companies, and what they sell in the news."

It was a full academic battle. "The implication is that they paid the news for such coverage."

Pierce rose to the challenge. "We made no such implication. We only illuminated what's covered, and that such types of coverage are increasing in the news."

"Ah, yes," Kirby smiled, sensing an opening. "And how do you know that?"

Where is this going, Pierce wondered. "A student of mine wrote an algorithm…"

"And did you test his algorithm?"

"Hers'," Pierce responded. "I couldn't. Nobody can do what she can do. But she's an honest…"

"So you don't know if she really found the data she claimed to?"

Now, Jackson rose to his feet. "You don't have proof of any errors she might have made?"

Kirby played his trump card. "Do you know why she sought psychological counseling?"

The professor flushed. "Well, do *you* know why?!"

"Not unless you care to share with us," *Kirby's toothy, confident grin was getting annoying,* Jackson thought. "But it does lead us to question her judgement… and perhaps yours."

"Wait… how do *you* know that she sought counseling? Aren't there privacy regulations and HIPPA rules applying here?"

Now it was Kirby's turn to adopt a worried look. Both Doris and Peter zeroed in on the esteemed guest panelist.

Dr. Kirby attempted to shift the attention back to Professor Pierce. "One of the few papers that did not retract your column is run by your sister-in-law. And your wife teaches here at PSC. It sounds like there's a fair amount of nepotism going on in Georgia."

Arbell stood up. "Gentlemen, and Madam President, the hearing has run out of time."

"Now there's a time limit?" Jackson gasped. "When the hell did that…"

"Professor Pierce, please wait outside while we confer to pass judgment," the Higher Education Dean announced.

Thirty minutes later, Dean Franklin Arbell ordered Professor Pierce to return and informed him of his suspension from all external activities. Suzanne LaFleur, the secretary taking notes, told him later that the vote was actually 2-1, with Peter Sheldon voting against his suspension.

"Therefore, Professor, you are forbidden to publish any additional articles, or to take students to any conferences, though I suspect the matter is moot."

Pierce pulled out his phone, glanced at the screen, and put it back into his pocket. "I understand, Dean Arbell."

There was no professor raging, or angry retorts, for his sentence. Just a quiet acceptance. That surprised Arbell. As the higher education administrator read prepared remarks thanking the committee for their service, Arbell paused to make a sideways glance at the guilty professor. Did he detect a slight smile? *No, it couldn't be*, thought Arbell, though he wondered what was going on. By the look on Kirby's face, the famed lecturer was probably thinking the same thing.

The Malek couple hugged each other. Their daughter was competing in an important scholastic event, and they had just brought in a fair amount of money for their hotel, which took in many guests for the lacrosse tournament that Peach State College hosted. Their investments had increased to where they now had enough for Senami to start a coffee shop a block away on the site of a former real estate office. Then came a jarring phone call.

"This is Martin Connors with the U.S. Immigration and Customs Enforcement," the almost mechanical voice intoned. "We have questions about your original asylum application, before you applied to become U.S. citizens."

Sadik put the message on speakerphone. "Wha-what questions?"

"We are reviewing why you came to America in the first place."

"We came over during the Lebanese Civil War!" Senami insisted, her voice almost quaking. She remembered the truck bombs, kidnappings, assassinations, foreign occupation, the American Embassy destroyed, along with all of those brave U.S. Marines.

Martin Connors seemed unsympathetic. "And that war has concluded."

Taira's parents remained speechless. "So, you are free to go home," Connors added.

"But we are Americans now," Sadik pleaded. "All three of us are U.S. citizens. We passed our test, and did the appli–"

"That remains to be seen," the voice cut him off. "We are still reviewing your status."

"Lebanon remains a dangerous place," Senami attempted to explain. "Last week, a car bomb killed the Speaker of the…"

"Your daughter is doing research in college," Martin took a different tack.

"Yes, she is very important." Sadik smiled, despite his wife's distress. "She is currently with her classmates in a special competition."

Again, the ICE agent interrupted. "Her work is very problematic. If you were to persuade her to stop, perhaps this review would not be necessary." The phone went dead.

CHAPTER 36:

Wednesday, March 26

"We're never going to win," Trey Bradford whispered to his teammates.

The six Peach State College students admired the surroundings in the Hyatt by the Superdome, which had been transformed into a sea of scholars. Professors and graduate students zipped about them with conference booklets, looking for the next panel at the annual meeting of the Southeast Communications Conference in New Orleans.

"There aren't many people our age here," whispered Taira Malek.

"But there are other undergraduates," Dr. Elena Pierce insisted. There were clumps of formally-attired students, perhaps looking a little fancy among the regular academic crowd, who opted for something more like church casual. Some participants from other schools even looked like they were wearing matching outfits... as if they were going to prom.

"Think we're a little...underdressed for the occasion?" Nat Holman wondered aloud.

Dr. Elena Pierce laughed. "Hardly. Some of these teams look like they're ready for a wedding photo."

"Some brought... like... an entourage," Paul Herrera gasped. He pointed to two groups. College presidents, provosts... one school even had a mascot and cheerleaders.

Sylvia Wright threw up her hands. "Is this a pep rally or a conference panel?"

That seemed to break the tension as they gawked at their competitors, who were perhaps trying a little *too* hard to impress someone.

"Still," Alicia Ina Sheehy noted. "Our college isn't even funding us."

"At least Pyramid Coffee came through with money," Elena replied. She pointed at the kiosk. "We should get some of their coffee while we're here."

A few minutes later, they had their mugs and room keys.

"Guys in one, gals in another," their new chaperone ordered. "I get the one with the softest linen!"

The PSC students and professor rode up the glass elevators.

"Now this is real nice… a flight from the ATL to NOLA… and this ain't a Motel 6!" Sylvia crowed.

"We can meet at Starbucks for planning," mused Taira.

"Just don't tell Pyramid!" Elena insisted. They all laughed.

An hour later, the six PSC students headed to the Starbucks café, where Elena met them and started on their plans.

"Let's go up to one of the unused conference rooms. I've booked one, now that the last of those panels is done before dinner. We can all go up and simulate the real…"

She caught their expressions. "What gives?"

Sylvia lowered her eyes. "This is kind of stressful."

Dr. Pierce looked quizzical. "Didn't Jackson teach you how to present?"

"Sort of. He's a nice professor and all," Nat insisted.

"But he's mostly about the statistics, the research, the findings," Trey contended.

"And he tries to get us all inspired and all…" Taira defended her teacher.

"But… he doesn't really teach us *how* to present," Sylvia stated.

Elena rolled her eyes. "I can see my husband doing that. He's a shameless extrovert. He loves to chat, so he probably assumes anyone and everyone can present… am I right?"

All nodded.

"Well, that is something I can teach you," Elena said. "Before I was an English professor, I was in theater."

Again, all of them nodded. "Professor Pierce… the other Professor Pierce always brags on you," Taira explained. "He said you were the best actress at Tulane while you all were there."

She blushed. "Well, I don't know about that, but I certainly did have fun in plays. Want me to give you some tips I learned from the stage?"

"Hell yes!" Paul boomed, which got all of them talking at once.

"They say more people are scared of public speaking than snakes or spiders," Sylvia commented.

Elena nodded. "There is some truth to that. And though I loved reading plays as a child, I was terrified to get up and speak before an audience. Once, in a play version of *The Hobbit*, a big guy in the front of the audience yawned. It got me thinking that our performance was boring, and it threw me off my game. So, I realized I couldn't deliver a line while looking at the crowd. Instead, I would present to the doors in the back, or the camera with the lighting, or even someone's duffle bag next to them in a chair."

"But shouldn't you look someone in the eye when you speak to them?" Trey responded.

"You're looking near them, but not directly into their eyes," Elena explained. "I learned later that the big guy in the front who was yawning was my friend's dad. He had stayed up all night with his youngest daughter, who was sick. He would have nodded off during a nuclear explosion."

The six laughed, catching the attention of others in the café.

"So, present to that silver pitcher of water, or Sylvia's purple notebook, or Paul's coffee mug, or Trey's political tie."

A.I. raised her hand. "Why couldn't the other Dr. Pierce be here in New Orleans?"

"You didn't hear?"

"I knew he couldn't come. I just don't know why."

"PSC's Higher Education Dean, Franklin Arbell, scheduled a Peer Review Committee full of some cronies he recruited to get Jackson suspended for the project you're working on," Elena explained. "And that scheduled hearing finished earlier this week."

Sylvia switched gears. "Is it true you took your husband's place right under the nose of Dean Arbell?"

Elena laughed. "Yeah, we pulled the switcheroo. Pyramid was cool with the change, and the conference only required that you have a chaperone. Arbell was so obsessed with suspending my husband that he didn't consider we would simply change advisors. I think Franklin's a little sexist; he didn't think a woman could coach you."

Trey looked up in alarm. "Won't he go after you, too?"

Elena waved him off. "Unlike my husband, I've got tenure. Besides, Arbell is already targeting any teacher who's trying to teach you kids something. We've crossed swords before, and we'll probably do it again, so as long as he's at PSC. If it were up to Dean Arbell, all of us professors would be replaced by video lectures, Scantron 'bubble-in' tests, and some computers to automatically grade you."

The students shuddered.

"Now let's get some practice in now, before…."

"Uh, Professor Pierce?" Nat began.

"What?"

"You're kind of… taking this a bit seriously," Sylvia jumped in.

"Well… I want you to win!" the English Professor insisted.

"Why?" Paul asked. "It's not your class."

"S-she… wants… tohelpherhusband," A.I. blurted.

"Is it that obvious?" Elena rolled her eyes. "Did my husband tell you about my high school experience? I had perfect grades, more extra-curriculars than the entire top four combined. But I didn't make valedictorian, or even salutatorian!"

All looked at each other. The confusion on their faces was obvious.

"Why?" Trey couldn't resist.

"I would have been the first female graduation speaker in St. Paul's Academy history," Professor Pierce snapped, showing how fresh the mental wound still was. "So maybe I do want you to win, so you don't have your hard work stolen from you, like my high school did to me."

All stood looking at her in shock, finally understanding why she was passionately pushing their team to success.

"Okay… time's wasting. Let's get that run-through of your presentation out of the way so we can watch some late afternoon panels. You can critique their performance, and then I'll take you to one of the oldest restaurants in the French Quarter, where Jackson and I used to go out in college. It serves the best Cajun food in Louisiana!"

———

The phone rang, and Nat's dad called out, "That's probably our boy telling us he made it safely to New Orleans."

But when his wife reached the phone, she heard a different voice. "Are you the parent of Nathaniel Holman?"

"Speaking…" Nat's mother seemed confused.

"This is Samuel Ross, the assistant to Higher Education Dean Franklin Arbell at Peach State College. I am sorry to inform you that your son's membership on the PSC Sabers team and his athletic scholarship have been suspended, pending an investigation into his academic activities."

Shawna Holman pushed the button to put the call on speakerphone. "My son does not cheat! He hasn't done any…"

"Mrs. Holman," Ross interrupted. "I'm merely informing you of the facts. Dean Arbell is looking into whether Nathaniel Holman and his classmates, who were working on a project with Professor Jackson Pierce, broke any Peach State College rules. Their columns have been retracted. Apologies by newspapers have been made. We feel such actions are unbecoming of a student representing the college, hence the suspension. And, unfortunately, we will have to announce the suspension to the NCAA, which could affect your son's draft status."

Willie Holman yelled from his bed where his injured body was forced to remain. "What do you have against my son? He and the other students didn't do anything wrong!"

"I'm sorry, Mr. Holman," Ross replied. "But I received word that Dr. Pierce has been suspended from external activities. Of course, if your son were to quit the project, his suspension would be immediately lifted, and he would be reinstated to the team. In fact, the NCAA wouldn't even know about the suspension, and he would be free to be chosen by an NFL team with no cloud of suspicion over his head. And you would not owe the balance on the athletic scholarship's suspension. Just keep that in mind when you talk to Nathaniel."

Then the line went dead. To the Holmans, it seemed their son's academic and athletic dreams did as well, unless they "played ball".

CHAPTER 37:

Wednesday, March 26-Thursday, March 27

"Okay, so we might win," Trey announced to the group at Tujague's, the Cajun restaurant on Decatur Street in New Orleans.

Sylvia smiled. "What happened to all of that earlier pessimism, Trey?"

"Well, that was before our 'drama professor' taught us how to present," he announced. "Cheers!"

Elena smiled wryly. Their practice presentation had gone well. They didn't seem to fear the big stage nearly as much, and appeared eager to speak before an audience tomorrow, even Alicia Ina. Elena gave her an encouraging hug after the computer-science wizard completed her lines without a single stutter or stumble.

"Practice, practice, *practice* what I taught you," Elena insisted. "It's going to help you a lot in this conference."

"Now, that's something your husband *does* make us do," Nat explained. "We just needed to learn your trick about presenting with confidence. For example, I informed the thermostat in the back of the room about our important hypotheses!" Guffaws and giggles came from the others.

"And Sylvia's going to have the most well-educated notebook," Paul noted.

"That notebook has seen a lot!" the future lawyer admitted. "I save it for all of my communications and political science courses on judicial politics."

=

"Helen Ridgefield?"

"Speaking," the history teacher evaluated the gray-suited man approaching the porch she had just finished sweeping. He was too well-dressed for the warm Tallahassee afternoon, which made her suspicious.

"My name is Irwin Weldon, National Parks Service in the Department of the Interior. I congratulate you on your home, which will officially be designated a National Historic Site."

While Helen was pleased to hear her residence was to be so honored, there was nothing that suggested "good news" about this guy.

"It seems some retired educator found that a relative of Napoleon's lived here."

"Achille Murat, you mean," she corrected. "There's no evidence that the former Crown Prince of Naples and Postmaster of Tallahassee took up residence here."

"Well, the Department of the Interior thinks otherwise…"

"I'd like to see the evidence," she snapped.

"During this legal dispute, you are to vacate the premises," Weldon replied. "And those begin next week. So, find alternative lodging until—"

"Wait, you can't throw me out of my home!"

"Actually, I can." The bureaucrat handed her a document. As he turned to walk away, he spun on his heel. "Do you have a relative named Alicia Ina Sheehy?"

"Yes. What does this have to do with…"

"And she's at Peach State College?"

"What's this about?"

"She's been engaging in some very troubling research at PSC. Have her terminate her participation in that project so it won't affect her graduation there." Then he smiled. "If she would do that, perhaps you would not have to leave this house. My number is on the papers I just handed you. Call me if you can persuade Miss Sheehy to leave the research team."

As he departed, Helen contemplated hurling a few acorns at the back of his head. What was going on here?

....

....

The Southeast Communications Conference undergraduate research competition began early on the second day, with four panels of three presentations each, a marathon event for the nine judges. Elena was relieved that Dr. James LeBlanc's team from Louisiana State University was on a different panel. They would all still be in the same competition, of course, but they wouldn't go head-to-head. Jackson had warned her about the LSU team and how they usually dominated regionals.

"Wow, this ballroom is huge," Paul mused, looking around the main room of the Hyatt. "It could seat the entire Georgia conference in one room."

"Is that a lot?" A.I. gaped.

"Compared to most academic conferences, this is like a Journey concert," Elena mused.

"Who's Journey?" Taira asked.

"You... don't... know... who... Journey... is?" the English professor spluttered, before she caught all of their expressions, in on the same joke.

"Don't stop believin', Dr. Pierce," Nat joked.

=====

Elena looked at the other competitors, a who's-who of schools, all joining LSU. Most were among the most highly ranked schools in the Southeast. PSC, on the other hand, had a mix of nontraditional students in evening colleges and professional program kids, along with a few scholars in the liberal arts. *One of these things is not like the other*, she mused, noting how different her team was in comparison to their competition.

"Well, you've seen what the professors and graduate students do in the panels," she told the PSC students as they clumped around her, craning their necks to see the posted schedule, rooms, and times. "Let's see if you learned anything from my presentation suggestions."

In the first round, Florida State University students started with a focus on citizen blogs, and the undergraduate research conference was underway. Elena watched the proceedings, as Team Wofford investigated who downloaded Wikileaks material, with a little bit of jealousy. *I wish we had something like this for our PSC students*, she mused, given Wofford's impressive computers that displayed their results.

Her students were taking notes and whispering quietly, a half-hour later, as Duke took the stage to present with something known as "developmental journalism". It was good to see that they were engaging in "active learning", which was something both Professor Pierces' preached.

When their scheduled midmorning time slot arrived, The University of Alabama students walked in, with the guys in crimson tux jackets, bowties, and pants, along with white shirts, while the ladies wore white dresses with red hats. Elena smacked her forehead at the ostentatious display of formal wear, like this was a wedding reception or tailgate party. Thankfully, their presentation wasn't as fancy. The Crimson Tide faithful stumbled through a presentation on how news anchors ran for public office. *Why was that such a big deal,* Elena wondered. She noted the judges frowning, not sure whether it was directed toward their garish outfits or their presentation. She hoped it was the latter.

Vanderbilt went up next, and the pride of the Commodores performed much better. They looked at whether newscasters were more likely to work their way up from internships or slide straight in from graduation to the TV news broadcast. She found herself engrossed in their topic and findings, actually wanting to know their results. *Hey, wait a minute, girl… that's our competitor*, she glumly noted. The smiles from the judges revealed that the team right before them would be a tough one to top.

Then, it was time for Peach State College to take the stage. Now *Elena* was the one who was worried. Vanderbilt's presentation was quite good. A win could help her husband get tenure, while a loss might doom his chances. She had done her best, but now it was out of her hands.

But her fears were unwarranted. Taira, Trey, Nat, A.I, Paul, and Sylvia each stepped forward, showing improvement even over their afternoon practice and post-dinner rehearsal. Even though she had heard their topic before, they still managed to make it sound interesting.

The judges weren't even writing… just staring at them. She hoped that was a good sign. Everyone in the room seemed to hang on every word. And A.I., the weak link on stage yesterday afternoon and evening, spoke so calmly and understandably that anyone could run the algorithm themselves. Sylvia did a fist-pump toward her classmates at the table as she turned, having delivered the final words. They were all smiles.

The chair, a professor named Terry Lightner, complimented the presenters before opening up the questions to judges and the audience. She watched how Trey, Sylvia, and Taira deftly handled each query; Nat even elaborated upon one of their hypotheses, while "Sarge" Paul Herrera brought back up the slide with tables to reveal whether one test was statistically significant or not. When Professor Lightner adjourned the panel, they all ran over to Dr. Pierce, excitedly telling them what each focused on during their talk. Lunch at GW Fins was even more celebratory than the prior night.

———

On to the afternoon panels, Virginia started off with a piece on documentaries, almost as good as Vanderbilt's. The students from the Texas Longhorns went with a presentation on teaching journalism, which sounded more like it was written and designed by their instructors. Several professors began a heated argument about their findings, distracting from the students' work.

Then, it was time for LeBlanc's LSU Tigers. As the students launched into their topic of who gets sued more… print, broadcast, radio, or internet journalism sites, Elena could see why the aged scholar's team was one of the best in the country. Jackson had warned her that LSU would be their strongest competition. There was hardly an "ah," "um," or "er" in their talk, and they handled each answer with the precision of a presidential press secretary. That early enthusiasm of the Peach State students turned to anxious looks as they exchanged glances with her and each other. That trophy and spot in the nationals looked less likely now.

In the last panel, the presentations by the final three schools were also fairly good. Hendrix's was a comparative analysis of BBC and ABC News, while the undergraduates of Louisville turned in an acceptable lecture on the impact of women in journalism like Nelly Bly, Gloria Steinem, and Katie Couric. Millsaps went last, with a critique of the Telecommunications Act of 1996, and how it let local markets compete in the national markets. All were good, but none of them seemed to generate a top-notch analysis.

According to Dr. Pierce's notes, it was a four-school race. She only hoped the judges would give PSC a shot. Her competitive nature was kicking in, and she could see why her husband got into research and this competition. Now they were critical to her family's future that Jackson get that job security, which looked increasingly less likely each day.

———

At the luncheon the next day, the organizers announced that Virginia, Wofford, and Vanderbilt had received Honorable Mentions Awards. Chair Terry Lightner then declared the third-place winner was Duke University. Cheers broke out among the large crowd of blue and white faithful, the academic equivalent of the "Cameron Crazies," their rabid basketball fans.

"Second place," Lightner continued as the cheers eventually tapered off, "is the Louisiana State University!"

Cheers were still loud, as LSU was the "home favorite," with Baton Rouge just a short distance away. But there were also some mixed emotions, as plenty of the local attendees had hoped their team would win yet another first-place award, and a shot at taking nationals.

"And in first place… Peach State College, with their focus on…" But the six students exploded into a wild celebration, leaving most of the larger and better-known colleges and universities in stunned silence. While the PSC kids hugged each other, Elena texted the good news to her husband, knowing she couldn't be heard over the chaos.

Unbeknownst to Elena, a graduate student several rows away was also taking notes. He messaged his professor with the details. The doctoral hopeful, Nigel Grayson, had no idea why Dr. E. E. Kirby wanted this information, but he knew it would not pay to ignore an order from his major professor if he wanted to pass his comprehensive exams later than spring.

CHAPTER 38:

Friday, March 28

"Good afternoon, Dean Franklin Arbell."

The speaker on the phone came through clearly. Dr. E. E. Kirby's voice was the only thing that could have frozen Peach State College's Higher Education Dean as he was packing his briefcase to leave early for the day.

"To what do I owe the pleasure?"

"I'll get right to the point," Kirby said brusquely. "Did the Peach State College team compete at the Southeast Communications Conference?"

"I don't see how," Franklin managed. "We suspended Dr. Pierce, didn't we?"

"Have you checked on him recently, as I instructed you?"

"Yes," Arbell insisted. "He's in his office grading papers."

"Really," Kirby's anger seemed difficult to hold in check. "Because my sources at the regional informed me that the PSC team did indeed compete."

"But that's impossible. Dr. Pierce…"

"You evidently didn't monitor the activities of *both* Dr. Pierces. It seems Jackson's wife was able to help them compete," Kirby snapped. "And your school's team *won* the competition."

"That's impossible! They can't…"

"Oh, but they *did*, Dean Arbell," Kirby said calmly, though with a strong hint of disdain. "We had a deal to stop the presentation. I see my faith in you was sorely misplaced."

Dr. Kirby hung up the phone. Jeremiah and the others at PPP wouldn't be pleased. He had to act fast to fix things. Perhaps it was time for a change in tactics.

———

Later that afternoon, Professor Jackson Pierce accompanied his son, Isaac, to East Georgia for the high school state quarterfinals. In the prior week, Isaac had upset two rivals, seniors who had underestimated the diminutive kid from Alexandria.

Kat and R.J. were also in attendance at the Savannah match, along with their kids, to add to the Alexandria Academy team cheering on their only remaining player, with the others being eliminated in West Georgia the prior week. But few expected that Isaac could defeat the top-seeded rival in his division.

The dark-haired boy from Augusta split the first two sets with Isaac. But something happened in the last game that would change the entire match. Isaac's opponent served a ball straight into the net. Frustrated, he smashed his racket into the ground, damaging it. The Augusta player requested a new racket and was given one from the tennis association. Realizing it wasn't his favorite graphite model, the top-ranked player in his division demanded that the match be delayed until his coach could find his personal favorite at a local sporting goods store. Denied that request, the heavily favored player never seemed to recover and eventually lost the third set to Isaac, 4-6.

In the last of the quarterfinals matches, Isaac faced the second-ranked player in his division for a spot in the final four for the state tennis tournament. This player was known for having the most wicked serve in the state. In no time, Isaac had dropped the first set 6-0.

During the break, Isaac and Jackson got a minute to chat. "Coach told me to hang in there, but I don't see how I can beat that serve."

"You don't need to, Isaac."

His son registered shock. "What do you mean, Dad?"

The PSC professor suggested a new strategy. "Just put it back into play instead of having a killer response. Keep volleying him until he eventually tires himself out."

His son gave a thumbs-up, puffed on his inhaler, and went back in. Isaac was able to return the serve just well enough to set up a volley. Little by little, the "super-server" was worn down. The ranked player dropped the second set 5-7 to Isaac. In the third set, "super-server" was drooping in the humid afternoon. Unable to keep volleying with Isaac, he sought to smash his serves harder, which made those hits erratic. To the surprise of nearly all in attendance at that Savannah match, Isaac prevailed in the third set, 6-2. It was on to the Final Four for the State Tennis Tournament in Atlanta for Isaac.

=====

As Isaac joined Kat, RJ, and their kids watching a movie, Jackson headed to the lobby to get a drink.

"I saw your boy play today," said a familiar voice from the lounge in the Historic District Doubletree Savannah. *It couldn't be...*

"Dr. Kirby?"

"Yes. I've played a little tennis myself. And I'm impressed with the way he dispatched that kid with the killer serve by outthinking him. Brains over brawn, it seems. That's why I'm looking to chat with you."

When he could sense Dr. Pierce's reticence to chat, Kirby continued. "I think we got off on the wrong foot. I was impressed with your defense at the hearing. I now think I have 'the measure of the man', so to speak."

Jackson nodded. "Maybe we can bury the hatchet."

Edward Edmund Kirby grinned. "Perhaps we can do more than that... form an alliance, even. I am *sure* you know who I am."

True, Kirby was known nationwide, unlike a certain PSC professor struggling to get tenure. Jackson wondered what he had in mind.

"The same can happen for you, Professor Pierce. I am looking for someone who can do lectures on my behalf when I am unable to handle all of my many speaking engagements. The opportunity can certainly raise your profile."

The Peach State College professor was surprised at such a generous offer from the egotistical speaker.

"And these speaking opportunities pay handsomely," Kirby added, flashing a watch that may have cost more than the Georgian's annual salary.

"Thanks for the kind offer," Jackson began. "I assume this would be in exchange for something I would be expected to do on your behalf."

"You assume correctly, Dr. Pierce."

Wow, now I've been promoted from the title of professor to doctor.

"This is a *quid pro quo*," Kirby added.

"And you want me to…"

"I think you have a good idea of what has to be done," Dr. Kirby lowered his voice so the other patrons in the lounge couldn't hear them. "Just end the research. Blame Arbell for why your students are dropping out of the national competition. Give them all automatic A's. The kids at your school will all graduate and get good jobs. And I would write you a letter in support of your tenure file."

As Jackson was too stunned to respond, Kirby continued. "What would you get out of continuing, except a line on the vita? And that's only if you prevail again in Washington D.C., at that national competition? You're not even guaranteed tenure if you win the nationals. On the other hand, if you persist, you'll be turning down a generous financial offer and will earn the enmity from a superior."

"Oh, he'll be around to make my life miserable, no matter…"

Kirby smiled a bit wider. "I can perhaps arrange it so that you replace your antagonist, and become the new Higher Education Dean of Peach State College. Franklin Arbell sought to have you dismissed, yet you can turn the tables on him. You seem a lot smarter than he is. You and your clever wife certainly outfoxed him to compete in New Orleans. And he *does* want you gone. It's you, or him. And we can help *you* defeat *him*."

Jackson stared at his drink. "Sorry… it's all rather sudden…"

"You probably want time to think it over, consult with that crafty wife of yours."

Kirby motioned for the bartender and pointed at the two drinks to cover them. Then he added, "You could also escape Peach State College for the Northeast, where so many schools would pay generously for your services. That's something else a word from me could help. I'm sure we could find something for Elena as well, and your kids could study in the most prestigious prep schools in the country."

It was a good offer.

Too good, perhaps?

I would become just like you, Jackson thought. It seemed just weeks ago that he'd do anything for tenure. Now, with his values at stake, he debated what he should do. He thought of his daughter… *there was a right and a wrong*. And this was clearly trending in the wrong direction.

But before Pierce could speak, the famed communications professor Dr. Kirby jumped in. "I mean, what you've accomplished with *your type of student* is quite impressive, all things considered. But imagine what you could do with the children of the elite in the New England area. You would be competing for that national award annually with the right sort of students."

Jackson barely contained his anger. He now had his answer, and it wouldn't be the one Professor E.E. Kirby would like, even if it would likely cost him tenure. But he held his tongue. The more he pretended to keep his options open, the more time he would have to formulate a plan for his family and students. *I can do more than outthink Dean Arbell. I might outsmart the great Dr. Kirby*, he thought.

"I will consider your generous offer, Dr. Kirby."

———

Dr. Kirby joined Hap Dixon, who was waiting by the door, and crossed the street from the Doubletree to the Hilton Garden Inn, where PPP's Second-in-Command, Wallace Bragg, awaited them.

"So, will he take the deal?" Wallace asked without any formalities.

"I believe he will," the professor explained. "It's the *rational* decision to make, with his career and tenure at stake."

Dixon shook his head. "I'm not so sure. He looks like one of them crusading liberal hippie-types who want to be do-gooders."

———

"Aunt Kat asked about your dinner plans," Isaac explained as Jackson finished his drink. "They're having pizza, and I'm sick of pizza right now."

"Since you won, what spoils do you desire?"

"Thai food!"

"I'm not sure if there's a Thai place in Savannah, but let's see what we can scrounge up."

At that moment, a stranger sat down next to Jackson. "I know a good place where we can go."

Pierce evaluated the middle-aged man. "Who are you?"

"Your sister-in-law said you might be here. I work with her. My name is Bob Carlson, and I am a reporter with the *Savannah Herald-Post*."

CHAPTER 39:

Friday March 28-Saturday March 29

"Did you see that?" Dr. Edward E. Kirby gasped and pointed as they looked out from the Hilton Garden Inn lounge across the street to see Professor Jackson Pierce, his son Isaac, and a third man, on Bay Street hailing a cab.

"Who is that other man?" PPP's COO Wallace Bragg frowned.

Hap jumped to his feet. "I'll find out." He dashed across the lobby, narrowly avoiding knocking down an elderly couple struggling with a suitcase.

———

"This is a nice spot!" Jackson said as they settled into the Thai restaurant, which featured excellent service and menu options. The aroma of the food was intoxicating. "What's on your mind?"

"Information," Bob Carlson responded. "You sent that article about product placement."

"Yeah," Jackson admitted. "Caused me a lot of trouble."

"And Kat, too," Carlson added. "A lawyer just threatened her with a lawsuit if she didn't pull your original article from the website, print a retraction, and an apology. She was told to refuse to run a rumored follow-up article."

"Wonder why people are going crazy over that column," Jackson sighed. "It's not as if we targeted any individuals by name."

Bob Carlson stopped eating his Pad Thai. "I thought you could tell me why."

"It's the Illuminati!" Jackson's son announced dramatically.

The Savannah reporter chuckled. "You may not be that far off, Isaac. Someone powerful feels threatened by what you found, or were going to find. Didn't you promise a sequel?"

"I did."

"May I see it?" Carlson asked.

"I was going to send…."

"To Kat?" The journalist jumped in.

The communications professor eyed him suspiciously, as did Isaac. "I'll check with her first. You'll understand, of course, given all that's happened just this semester alone."

Carlson tried not to look hurt. "Okay. But could you do it now? I really need to get after that lead. I'm on a deadline. And these people went after your story…"

"You don't know the half of it! Some at our college are in on it. Earlier they tried to block us from attending the Georgia Communications Conference in Savannah, as well as the regional conference in New Orleans, even suspending me."

Isaac chimed in. "Good thing Mom and Pyramid Coffee bailed you out."

Carlson looked outraged as if it had all happened to him personally. "Let me help you get back at whoever is doing this to you."

"Bob, I'm not interested in revenge. I just want the truth…"

Pierce checked his cell phone. "Kat just texted me. She's good with me giving you my follow-up story."

Jackson hit send, then went back to his chicken curry while Isaac related one of the better volleys of the day in his tennis tournament to their guest. Ignoring his meal, Bob read Pierce's article intently.

A few minutes later, the reporter gasped. "So, it's Preston Powell Partnership behind all of this?"

Jackson hesitated. "I'm taking that out of the article, so the college, the students, and I don't get sued…"

"Take it out if you want. But thanks for the big lead!" With that, Carlson dropped two twenties on the table and bolted from the chair. "Sorry I have to run, but… you know, deadline." He exited the restaurant rapidly. A patron watched him go, then resumed eating.

Jackson began to wonder if he'd done the right thing. Isaac broke the silence. "Well, Dad, that's the press for ya!"

The CEO of the Preston Powell Partnership, informally known as Product Placement Partnership, checked his tie and teeth in a mirror, just before one of the secretaries ushered Giselle Robideaux into the office, flanked by Darcie Matthews and Preston Powell himself. Giselle wasn't dressed up, or made-up like her Hollywood persona. Now she just looked scared and vulnerable… just what Jeremiah Calhoun liked to see in a woman.

"Miss Robideaux, it is a pleasure to…"

"I don't want to finish this movie, after what *that man* did to me!"

"Don't worry, my lady. Someone who just looks like him will replace him," Jeremiah Calhoun promised, with a smile.

"That was a very scary event, being kidnapped," the actress explained. "I have had nightmares about it!"

Jeremiah didn't know which he found more alluring, her tale or her French accent.

Darcie tried a different tack as her boss seemed mesmerized. "But Miss Robideaux, you're the talk of Hollywood! The news media is begging for more. And you're number one, trending on all social media accounts!"

Jeremiah folded his fingers together. "Perhaps Summit Studios can provide some 'hazard pay' for this little *change* in the script."

"I don't need any more money, Mr. Calhoun." The madder she got, the thicker her French accent.

"Actually, Miss Robideaux, you do."

Jeremiah pressed a button, and the door opened. Chip McLane came in with a manila folder, marked "Confidential," and slid it across the table to his boss.

"My associate, Mr. McLane, has reviewed your financial records. It seems you spend a lot more than you can afford to pay in taxes. And if you lose work, you'll lose your mansion."

"Wha-what do you mean?" she stammered.

Flirtation was over. Now, it was business for Jeremiah Calhoun. "I'll see to it that you'll never work in Hollywood if you won't finish the picture with Summit Studios, Miss Robideaux!"

She held her hand to her mouth in shock. "I-I'll finish it." Then her eyes became slits. "You're meaner than Dale Travis!"

Jeremiah smiled. *She was right.*

———

"So, what shall we talk about today, Mr. Dixon?" Jeremiah began at a meeting of several PPP employees and leaders the next day.

PPP's security specialist was rarely worried. Today was an exception.

"Jackson Pierce, that Georgian professor we've been tracking, had dinner with Bob Carlson, Mr. Calhoun."

Jeremiah spat out his Frappuccino. "That little *snake* has been a thorn in my side for too long!"

"Dr. Pierce?"

"No! I'm talking about that slimeball reporter!" Jeremiah explained to the PPP workers assembled. "Carlson. He's dangerous. We set him up in Washington D.C. years ago, but it seems he's trying to make a comeback."

Wallace Bragg weighed in. "He now writes for the *Savannah Herald-Post*, one of the few papers that didn't retract Pierce's story. We've got Dewey Symington preparing to sue them."

Calhoun reached over to pick up the photo that Dixon took. "Hap snapped this photo at a Thai restaurant the other night," Wallace explained, "where Carlson joined the Pierces' for dinner. And they had a long conversation."

Ray Maillon, who had been fiddling with his cell phone, looked at the image Calhoun was studying. "Hey, that's Kimber's new boyfriend."

All turned to stare at him. Calhoun squinted skeptically. "Are you sure, Mr. Maillon?"

"Well, I don't know if they're officially dating, but I saw Carlson escort her to her car earlier today."

Calhoun looked at Darcie, expecting a response.

"She hasn't said anything to me about a new boyfriend," his employee stated nervously.

Jeremiah's face could not betray his anger. "First, a Savannah paper doesn't pull their story on us. Now, their star reporter is meeting one of my employees?! I don't like it!"

Darcie tried to calm her boss. "Let me talk to her. I'll…"

"Sorry, Ms. Matthews," Calhoun snapped. "She kept this from you. She betrayed our trust."

Then he pointed a finger that shook with his fury. "You'll say nothing to Kimber, Darcie. I don't care if she is your friend. Mr. Dixon, you and Mr. Turosz follow Kimber tonight. We can't take the chance that this could be anything but cooperation with our enemies."

After allowing his anger to subside, Jeremiah returned to the agenda. "So our enemies from Peach State College prevailed in New Orleans at that scholastic competition." His fury then turned on Edward Edmund Kirby. "Dr. Kirby, you told me they had no chance of winning this thing!"

Kirby spluttered. "I thought it was unlikely that a glorified community college could compete against the likes of Duke and Vanderbilt."

"Who gives a *rip* what you think!" Calhoun snapped. "I'm more interested in what we're going to do now about the professor and his undergraduate students."

The Spider rarely spoke at meetings, but that would change today. "We've already hit the families hard. And we've told them how the pain can end if their kids drop out of the program."

"And we got Jackson suspended," Kirby pointed out.

Calhoun threw up his hands. "Then how could they win in New Orleans?"

Kirby hated the words that would follow. "Our man at PSC, Dean Franklin Arbell, did not anticipate that Pierce's wife, also a professor at the college, would replace her husband, take the students to New Orleans, and lead them to victory."

Calhoun slammed his hand down. "We've been too easy on them! The gloves come off now. This time, we hit the kids where it really hurts."

After a pause, the PPP founder added, "Perhaps it's time I departed for the day."

As Preston Powell exited the room, discussion resumed on how to increase the stress on the college students and their professor.

"One kid is going out for the NFL," Vinny Moro offered.

"Figure out who is scouting him," Jeremiah ordered. "Then make sure he doesn't stand a chance, unless he 'plays ball' and drops the research."

"Some of the kids are applying for graduate school and law school," Wallace Bragg, his second-in-command, stated.

"Ensure they get rejected unless they quit the project," Jeremiah insisted. "Next?"

"That Middle Eastern kid is going for a USBC internship," Darcie checked her notes.

Calhoun smiled. "Have them reject her. Make sure other networks and TV stations follow their lead, until she abandons the research project."

Spider raised his hand. "One of their's is a hacker. I'm sure…"

"We have contacts that can leak her to law enforcement. She can side with Jackson and go to prison, or listen to us."

"But what about the professor?" Kirby pressed on. "I mean we can have Dean Arbell suspend his wife Elena, too…"

"And get some friends on campus to step in and lead them?" Calhoun retorted. "What I have in mind is a more permanent solution, for all of them, perhaps…"

He snapped his fingers at Ray Maillon. "Get your buddy Larry Murray in on this plan. We're going to take care of this problem once and for all, and get a new client in the process."
"What product is that?"
Jeremiah Calhoun grinned. "Guns!"

April–May

CHAPTER 40:

Wednesday, April 2

The wide receiver chucked his video game console, dove across his dorm room, and swiped the campus phone on the second ring.

"Nat Holman? This is Guy Van Zandt..." a voice rasped on the other line.

The Peach State College wide receiver knew exactly who the assistant GM for the New York Jets was. The team had invited him for a tryout that was to take place the following week.

"...I'm sorry, but we have to cancel."

What? This was bad news.

"We heard about a scandal involving your academic record, where newspapers are pulling an article you helped write for a class."

"I can explain..."

"I'm sorry, but there have been too many incidents of player misconduct in the National Football League for us to take a chance on you, especially in a draft where there are so many talented receivers available."

Nat's mouth moved, but no words came out. The line on the other end went dead. This was terrible. His only options now were the Packers, maybe the Titans, and hopefully the Falcons. Then his cell phone vibrated, displaying a Nashville area code.

No... no... he pleaded.

———

Down the hall, Trey's phone also rang. It was his dad.

"Hey, Trey, know what's going on over at Peach State College involving our Edict?"

"No… what happened?" The PSC student was now getting nervous.

"I got a call from Sam in purchasing," the CEO of Bradford Communications explained. "It seems your college cancelled their order for Edicts from all of the coaches."

"What? No… Dad… let me talk to Coach Wesley…"

"A 'Dean Franklin Arbell' issued the order the other night, effective immediately. They're going with 'The Miracle'."

"Arbell is the guy who has been giving us so much trouble, Dad," Trey replied. "He tried to block our funds and got Dr. Pierce suspended."

"Well, he's now cutting into our business," Bradford complained. "I have no idea who you kids and your professor ticked off, but they're going after us, as well. We've got to do something about this, and sooner rather than later. I'll be damned if I lose out to that holier-than-thou…"

———

The letter from the University of Southern California was a little thin, Sgt. Paul Herrera noted. Their prior message was a thick packet with an acceptance letter and a stack of graduate school information, which he proudly showed to his class. *California Dreamin',* he thought at the time.

This mailer was only a page long. But it only took two sentences to convey the bleak message.

"Bad news too, Sarge?"

He shielded his eyes from the sun, taking a second to adjust, to see Sylvia Wright, hands on her hips, a crumpled note in her hand.

"Yeah… wait, what happened to you?"

His classmate related her tale of her morning. That paid internship for the law firm of Stone, Richey, and Taylor up in Atlanta, which she just won last week, had disappeared.

"They told me that because of our 'tainted' research project, they couldn't 'trust me with legal research' anymore. Nashville School of Law rescinded its acceptance. Well, I'm gonna…" Sylvia's rising voice stopped suddenly as she checked her buzzing cell phone.

It was a text from A.I.

"I'm in big trouble."

———

They raced over to her dorm, where they got the whole story. A.I. received an encrypted email. After checking it for viruses, she opened it. It came from some anti-hacker group, she explained. "They told me they would be after me for all my computer activities, and then they'd turn me into the Department of Homeland Security. While I was emailing them back that I hadn't really done anything… well, anything violating national security… this card was slipped under my door."

Paul and Sylvia looked at the image of a famous graveyard, maybe in Salem, Massachusetts. The typed message on the back, with no address, simply said "Drop the research project."

"Anyone heard from Taira?" Paul asked.

Sylvia looked over from the chair where she was sitting. "I've tried calling and texting her this morning, but no answer."

A.I. surprised everyone with her boldness. "Call Nat and Trey… let's g-get over to her place, and fast!"

———

While most PSC students lived in the dorms, Taira opted for a small apartment just off the edge of campus, so she could throw the occasional party. Since all five of her classmates had been to those, they knew exactly where to go.

The students sprinted up the stairs to the second floor. After a knock, they heard a gasp. "Go away."

"Taira, we've got to talk. There are a lot of bad things happening…"

The door swung open, almost ripped from its hinges. Taira stood there, red-eyed, tears staining her makeup. Her hair was a mess, and she was in a bathrobe and slippers, even though it was almost lunchtime.

"I *know* about bad news!" she snapped. She then told them her dreams of making it in broadcast journalism were all but gone, as USBC canceled their internship, and threatened to tell other broadcasters why, noting their class research for the article.

"Then I got this shoved under my door," Taira flung the postcard at their feet. It was identical to the one A.I. had just shown them.

"I got one too," the computer geek said.

"Me too," Nat and Trey said as one.

Sylvia looked at Paul. "I am guessing there's one waiting for each of us back at our dorms."

"Don't you think it's odd-ddd that they didn't send it in campus mail?" A.I. ended the moment of silence.

"It's so they can't be traced," Nat offered.

"That's not the point I'm making," their resident computer hacker replied. "It means they had someone on campus hand-deliver it to each of our rooms. They know where we live and are close to us."

Sylvia waved off her classmate's ominous comment. "Well, they could have looked us up on the..."

Taira gasped. "But I'm unlisted!"

All froze, looking toward her door.

"We'd better tell Dr. Pierce right away," Trey stated, a quiver in his voice.

———

"Sorry for meeting like this," *Savannah Herald-Post* reporter Bob Carlson apologized to his interviewer on the dark street a few blocks from the PPP headquarters, though he wasn't really sorry. This evening's rendezvous reminded him of when he was in Washington D.C., going after politicians, looking for the next "Deep Throat" source, seeking that elusive

Pulitzer. If Ms. Elliot was being honest with him, it would put him in the running for an award and maybe get one of those big-time jobs in the nation's capital, or even New York.

Kimber Elliot bit her nails. "It's okay," she managed. "My conscience has been killing me about what's going on at PPP, where I work."

She detailed the recent events at the Preston Powell Partnership and named their clients. Some of it she had seen, and some of it came from Darcie. The rest she overheard in a conversation between Calhoun and Bragg.

Every sordid detail came out, from sleeping pill deaths, to car crashes, to computer hacks, to movie scandals. Carlson was glad he was secretly taping everything. The material was so shocking that he could only gape at some of the stories. SRD, Talladega Motors, Miracle, Summit Studios, USBC News… *A lot of heads were going to roll*, he thought.

"And the next company has something to do with guns!" Kimber blurted.

"Miss Elliot," Carlson managed. "I have to step out and contact my editor, okay?"

She weakly nodded.

Kimber felt better after getting these awful secrets off her chest. But what if Jeremiah found out that she was the source? She would have to get out of town, possibly out of the country. *I'll pack later tonight*, she thought.

Carlson smiled as he uploaded the audio file to Kat in Savannah. As it traveled electronically, he thought about giving it to New York or Washington D.C. instead, for more pay and even his old job back.

As he glanced up from his phone, he had only a moment to see the pickup truck and headlights zooming toward him. The vehicle slammed into his body and hit the truck so fast that neither he nor Kimber had time to so much as scream before the crash.

CHAPTER 41:

Thursday, April 3-Friday, April 4

Hap bolted from the shotgun side to dash over and try to track down Bob Carlson's cell phone on the dark street. Jeremiah was quite insistent on retrieving it from the reporter. But it was crushed beyond further usage.

Kimber was slumped over, bloodied and unconscious, but her body was still moving.

"Hey, she's…"

Oeznik flicked a lit match at the gasoline spread all over the road. He gestured to Hap, and the two bailed from the crash scene. *Sorry, kid,* Dixon thought. *But she talked. And they had a client to please.*

USBC would surely tell the tale of the deadly crash and how flammable Bob's rental truck, the Marshall Pioneer, was. The Spider had done well at tracking the Savannah reporter, not far from the PPP HQ, ensuring what he would be driving when he landed at LaGuardia by hacking the rental vehicle company Bob regularly used…

"I called in some favors and put some pressure on the kids and their parents," Wallace Bragg bragged. "It should be enough."

His superior at PPP, Jeremiah Calhoun, shook his head. "It's not enough, Mr. Bragg. Here's my plan. Call in Larry. Meet in my office in five minutes."

When the COO departed, Jeremiah waited in his office for his two employees to enter. Hap Dixon and Oeznik Turosz entered through the other door.

"Report."

"We did it," Hap replied in a low voice, so others outside wouldn't hear. "Both KIA."

"And their cell phones?"

His security chief produced a mangled piece of metal. "That's Bob's. Kimber's was fried in the fire."

Jeremiah frowned. "Bad luck."

Then he looked at the two responsible for the mission, more of an expression of pride that replaced the anxiety when he first heard about the reporter and Kimber. "But the matter has been taken care of. Thank you, gentlemen, for your service."

Oeznik and Hap smiled.

———

Wallace removed his glasses. "Jeremiah, I think we need to discuss this…"

"There's nothing to discuss, Mr. Bragg. Richmond & Webb have agreed to the deal."

"But… if we're found out…"

"Mr. Bragg, there's nothing to worry about," Jeremiah barked. "Think about what happens during a mass shooting. Everyone wants to know who the shooter is, why he did it, how many died, and… most importantly for us… what gun he used, which will be the RW-29, or 'The Rebel Yell'. Congress will want to outlaw it. Folks will want to sue the company. Neither the lawsuits nor the legislative ban will ever work. And we'll make more money than we've *ever* made in the past. What's so bad?"

Wallace slumped into a chair. Calhoun ignored his negative body language.

"So, Mr. Murray, any leads on our preferred perpetrator?"

The two ruled out skinheads, supremacists, and separatists for fear that the media would focus more on their extremist ideology than the gun.

"I can't believe we're contemplating this," Wallace gasped.

"I'm also working on an 'Incel' person at the target location you gave me," Larry said. "He can't get a date, hates women, is jealous of classmates, struggles at school, has few friends… a loner. I've already got him to do a job for us on PSC's campus. I can get him to do exactly what you want, for fame and notoriety."

"Target location?" Wallace's expression swung from Murray to Calhoun. "Where do you expect him to strike?"

"Why, Mr. Bragg, that's the best part. We'll kill two birds with one stone for this client and eliminate an enemy!"

———

Franklin Arbell entered the president's office at three that afternoon, as directed. Expecting to be briefed about the upcoming SACS review, the Dean was surprised to see President Sullivan with professors Jackson Pierce and Elena Pierce, as well as college attorney Jerome Baker, who also doubled as a local judge. Also there were Biology Professor Walt Diehl and Math Professor Mimi Grey.

President Sullivan wasted little time. "I'm told that, in my absence, you convened some ad-hoc Peer Review Committee to punish Professor Jackson Pierce."

While Dean Arbell fumbled for an excuse, Sullivan pressed on. "Who authorized that? I certainly didn't. Did you go through the Faculty Assembly?"

"You were busy with SACS…"

"Not even an email?"

"The charges were too serious to share in an email, President Sullivan."

"And your 'Peer Review Committee' actually suspended a professor?"

"Only from external activities," Arbell managed. He didn't like the direction this was going.

Dr. Elena Pierce stepped forward. "One third of our annual review comes from those external activities."

Sullivan glanced over at Baker. "Judge, what's your assessment?"

The college's legal representative shook his head. "If Jackson's suspension could impact his ability to fulfill his contract obligations, it would indeed be problematic."

"Could he sue?" PSC's President wondered aloud. Arbell gasped.

"He could," Baker concluded.

Before Arbell could speak, Jackson jumped in. "One of the committee members brought up that a PSC student was seeing a psychiatrist."

Sullivan held his head in his hands.

Dr. Diehl stepped forward. "President Sullivan, the Faculty Assembly is prepared to meet tomorrow on this matter."

Dr. Grey glared at Arbell. "We plan to call a vote of no confidence in you. Based on the way you've treated our professors, it should pass easily."

Hemmed in on all sides, Arbell stormed out of the room and slammed the door.

PSC's leader turned to Dr. Jackson Pierce. "My sincere apologies. Your suspension is lifted, of course."

Then Jackson Pierce thought back to Dr. Kirby's offer. *Looks like I don't need to compromise my morals to fight my own battles*, he concluded.

———

An hour later, Elena knocked on the classroom door. As Jackson answered, several members of the senior class at Peach State College applauded their mentor from the regional competition.

"No offense, Professor Pierce… you've taught us lots about research and statistics…" Nat began, referring to Jackson.

"But Professor Pierce… Elena… you showed us how to give better presentations!" Sylvia finished.

Elena waved them off. "You all can now begin your careers on Broadway or in Hollywood!" All laughed.

Then the English Professor added, "I just came by to tell you all that according to Suzanne LaFleur, the secretary, Dean Franklin Arbell is in his office, writing what looks like a resignation letter."

That brought cheers from the class, though it was replaced seconds later by what sounded like fireworks, amid a whistling, screeching metallic sound. The students looked around nervously while Jackson sprang for the door, locking it.

"Get all the chairs and tables you can and help me barricade the door!" he shouted to his students. "That's the sound of a gun out there!"

=====

Sgt. Paul Herrera was almost never late to class and hadn't pulled a tardy in his senior year. But he was amazed to find a fellow vet on campus who had also served in Iraq. While Herrera had patrolled the streets of Baghdad, Private Chris Jacobson had battled insurgents in the Anbar Rrovince. Now, as Herrera was hoping to graduate, Jacobson was splitting time between his courses in civil engineering and providing campus security. Paul and his fellow trainee from Fort George Thomas shared a Pyramid Coffee cup when...

The two heard the awful sounds that could not be mistaken for a car's repeated backfire. The nearly empty cup fell from Herrera's hands, and Jacobson reached for his holster. The shots were loud and constant, having a scream to it... *Perhaps that crazy new automatic weapon*, Herrera thought.

"What are you doing with a gun?" Jacobson gasped. "I thought they were illegal for students!"

"Got threatened the other day," Herrera responded.

"Well, come on, Sarge," the security officer insisted. "We might need your help."

They sprinted toward the sound of the gunfire, near the Beauchamp Building. Several students either hit the dirt, or *were* hit. A few stood like statues.

"*Get down*," Jacobson yelled. Half did. Herrera tackled a maintenance worker and knocked aside a stunned undergraduate, falling to the ground in the process. Next to him lay a female student in a sorority t-shirt, motionless, with a vacant expression on her face. Blood ran down from a massive chest wound. *No way to help her right now*, he thought.

Jacobson pulled at the door to the Beauchamp building, but immediately ducked back as a hail of bullets flew out the door. The rest struck the door itself. The security guard fired a round inside in the direction of the shooter. No reply. Jacobson, covered by Herrera, did a "turkey peek" to try and confirm the killer's location, but the shooter had made his way up the steps. Several shots followed with that high-pitch whine, and a male body slid down… looked like a professor, whose white shirt was now mostly stained red. Though Herrera wanted to help him, he couldn't do much good with an active shooter firing at him. He followed Jacobson up the steps. On the second floor, a burst hit Jacobson just as he discharged his pistol, and his fellow veteran staggered back into the stairwell, hit at least twice.

Tamping down his rage, Herrera remembered his training and quietly peeked around the door. The shooter, with that "Rebel Yell" gun, was peering through a window of a classroom, as if looking for something or someone. Then, he moved toward the door of the classroom where he and his fellow seniors met, glancing inside. Then the shooter pointed his gun at the door.

Herrera squeezed the trigger, just as the gunman fired a burst through the door.

CHAPTER 42:
Friday, April 4

Bodies and blood littered the floor. Weeping college kids and professors stood about, the police kneeling alongside the shocked survivors, all the subject of jarring graphic imagery that were now headed to anti-gun groups and politicians, courtesy of The Spider's algorithm.

But Evan Gordy knew his boss wouldn't be mad.

Nothing spiked gun sales like mass shootings and calls to outlaw these weapons. *Such opponents of firearms never learned,* Evan Gordy mused. Showing where gun regulations worked built support for the cause of gun safety. But no, firearm regulators preferred to wave the bloody shirt. And *that's* why Americans owned millions of guns.

But The Spider's web wasn't fully woven. There was more chaos to spread. Pro-gun groups needed to know that the government was coming for their guns. That would freak them out, as usual. The name Rebel Yell gave him an idea. What if those "New Confederate" groups were encouraged to buy these, and maybe start a new rebellion of their own?

———

When he awoke, PSC security guard Chris Jacobson found himself in St. Charles Borromeo, the Catholic Hospital on the east side of town. He was staring up into the eyes of his college president, Alex Sullivan. There was also Alexandra's police chief, as well as a woman with an ATF cap. There was also a bald guy with shades and a dark suit whose outfit practically screamed FBI. Coming over was a professor from Peach State College whom he recognized. Sgt. Herrera was there too, looking relieved.

"PSC owes you a debt of gratitude," the president said.

"Wish I could have been there sooner," Jacobson rasped. *It hurt to breathe.*

"No one could have done better," admitted Police Chief Drew Hekmayer.

"Several must have died," Jacobson croaked.

Chief Hekmayer nodded. "Dr. Michael Clausen of Data Science and Hayley Terrell, an undergraduate student. Her twin sister, Harley, and several students and staff are here at St. Charles…"

A nurse and doctor tried to shoo them away, but the security guard said, "I have questions."

The nurse threw up her hands in disgust, but the doctor nodded.

"Who… was the gunman?"

"It was a student… Randall Rodes," President Sullivan explained. "He had withdrawn from all classes a few days ago. We don't know why."

Jacobson didn't ask about Rodes' condition. The past-tense reference cued him in that the shooter didn't make it. *Had his shot connected?* The security guard slipped into unconsciousness before he could remember.

"Jacobson will likely make it, President Sullivan," the doctor stated. "He's in serious, but thankfully stable, condition."

═══

The others in the patient's room turned to Herrera.

The ATF woman asked the first question.

"What was he doing when you got on the second floor of Beauchamp?"

"He was trying to shoot his way into Room 204."

"He wasn't going up and down the hall?" The FBI guy asked.

"He wanted to get into Room 204. No place else. He acted like he wanted someone in there dead. And I was supposed to be there in that room too, but I was running late."

"Why did you have a gun?" the ATF agent asked Herrera.

The ex-military communications student held up his hands. "Everyone in the class got a threatening postcard the other day. They even left one at Taira's unlisted address, so I thought somebody must be stalking us. I'm sorry, President Sullivan. I know it's against the rules…"

The FBI agent asked, "Do you still have that threatening postcard?"

Jackson handed one to the man in the shades. "Sylvia brought her postcard to class to show me."

"Yeah, that's what mine looked like," Paul added.

President Sullivan shook his head. "Normally, the rules call for…" Then he paused. "Can the official report say our security officer shot him?"

"Well…"

"Maybe if someone else is involved, it won't tip them off about the investigation," Jackson suggested.

"Okay," the ATF agent agreed. "For now."

———

Elena was waiting outside Jacobson's room, with Vivian and Isaac. President Sullivan acknowledged the English Professor and then invited the Pierces' to go to the waiting room. She whispered to her daughter. Vivian looked at Isaac.

"Let's see if we can find a vending machine that has Cool Ranch Doritos." The two of them bolted for the elevator.

The law enforcement officers joined them in the waiting room. "Sorry, I didn't want to alarm your kids," President Sullivan explained to the Pierces'. "But I thought you should know something about today's shooting."

"You were both in Beauchamp Hall, Room 204, right, professors?" Chief Hekmayer asked.

Jackson nodded weakly. "I wasn't normally going to be there," Elena said. "But I had news to share."

The FBI man replied. "Could you hear the shooter at your door?"

Elena shuddered. "Yes."

Jackson explained. "He peered inside the doorway. Then, he fired back at the security guard. A few seconds later, he fired into the door and fell when another shot rang out. We were pinned down behind the table, and fortunately, none of us were hurt."

The woman with the ATF cap stepped forward. "Do you know the name Randall Rodes? Have you ever interacted with him? Did he take any classes with you?"

"I've never had him in my class, nor have I heard of him until today," Jackson said.

"He's never taken any of my courses, either," Elena added.

ATF and FBI nodded at each other. "We're interviewing your students right now, Dr. Pierce," Chief Hekmayer noted. "One of them, Taira Malek, thinks his name sounded familiar."

"Rodes took down his social media and email accounts," the FBI agent admitted. "We're having some trouble figuring out how to get into them."

Jackson brightened. "One of our students, A–I mean Alicia Ina Sheehy, is as good a computer geek as I've ever seen. She probably knows how college students cover their tracks in ways your agencies may not know."

The two government agents looked at each other. He jotted down something while she nodded.

Chief Hekmayer persisted. "So, you can't think of a reason Rodes wanted you dead?"

"Sorry, Chief. I have no idea."

President Sullivan shook his head. "He shot his parents and sister at his house near Tifton. He gunned down a student and hit a few on the way to Beauchamp, but it seemed more to scatter them. He killed Dr. Clausen on the way up the stairs, but that's because the professor tried to stop him. On the second floor, he passed Rooms 201, 202, and 203. And Dr. Eugene Bullock, who was in Room 201, suffered a heart attack..."

"He died?" gasped Elena. "He and I are on the Curriculum Committee!"

"He's still with the pulmonologist, but doctors think he'll probably make it," President Sullivan reassured her.

Hekmayer clasped his hands together. "Rooms 201, 202, and 203 were unlocked. When Bullock went down in 201, his students focused on trying to help him rather than securing the door. In 203, they hid under their desks, but forgot to keep the intruder from entering. Each of these rooms would have been easy pickings for a shooter intent upon creating a mass casualty event. Rooms 201 and 203 had glass windows... making it easy to spot victims. But Rodes ignored them."

The police chief looked at the professors with concern. "He wanted someone dead in Room 204. Why pass up easy victims to go after a locked door with no guarantee of casualties, unless someone was targeted?"

The question that nobody knew the answer to hung in the air, as Vivian and Isaac reentered the room, with a compromise: Nacho Cheese Doritos.

"What?" the youngest asked, as the room fell silent.

"That's right," the TV blared in the waiting room, set to USBC, everyone's new favorite news channel.

"It was a 'Rebel Yell' assault rifle, made by Richmond & Webb, whose trademark is that eerie scream that puts fear into the victims," explained lead anchor Mick Camden.

"Authorities are looking into how Rodes procured the weapon that killed the professor and the student at Peach State College," co-anchor Paige Glass continued. "It may also be the same gun that killed his family."

The two anchors then shifted to the Congressional debate over whether the "Rebel Yell" should be banned or not.

Chief Hekmayer stared at the screen in disgust. "Looks like they care more about the gun than they do the victims!"

Both Pierces looked at each other.

"Something jog your mind?" the FBI agent inquired.

"Nothing you'd believe," muttered Jackson.

The ATF agent frowned. "Well, if you change your mind..." She handed a business card to Elena. "Call us if the situation changes."

The two departed with Chief Hekmayer. Elena's cell phone rang.

"Dr. Pierce… it's Donna Macklin," her neighbor began. "Your house is on fire."

———

Nothing prepares you for "your house is on fire," Jackson thought. *It's not just your shelter. It's your possessions, your memories, things that can't be replaced, and others that insurance just can't pay for. Thank God they didn't have a pet anymore, and that they were putting off getting a cat until the summer. And the insurance premiums were paid up.* But everything he would lose raced through his mind on the fast drive home from the hospital.

Alexandria was a small town where everyone knew each other. Neighbors like the Macklins, the Tates, the Laynes, and Lambeths were there already, carrying dishes and even some furniture away, as the last of the fires were put out by the local firefighters.

"I got a 'Deer Cooler' and no deer in it," Mark Lambeth said as he and his wife, Mindy, and the kids had armfuls of their refrigerator food in their arms. "We'll be glad to hold it for you, as your fridge looks fried."

"Much obliged, Mark," Jackson managed, exhausted by the day's events.

"At least the back rooms didn't burn," Mindy offered. She was holding a piece of Vivian's artwork, the second-place ribbon from the city contest still trailing behind it.

Inside, Fire Chief Chuck Woodward gave the tour. "Fire damaged your kitchen, laundry room, and more than half of your family room," he began.

"How did it start?" Elena asked.

"This was no ordinary fire," the chief replied. "It was arson."

All four Pierces' jaws dropped. This was not what they were expecting to hear.

"The perps were pretty clever," Chief Woodward began. "They didn't use an accelerant, as most amateurs do. Instead, they malfunctioned your toaster oven."

"We haven't even used that since we fixed the microwave," Isaac claimed.

The fire chief eyed him. "They knew what to do to make it look like an accident. You'd miss it if you didn't know what to look for. But I worked the detail when they burned down the home of that civil rights guy in Clifton, Ernie Curtiss."

Jackson frowned. "But why did you even suspect arson?"

"I'll show you."

The mustachioed man gestured for them to join him in the back bedroom.

"The rooms were all ransacked. They were looking for something." All could see the adults' room had clearly been tossed, while the kids' rooms looked like normal kid rooms.

"My room's messy enough to look like an intruder worked it over," Isaac joked. "Probably looking for my baseball card collection." He exited the hallway, to check.

"Is someone targeting us?" Vivian shivered. Elena put her arms around her daughter, going full mama bear.

"They didn't go for your TV or DVD player," Chief Chuck pointed out. "So, it wasn't an ordinary burglary. They did seem interested in your CDs and computer stuff. Do you notice anything missing?"

Elena detached herself from Vivian to join Jackson in his search. He knew his laptop was still in his car, and he had been keeping the flash drive in a tiny metal tea box… Viv's idea… in his jacket pocket.

"Nothing… that I can see," Jackson mumbled.

"Know what they might have been looking for?" The chief persisted.

"I'm not sure you'd believe me if I guessed at what it could be," the communications professor claimed

"Well, at least let Hekmayer know… trust me, he'd help you if you told him."

While the Pierces' mulled it over, Fire Chief Woodward added. "I gotta tell him anyway, 'cause of the arson."

The silence was interrupted by a cell phone call from President Sullivan. "I heard about the news… so sorry… Christine and I send out our prayers. Was it a total loss?"

"No, Alex," Jackson replied. "But it's pretty close to it. The whole place reeks of smoke, and the half that technically survived isn't habitable. Someone seems to have set the fire to cover the fact that they ransacked our back bedrooms."

"Think it's about your research project?"

"As crazy as it sounds, Elena and I are thinking the same thing."

"Well, as for a place to stay, even to hide, you can stay in one of our dorms with a suite. One set of occupants got an apartment for the summer. And you can use your IDs to eat in the cafeteria, grill, and coffeehouse," Sullivan replied. "But please keep a very low profile."

"Thanks," Elena called out over her husband's shoulder. "We really appreciate that."

"Well, I hate to be the bearer of worse tidings for you two, but there are several students and parents from your senior class on campus, in my office. They want to meet tonight."

CHAPTER 43:

Friday, April 4-Saturday, April 5-Monday, April 7

The Lakken Room in the Peach State College Administration building, one floor below the President and Higher Education Dean's office, was where prospective students and their parents would meet with an administrator to make the official decision to commit to PSC. When the college made a big signing, the media was invited. But there would be no cameras tonight. In fact, President Sullivan took the unprecedented step of bringing on two police officers from APD, a request Chief Hekmayer was more than happy to grant.

All of the communications students were there: Paul, Sylvia, Nat, Trey, Taira, and A.I. Jackson recognized several of their parents, as he had invited them to his classes and conferences.

Given the expressions on their faces, which ranged from worried to angry, he was glad he wasn't meeting them for the first time. This was not going to be a pleasant session.

One by one, the parents listed their complaints. Their children lost scholarships, internships, acceptances, tryouts, and job offers. Some had been threatened with investigations. For the parents, houses, jobs, businesses, churches, and even citizenship were in jeopardy.

Elena shook her head in dismay. It was one thing to get around that damned Dean and his toadies to get the money to present at a conference. But this went well beyond Arbell and his cronies on campus. He didn't have that kind of pull. Whoever was targeting them was powerful. She wondered whose hornet's nest Jackson and his students had actually kicked.

Jackson staggered to his feet, like a boxer who had been knocked down in late rounds. "I hear you all… no, I really do. You may not know this, but our house was ransacked, and whoever did so burned down our place to cover their tracks."

Anger was replaced by shock among his students and their parents or caregivers. He thought he even spotted a minister among the group.

"I swear to you that when I started this whole thing with my students, Trey, Paul, Sylvia, Taira, Nat and A… Alicia Ina, we had *no* intention of causing trouble. We were just interested in how some products were being covered in the news. And we hoped to win an award or two at a conference, get some lines on a resume. And I was kind of hoping a conference win might help get me tenure. Nothing more than that. And now we've clearly ticked off someone powerful nationwide, and they've come at us with everything they've got."

Jackson took a deep breath. "Since I've started this, I've been suspended, lost my house, and most of my possessions. Tenure is now off the table. And you may not know this, but according to the police, we may have been the targets for that shooter today."

Several parents and some of the students got to their feet, shouting angrily. Jackson saw Sylvia's mom slump over, as if she'd fainted. Others gathered around to revive her. Everyone was talking at once. President Sullivan raised his hands in a vain attempt to calm things down.

Jackson looked into his students' eyes. "Each of us has been given a message one way or another… drop the research, or else. I even had someone on the board that suspended me give me a job offer and opportunities to make several times more than I make here… if we all just, you know, play ball, and stop the research."

The communications professor hugged his kids and Elena. "Several people died today in the shooting. Our research isn't worth even one life. For once, I'm not even interested in tenure anymore. Let's vote whether to continue or end this project. I'll get some paper…"

Senami Malek bowed her head before replying. "We've been threatened with deportation."

Everyone gasped as they looked in her direction.

"Okay, that's it," Jackson sighed. "I'm pulling the plug…"

Sadik, her husband, cut him off. "Wait a moment, Professor Pierce. We came to this country years ago to leave dangerous people. But we love the United States and don't want to see it turn into the way it used to be in our former home country. We decided, as a family, that we will risk it." He hugged his daughter, who took it in stride.

The tallest man present stood up, walked to the front so that he was nearly eye-to-eye with Jackson. "My name's Major George Herrera. I just drove up from MacDill Air Force Base in Tampa. I was gonna remove Paul from this place. But before you got here, we all talked." He indicated Carmen and the rest of the families.

"In the military, you do your job," the Major continued. "You don't cut-and-run… even when it's dangerous. People have died because of whatever you're looking into. And that's not right. This mission sounds more important than anything. I say we fight those bastards who've ruined or killed people!"

"Hear, hear!" announced Rick Hinton, Nat's older brother, clapping the football player on the back.

Lyndsey Bradford stood from her chair. "We're all trying to give our kids a good education… teach them something more than just memorizing some text from a book. Life beyond college may not be this hard, but it won't be easy. I'm sure the Reverend here could say something from the Good Book to fit this occasion."

Rev. Braxton Quincy pulled out a book, but not one the others expected. It was a collection of poems by Robert Frost. "We must take the road less traveled by. That will make all the difference."

It almost sounded like cheers, a bewildered Jackson observed, as the students and families reacted to those words.

"But what do the students think?" asked Helen Ridgefield, A.I.'s caregiver.

"We've already talked about it," Sylvia began.

"We're ready to go as far as you'll take us, Dr. Pierce," Trey croaked. "We don't want Hayley and Dr. Clausen to have died in vain."

"Something tells me they won't stop trying to silence us, even if we say nothing more," Paul pointed out. "We already know too much."

Nat stood up. "All this time, we've been playing defense. They've been going after us. It's time to play a little offense and take the fight to *them*."

"If we present our work… maybe others at nationals will learn the truth. Authorities might go after whoever is doing this," Taira added enthusiastically. "If everyone knows, it won't matter if they silence us."

"On…to Washington!" A.I. shocked everyone by speaking. The resulting applause let Jackson and Elena know all they needed to about where everyone else stood on continuing with the research project and the national competition.

———

With only a few days before the National Communications Conference, there was still the matter of Isaac's tournament. Now in the Final Four, Jackson's son had gone further than he, or anyone else in his family and school, could have expected. Fortunately, his gear and equipment were in a locker room at school, and not burned.

"Rumor is that your opponent, Max Early, narrowly missed qualifying for the U.S. Open," Uncle R.J. explained, having driven his own family up to meet the Pierces'. "Our kids read about him in *Sports Illustrated Teen*."

"Looks like he has his own entourage," Aunt Kat groaned.

Something suddenly occurred to Isaac. "Dad, where's my inhaler?!"

"It's in your bag, Isaac."

"Yeah but… Oh, crap… wrong bag!"

Kat spun around. "R.J. and I will get it!"

They prepared to leave, but a judge held up his hand. "You can't give anything to a player once the match starts, so unless you make it back in five minutes, don't bother."

"That's completely unfair," Jackson protested.

"I'll make sure the press hears about this!" Kat threatened.

The judge threw up his hands. "Take it up with the Georgia Youth Tennis Association, lady!"

Isaac trudged toward the court, looking defeated before the match even began.

Jackson, Kat, R.J., and the kids made their way to the stands. Sure enough, Isaac lost badly, 6-1 in the first set. He put up a valiant effort, but the outcome was a foregone conclusion this afternoon.

In between the sets, Jackson went down to see his son. Isaac was slumped on his chair, looking drained as his coach tried to find the right words to inspire his player.

"Any advice, Dad?" he asked as his father came over.

"The odds are against you," Jackson admitted. "And you don't have your inhaler. Nobody expects you to win a single game, much less a set. Nobody would blame you for losing."

"Great pep talk, Dad," Isaac smiled weakly.

"But I've never seen you quit," his father told him. "And that's helped keep me going through all of this with the research project, the loss of the house, the shooting, the suspension…"

"Really?" his son perked up. "I was your inspiration?"

"The persistence part," Jackson explained. "I get the 'do the right thing' part from your sister these days, and your mom knows how to get things done. But your tenacity has rubbed off on me. I'm going to see this to the end."

"Time to get back on the court," barked a judge.

"I'll give everyone something to remember," Isaac promised. He gave his dad an elbow bump. Jackson noticed a new spring in his son's step.

"I got this," he muttered.

Sure enough, Max did go up 2-0, but he had to fight for every game. Eventually, Isaac broke through to make it 2-1. Going into the afternoon, the seesaw battle continued: 3-1, 3-2, 4-2, 4-3, 4-4… the crowd went wild when Isaac tied it up. He even took a 5-4 lead until Max battled back to make it 5-5. Then 6-5… 6-6. The set dragged into the afternoon. Several times, Max hit a kill shot, only to have Isaac manage to track it down, keeping it in play. The lights came on, and everyone still at the courts had their eyes on this titanic battle.

Finally, as the set went 34-33, Max hit an incredible backhand just beyond Isaac's reach to take the second set, and the match. But the angry favorite stormed into the locker room, blowing past his girlfriend, coach, agent, and publicist, showing only his back to the photographer.

The press, however, did not pursue Early as he stomped off. Instead, they swarmed an exhausted Isaac who, despite his condition, was smiling, even adding a few quips about his great set.

"That little kid was like Rocky out there," one journalist proclaimed.

"He's a smart guy," another sports reporter noted. "He interviews even better than he plays."

"He's got a future in tennis for sure," a third remarked.

Isaac grinned weakly at his dad as Elena, Kat, R.J., and others joined the crowd around him.

"Glad I could *inspire* you to keep going with that research."

CHAPTER 44:
Tuesday, April 8

"So, who do we face at the National Communications Conference?" Sylvia asked, looking up from one of the small library study rooms at Peach State College.

Jackson looked up from his laptop. In all of the chaos from the shooting, the destroyed home, and additional threats, he hadn't devoted much time to those details. He shifted over to the conference website and opened a link.

"All of the finalists for each region are invited, but only the four regional winners will compete to determine the overall winner. Let's see… the University of Pennsylvania took the Northeast region. Wisconsin won the Midwest region, and USC was the clear winner out West. The second and third-place finishers from each region will go to D.C. But only the four winners will be on the final panel."

Paul Herrera winced at the mention of USC. He had been hoping to attend their graduate school before someone convinced their department to change the acceptance to a rejection. "Are you both coming with us, Dr. Pierce… and Dr. Pierce?"

Elena looked at Jackson. "I will be there to make sure you all present well. Vivian and Isaac agreed to stay with Kat and R.J. in Savannah. Under the circumstances, that's probably the safest thing to do."

"Yeah." Her husband nodded. "Their kids are camping that week, and Isaac can join them… he needs a few more outings for a merit badge. And Viv can look at the area around the Savannah College of Art and Design."

"But how are we going to get to D.C.?" The anxiety in Taira's voice was unmistakable. The strain was clearly taking its toll on her nerves. She hugged her knees to her chest on the library chair.

"Whoever is after us will probably be watching the airports and the roads, trying to spot any van with a PSC logo," Nat pointed out. "And I bet they can check for hotels and rentals."

"It's like those spy movies you watch," Sylvia grinned. "I swear you see more of those than game films."

President Sullivan looked up from his cell phone. "Just got a text from Rob Vidale. He told me that our college just bought a van from ABAC to replace the bus with a leaky radiator. The van still has the ABAC logo and school colors."

Paul laughed. "So we'll pretend to be from Abraham Baldwin Ag College? Going incognito! I *like* it."

"How many can it fit?"

"A dozen." Rob's familiar voice came through Sullivan's speakerphone. "Plus, two coaches and a driver. You'll be plenty comfy, even if you take the kids the whole way."

"Thanks. Sounds good." Jackson smiled. "We may get all the way to Washington D.C. before they even notice."

Elena pursed her lips, as she usually did when she was nervous. "But won't they be waiting for us at the conference?"

"Yeah… we gotta plan for that," Jackson admitted.

"Disguises?" Nat wondered aloud.

"Spy stuff again!" Sylvia laughed.

Trey glanced at A.I. "Does that stuff even work on security cameras and facial recognition?"

A.I. fixed Nat with a stare. "Probably depends on howgoodyour disguise is."

———

Jeremiah began the morning meeting, scheduled an hour before business opened, showing an increasing level of concern. After berating Juan for the botched arson and inability to find the Pierces" files, and then browbeating Larry when his shooter failed to take out the targeted students and professors, the CEO demanded answers. "How are we going to stop them from presenting at this D.C. conference?"

"Perhaps we should leave them alone," Darcie Matthews managed nervously. "The fact that PSC keeps winning is getting those students and their professors a lot of attention. Reporters are starting to look into those retractions and apologies that we made the newspapers write. Their appearance in D.C. is likely to be a big deal."

"And how is it that Professor Pierce still has a job… Dr. Kirby?" Calhoun growled. "Didn't you fix it so that he was suspended?"

Kirby stammered. "Yes… ah… well, his wife outsmarted the Dean. And now it seems the PSC President has overruled our Peer Review Committee, and Arbell is looking for a new job, under a lot of pressure."

Jeremiah Calhoun paced around the room. At one point, it seemed no one could touch them. Now, with that column and more to come, he could feel it all slipping away. *We have to regain the upper hand,* he said to himself.

Calhoun hatched a plan. Their employees would watch the PSC campus and airports, while The Spider would monitor computers for reservations and travel tickets.

Chip nervously raised his hand. "Mr. Calhoun… ah… er…."

"What, Mr. McLane?" CEO Calhoun snapped.

"I just want to know… well… what happens to the students and their professor when we catch them?"

"Mr. McLane, let's not think of such unpleasantries right now." Calhoun smiled, though it resembled one more befitting of a shark before its next meal. "Leave it to us, okay?"

———

The company founder, Preston Powell, was present at the regularly scheduled meeting time, eager for updates about the companies they served, but also the profits they made doing so.

"SRD is concerned about confidentiality," Chip explained. "They're afraid of leaks and bad publicity. They want to acquire Giant Px, the pharma chain."

Powell glared at Jeremiah Calhoun. "That's another reason why you can't let that professor and his students get that information out in the media about us... *and our clients.*"

"It's being taken care of."

"It had *better be*," the owner ordered his CEO. "I don't want details. I just want them gone!"

Everyone looked around the room. Veiled threats were becoming increasingly less transparent. Few had any illusions that Kimber's fate was another "accident".

Attendees learned that Talladega Motors was pleased with the negative news for Marshall Motors and their Pioneer Pickup. They even learned that Talladega was willing to pay a lot of money for a congressional investigation of their rival.

The Miracle company was so happy with the hack attack on Bradford Communications and Edict that Esther Ruth Harding offered, as a bonus, a brand new "Miracle 2000" communication device for every PPP employee, a recently created prototype. All accepted them eagerly, hoping they would be an improvement over other Miracle products.

The report on Summit Studios was also a good one. Darcie Matthews revealed that Giselle Robideaux agreed to finish the film, under protest. She also got Mitch Allen to replace Dale Travis.

"Trust me, Giselle would do anything to appear in a flick with Mitch," she insisted.

As for Knotty Scarves, all the information necessary for a juicy tell-all, including the role of the scarves in the abduction, would be in Roxanne Bainbridge's romance novel, which would soon hit the shelves.

"Giselle probably won't like it, but it'll help sales of those scarves," Darcie admitted.

Larry Murray gave the briefing on Richmond & Webb's "Rebel Yell". Because the shooting was so recent, it was too early to tell when it came to sales. But USBC gave the gun maximum coverage.

"I know, Mr. Murray." Calhoun beamed. "Folks know the weapon more than the name of the shooter, Randall… somebody or other…"

=====

"What did you say A.I… ALPRs?" Jackson wondered out loud as they ate their last dinner—takeout pizza—in the dorms before their early morning departure.

"Automated License Plate Readers," Sheehy explained. "They're on a bunch of interstates, and maybe a few highways closer to towns. Once someone knows your license plate number, they can track us."

"Who?" Taira spoke.

"Government… or someone who can hack the government," A.I. replied.

All exchanged looks.

"Anyone who can hack the Bradford Corporation can do the same to our government," Trey observed.

"We'll have to stay off the big roads," Jackson said after a loud exhale. "That'll add a lot of time to our trip."

"And we can't use our ATMs or credit cards, I bet," Nat gasped.

"Just like the spy films." Sylvia rolled her eyes.

Elena jumped into the conversation. "Well, we've got plenty of money. Ted Beauchamp from the Pyramid Foundation just came by with enough cash to cover our trip, and then some. And don't forget, we can always crash with 'Atari.'"

"Atari?" the students all said in unison.

"He's a buddy from Tulane, from our undergraduate days," the English professor revealed. "He owns a house near Elon College."

"A professor?" Paul asked.

Jackson and Elena looked at each other. "He's kind of a local historian." Jackson began. "Writes and teaches at Elon."

"And plays lots of videogames." Elena laughed. "That's how he got his name. He inherited an old mansion, where we can all stay."

Jackson looked at A.I. "Can *you* hack an ALPR system?"

She looked worried. "It wouldn't be legal…"

"Speaking of legal." Elena stood up to address the group. "We can't just give a presentation, tell the media our findings, and go home. We have to tell law enforcement something."

Jackson threw up his hands. "I can send them what we have, but these are regulatory issues, the kind of stuff that bureaucrats at the FCC and the Department of Commerce might like, but it's not like the FBI can jump on product placement with guns blazing."

"If that's true," Taira noted, "then this company is really wasting a lot of money just to make our lives miserable."

Sylvia tapped her forehead with a pencil. "You know, there may be more crimes going on than taking money and getting a company mentioned a lot."

"Like what?" Nat glanced over his shoulder.

"Well," Sylvia answered. "Think about how you might get someone to cover your product. With so many news channels and newscasters, it would be hard to get everyone to focus on your product. Even if you could, it wouldn't be economically worth it. You'd need to bribe a lot of people for that coverage, and that would be easily uncovered."

"That's a good point," Trey agreed. "You would have to do something shocking to make everyone cover whatever you want."

Paul held up his hand for silence. "Maybe, what they're doing isn't getting others to *cover* the news. They're getting them to *make* the news."

"I think we'd better go through the data," Jackson announced. "It looks like we have a lot more research to do."

Later that night, Jackson found himself in front of the laptop, composing what he hoped would not be his last will and testament, while his family attempted to sleep nearby in a mix of dorm beds and sleeping bags. As tired as he was from the stressful ordeal of recent events, he willed himself to stay awake, at least to write some message, explaining things to his family, his colleagues, maybe Kat and R.J., which would explain the story of what happened and what put them in that precarious position, hoping the reader would see their sacrifice was potentially worth it all.

But after a few false starts, he slammed his laptop shut. His wife, the kids, and his students were counting on him to be strong, project confidence, and see their quest through to the end. And anticipating a deadly outcome wasn't helping him do any of those things, even if the odds weren't in his favor.

CHAPTER 45:
Wednesday, April 9

Calhoun stared at the college map, surrounded by his security team, as well as computer experts and business specialists, designing a plan to grab the Pierces' and their college students.

They decided not to kidnap the students and professors from campus, especially so soon after the mass shooting, opting to intercept them on the road. White House Deputy Chief-of-Staff Nick Bradley promised to get someone to monitor the surveillance, especially the ALPR camera data.

PPP's CEO rubbed his hands, feeling more confident. "Sounds like we've got everything but walking and biking on lockdown," Calhoun said. "And with that national conference in three days, it's their move!"

———

Even though they had a long drive the next day, the quest for answers about their attackers kept everyone glued to the laptops in their dorm room, poring through the data.

"Look, PPP clients have had the most airplay on USBC," Jackson remarked to his students.

A.I. nodded. The algorithm she had written had discovered the link to the network and the public relations firm.

"I'm on the Talladega Motors case." Paul turned his head to the group. "They had their biggest spike on… hey, that's around when Pierre Bujols, the hockey star, crashed his car!"

"The media wouldn't stop talking about that fast car he drove… the Gyrfalcon," Taira noted. "But that would mean… PPP knew it would happen in advance?"

"If they happened to cause it."

Everyone looked at their professor. An argument broke out among those holed up in their dorm suite. Was the Gyrfalcon's brake line cut? Was Bujols drugged? Was the sportscar hijacked by programmers? Were cops bribed to chase him?

"We could make up a hundred ways someone could do it," Elena finally terminated the discussion. "But none of these could stand up in court or even trigger law enforcement without more proof."

"True," Jackson admitted. "But at least we could come up with a list of where to look, right?"

"Summit Studios is also on the PPP client list," Taira beamed, having made the discovery.

"Has USBC hyped their movie sales or upcoming releases?" Paul asked.

Taira shook her head. "No… but all Hollywood is buzzing about the movie "Strong and Free" and its controversy."

"Never heard of it," Viv said.

"It's the film where Giselle Robideaux was when she was kidnapped by her co-star, Dale Travis," Taira explained. "She just agreed to finish the picture, and the press can't stop talking about it."

"Oh yeah," Jackson's daughter admitted.

Sylvia looked at her classmate. "Say… ain't you wearing one of those Knotty Scarves?"

"Yeah? So?"

"Weren't those used in the kidnapping?"

Taira blushed.

"That product placement stuff works, I guess!" Nat laughed.

"Knotty Scarves is a client, too," Paul called from the other side of the room.

"So, what are we saying… that Giselle faked her own kidnapping?" Elena asked.

"She *is* an actress," Trey noted.

Taira shook her head. "She seemed pretty upset about the ordeal."

"Maybe Dale Travis was paid to abduct her?" Sylvia speculated. "A publicity stunt?"

Taira shook her head. "He's been fired… and jailed. Mitch Allen is replacing him on set. I'd come back to the picture, even after being nabbed, if he was my co-star!"

"Doesn't sound worth it," Jackson stated.

"Maybe somebody else tied her up and framed Travis?"

"Again, we're just playing the guessing game," Jackson sighed with fatigue. "We've got smoke, but no fire yet."

"And we need a smoking gun," Isaac added ominously.

Silence followed for the next twenty minutes while they scanned their laptops. "Not much on SRD, except that they're in merger talks with Giant Px."

"You know, before Dad's company and Senator Louis Boudreaux got hacked, PPP offered my dad a deal to get some good publicity," Trey explained. "But when Bradford Communications turned him down, the CEO went over to Miracle Communications and spoke with Esther Ruth Harding. And now, we can't catch a break."

Sylvia nodded. "And that South Carolina Governor, Ogden Stewart, gets a pass because he conveniently uses The Miracle."

Vivian rolled her eyes. "They seem to manufacture the news itself, not just the propaganda."

"We may not have proof," Sgt. Herrera pointed out. "But at least we're getting a better idea of where to look."

For the next half-hour, little more than a series of clicks or sips of caffeinated beverages could be heard.

"Jackson, remember how upset you were when Reginald Wald died of an overdose?" his wife asked.

"Yeah."

"What did he take?" Sylvia inquired

A pause followed. "The Access World News site said Kipenium."

Elena nodded. "Do they compete with SRD, that PPP client we were just talking about, that's doing the merger?"

Paul raised his hand. "Looks like Kipenium was in the running to buy Great Px… Then Wald's death from an O.D. from Kipenium's pills, hyped by USBC, ended that."

"This is too convenient for coincidence," Taira contended.

———

The next morning, PPP's conference room resembled a command center. Senior company officers and The Spider, with laptops at the massive table and other employees in the field, all worked to stop the Peach State College team from reaching Washington D.C.

They tracked a reservation Elena Pierce had made from Atlanta. Security teams monitored any vehicle that looked large enough to hold ten passengers, including a PSC van. Even a waste management vehicle did not escape security.

"Not many cars coming in this way," Larry Murray reported. "There was a van going off-campus, but it said ABAC on it."

"ABAC?" Jeremiah asked.

A few keystrokes and The Spider spoke "Abraham Baldwin Agricultural College."

"Must've played PSC in something last night," Jeremiah noted. "Keep your positions at the college."

Five minutes later, The Spider reported that a new reservation had gone in at Hartsfield-Jackson Airport… seven for a Jack Pearse from Atlanta to Washington Dulles Airport. *That's gotta be it*, PPP's CEO thought.

"Follow Mr. Moro to Atlanta," Calhoun commanded. "Have those TSA uniforms ready. You'll escort them to our plane when you plant those firearms on them in the security line."

"Good thinking, Jeremiah."

Calhoun looked up at the only man he'd allow to use his first name.

"Of course, Mr. Powell. Once there, we can come up with whatever scenario we want to keep them quiet. Put Operation Ghost into action."

═══

"Did you make it out of PSC?" Kat's excited voice jumped in almost as soon as Jackson put her on speakerphone.

"I saw a dark sedan parked by the entrance, lights off, and some guy with a camera…" Nat began.

Sylvia cut him off. "There goes Mr. Spy Guy again."

"It looked suspicious!"

"Miss Roemer, can you also back up Bob's computer hard drive?" A.I. asked. "It might help with decrypting his encryption."

"Sure!" Kat promised. "Can't wait to see you."

═══

As the PSC van pulled into Hartsfield-Jackson Airport, Vinnie Moro struggled to find a parking space in the crowded structure. He settled for a close pass. If he had to steal a handicapped spot, PPP could easily afford to pay the fine. He reported his position.

"Closer to the Dulles flight," Spider added.

"I knew it," Jeremiah grinned. "Mr. Dixon, Mr. Turosz, proceed…"

"Uh boss… bad news."

"What?"

"It's… not them. Looks like a bunch of Amazons… it's the Peach State College's women's softball team."

Calhoun kicked the wastebasket across the room. It wasn't only that they missed their chance, but he didn't know where they were.

"Check their rooms. Don't be shy this time. See if they're still on campus!"

A few minutes later, he got the bad news. Dressed as cleaning company staffers, his agents found the dorm places assigned to them on campus were deserted, as well as an empty apartment. The mood among the PPP team was grim until Dr. E. E. Kirby broke the silence in the conference room.

"I just got off the phone with Dean Franklin Arbell," the scholar announced. "I asked him about ABAC. Not only did that school not play any games against PSC, but he reported that his college purchased a van from ABAC earlier this semester."

"Does he have the license plate?" Jeremiah barked eagerly.

"He does."

"Give it to The Spider," PPP's CEO ordered. "They can't get to D.C. in time without going on some major roads. And if they do, he can track their movements via the ALPR system. We'll find them on the road and intercept them before they get too far!"

<h1 style="text-align:center">CHAPTER 46:</h1>

Wednesday, April 9

"Uh, oh!" Alicia Ina Sheehy announced and smacked her hand over her mouth to avoid saying something worse. The others soon learned from her that someone had hacked into the ALPR system and was scanning for the ABAC van's license.

"Will they catch us?" Professor Jackson Pierce asked, leaning over from the driver's seat.

She shook her head. "We're on a state road right now."

"But we can't stay on state roads the whole way," Trey pointed out. "We won't make the conference in time."

"And we can't go into Savannah with all those cameras," Sylvia concurred.

Elena Pierce whipped out her cell phone. "Kat? It's Elena. We're on our way to you, but… yes, they figured out our license plate… Evans? Yeah, we can do that. Goolsby's sounds good…"

A.I. jumped in. "Can you haveherbring the backupharddrive of the computer for the reporter who died?"

Elena relayed the instructions, asking her to get the data off Bob Carlson's computer, and turned off her cell phone. "Gotta stay off this thing, in case they hack it too!"

"Where's Evans?" Trey asked.

"It's outside Augusta," Elena replied.

"And Goolsby's?" Nat queried.

"BBQ." Jackson announced, which got a lot of cheers from the students. Elena repeated her warning to students after Taira pulled out her cell phone.

"You don't think…" Taira began, and then everyone looked at her.

"I hate to say it," Jackson ordered. "But stay off your cell phones from now on. We have no idea what they can do. When we stop, look for security cameras. Try and stay away from those."

═══

"No pings on the interstates yet," The Spider declared, as the PPP security detail prowled every southern interstate road and major airports.

In Evans, the Pierces" met Elena's sister Kat and her husband, R.J. Their kids, Mia and Hugh, bounded out to greet Vivian and Isaac, eager to talk about their upcoming camping plans.

"We'll make sure they're safe," R.J. promised. "We're heading up to my sister's place up North of Athens. There's a hike we can do for the merit badge."

"And we can tour the coffeehouses there," Vivian insisted.

"Promise me you'll send me updates for the *Savannah Herald-Post*," Kat begged. "Remember, we ran your research when everyone else bailed on you. And we're family, too."

As the sisters and RJ discussed the lawsuit against the paper, Jackson glanced over to see Nat, Paul, and Taira coming out of an antique store. "What did you three get?"

"Cobalt glass." Taira held up an item wrapped in paper.

"And we got our ticket to drive on interstate roads," Nat grinned. "Check it out."

He held out two Florida license plates with oranges on them. Paul then unscrewed the van's two plates from front and back and replaced them with the Florida ones. "Now they can't track us by that ALPR thing that A.I. was talking about."

"Just don't get pulled over, professor," Nat added.

"Hey," Trey broke in. "I've got an idea. Keep one ABAC license plate in case we do get pulled over. Here's what we can do with the other." He pointed to a truck. "We can put it there, next to the others."

Sylvia laughed. "I love it! Where's it going?"

Trey shrugged. "It says Tennessee on all the others. Let's hope they chase it there."

Taira yawned "So… perhaps we go on interstate highways now? I'm a little tired of the back roads, and it took so long to get here."

"Sure," Jackson promised. He plotted a course to Elon College and hoped their license plate gambit would work.

———

"Great news, sir!" The Spider announced. "Data shows their license plate got on I-75, heading north from Atlanta!"

There were cheers around the conference room. Jeremiah ordered everyone to converge on the road to Chattanooga.

"But what will we do if they try to drive the whole way up to D.C.?" Wallace Bragg asked.

"Mr. Bragg, I've given several of our associates law enforcement uniforms," his superior said. "We'll have them plant drugs in their luggage, make an arrest, and then get them somewhere where we can interrogate them, learn what they have on us, and who they've shared it with."

"And then?" PPP's owner asked, brows narrowing.

"We'll make sure they can't be traced to us, and they can't get us convicted."

"How're we going to do that?"

"Mr. Powell, I promise you, you don't want to know those details."

———

Three hours later, Jeremiah Calhoun was getting impatient. "Do we have a visual, Mr. Gordy?"

The Spider shook his head. "They've already gone through Chattanooga."

As the tracked license plate passed the airport, the CEO ordered all available vehicles to Chattanooga. The tense pursuit reached the suburb of East Ridge, where Hap exclaimed "Uhhhh…"

"What?!"

"It's… errr… on a truck."

"The ABAC van license is on a truck?!"

"Looks like it was put there, sir."

After a string of obscenities, Calhoun came back on the speaker. "We have no idea where the Pierces or the PSC kids are now. Everyone… fall back to D.C., the next flight, on the double! We'll catch them at the capital at that conference they're heading to."

———

In the late afternoon, the weary travelers arrived outside Elon College to meet the Pierces' friend at his elaborate, but eclectic home. The PSC students saw their professor's friend Atari had thick reddish-blonde hair, complete with a goatee. He wore an outfit that looked straight out of a Renaissance fair.

Jackson's friend promised them a trip to a nearby Revolutionary War battlefield and showed off his restored 1961 Lincoln Continental.

"Before you go," Jackson interrupted. "Got any paint? White would be best."

"Just picked up some at Home Depot last week, so I could paint the shed doors," Atari jerked his thumb out back. "You can have it, but what for?"

Jackson looked at his wife and Taira, then pointed at the van. "While the others get their history lesson, we've got work to do."

———

By the time Atari returned with the others, the ABAC logo had been painted over.

"Why'd you do that?" Paul asked.

"It's probably the only feature of our vehicle that they know about us," Elena explained, brushing some of the dried white paint from her cheek. "Now they've got nothing."

"As long as they can't track us from the make, model, and year," Trey noted.

Taira laughed. "How many of *those* might be on these roads now?"

"Good point," he conceded.

"What's the plan for dinner?" Sylvia asked. "I'm tired of tromping all over the battlefield."

"Got a couple of lasagnas in the ovens," Atari explained. "Terry's been inside baking them."

"Terry?" Elena's eyebrow arched slightly higher on the left side. "You don't mean…"

But at that moment, the Pierces" fellow college graduate opened the door. "Dinner is served!" Then her eyes narrowed. "*Elena*."

"*Terry*," hissed Jackson's wife. Their animosity was mutual.

"The two got into a huge argument as undergrads," Jackson whispered to his students as both women prepared to resume hostilities. "Terry thinks other people wrote Shakespeare's works. Elena thinks the Bard did it all himself. They fought over it at Tulane, where both were English majors and roommates."

"….and what evidence is there that they did…"

"No one person could write all that…."

"Ladies," Atari held up his hands. "Truce on that. Let's just agree…"

"To disagree?" Elena snapped.

"That *Romeo and Juliet* with Leonardo DiCaprio sucks?" Atari laughed. Both English majors rolled their eyes, which seemed to de-escalate the tension.

All sat down at the large table for sausage lasagna.

"You guys are getting a lot of attention!" Atari noted.

"How so?" Sylvia asked.

Atari pointed to a flat screen on the wall that was linked to a streaming site. They watched a CNN report, which covered their research, the forced retractions in other newspapers, Kat's willingness to stand up to the lawsuit, and questions by some about the research itself.

Dewey Symington was strangely unavailable for comment. The reporters noted the awards the students at Peach State College had won in the regional event and how they would present their findings in D.C. at a national conference. Their report ended by noting that the team had disappeared.

"Way to go, Kat!" Elena beamed. "She probably clued them into our study."

"And that doesn't even cover MSNBC, the other networks, and what's in the papers," Terry added. "Kat probably played the disappearance angle so national networks would cover the story."

"Or PPP did, to get people to call in tips about our whereabouts," Taira shuddered.

The others began discussing the possibilities of the news coverage and the excitement their work had generated.

After a few minutes, they noticed one chair was empty. "Hey, where's A.I.?" Trey asked.

As if on cue, their resident hacker bounded into the room. "Just decrypted it!"

Jackson looked over at Atari.

"One of Kat's reporters, Bob Carlson, got an interview with a PPP employee, the company we stumbled upon. Before both died in a crash, Carlson sent an encrypted message. A.I.'s got it open."

"It's avideofile, withthefull interview." A.I. blurted out excitedly.

"What's on it?" Terry asked.

"*Everything.*" A.I. grinned.

CHAPTER 47:

Thursday, April 10

"Jackson, I know you love to see your name in the press, but it's time to go to bed," Elena complained. "We've got another long day of driving tomorrow."

The communications professor shook his head. "Only a half-day at most. Plus, we need to let as many in the media know about this as soon as possible. If more folks know about this, that PPP company will have less of an incentive to harm us."

"Yeah," Elena pointed out. "But your theory doesn't account for the *revenge* factor those people will have for you letting half the world know about it."

"True," her husband admitted. "But if others hear about it at that conference, it might be important. Maybe law enforcement might go after them."

Elena shrugged. "I know you too well. You'll do what you were going to do anyway."

Jackson grinned in reply.

"I still don't see why you don't email them Carlson's file," Elena offered.

"A.I. tried that," Jackson insisted. "ABC News couldn't get it open. She decrypted it in a way that you can view it, but not send it. Not sure why."

He messaged every news organization he could think of, inviting them to his presentation, promising to give the second half of their findings at the National Communications Conference....

...In person.

Atari crept up the stairs with a few English Ales.

After a few swigs, Atari asked "Where are you staying tomorrow night? Not at the conference hotel, I assume."

"Too dangerous," Elena concurred.

"How about Andres from Tulane?" Atari smiled.

"I heard he's now the Rev. Figueroa." Jackson grinned. "Who would have guessed?"

Atari continued, "Well, you know how he helps Central American refugees and has a youth hostel attached to the church where he preaches. It's not far from the U.S. Capitol, and just a little further is the D.C. Metro." He showed it to Elena and Jackson on a computer map.

"Man, I wish I had thought of it!" Jackson exclaimed.

After finishing his ale, Jackson exclaimed, "He just responded to my text. No current refugees are staying there. We'll have the place to ourselves… and Andres, of course."

The three pored over the images of bunkbeds, the kitchen, game room, and television as Terry emerged. Then the four reminisced about their Tulane days.

===

Jeremiah Calhoun snarled something the others couldn't decipher and then devised a plan. Every bridge from Virginia to D.C. would be watched for the ABAC van, while the remainder prowled the nearby airports for flights from the south.

"I'll be at the National Communications Conference," added Dr. E. E. Kirby. "I'm sure I can convince the organizers to contact me immediately when they check in."

"I'll go to the database on facial recognition software through Reynolds Recon," Evan Gordy said.

Calhoun frowned.

"You know what, Mr. Bragg?" Calhoun observed. "We need to go down to Washington, D.C. ourselves. We've outsourced everything to a bunch of amateurs. We're going to need lots of eyes on hand, where we can spot them as they appear at the conference."

Bragg nodded, shoulders slumped, out of options.

———

The white van, missing an ABAC label and logo, cruised over the 14th Street Bridge on I-395, a day before their presentation at the National Communications Conference, having traveled six hours from North Carolina through Virginia. As the students snapped pictures of the Washington Memorial, the Smithsonian, and the U.S. Capitol, Jackson guided them off the interstate, down the side streets, to a church, and then proceeded to take their vehicle to a long-term parking lot, away from their lodging.

When he returned, he saw that Elena and the students had claimed their bunk beds and were already receiving the tour of the kitchen and TV room by another old college buddy. He gave Andres a hug. "Has Father Figueroa been telling you any stories about our school days?"

"No," Sylvia grinned. "But he promised to over dinner!"

But tales from Tulane would have to wait. Nearly every news network was focused on the upcoming media conference, especially the disappearance of two professors and several students. Even ESPN covered it, with the angle that one of the missing was Nat Holman, a potential draftee.

The thrill of being on television for a national story was soon replaced by a growing dread. Though they were the center of attention, they knew that those responsible for forcing them to go on the run were still out there and would be waiting for them before they could get in front of the conference and the media. Unless they could figure out a way to slip into the national presentation panel undetected and get the word out before it was too late, it would all be for naught.

———

A few hours later, the PPP leaders and their remaining workers were in their private plane, flying from LaGuardia to Dulles.

"Tell me about this conference," Jeremiah commanded.

"The National Communications Conference is the largest meeting for those who study the media in any of its forms," Dr. Kirby lectured. "One of the highlights is an undergraduate research presentation series of panels, which includes our targets."

Calhoun nodded.

"While all of the state winners would present their work earlier in the day, the real action would take place from 3:30 to 5:00 p.m.," the professor explained.

"The winning schools from each of the four regions will be on that last panel," Kirby announced, as if he were the emcee. "The University of Pennsylvania from the Northeast, the University of Wisconsin from the Midwest, and the University of Southern California from the West. And of course, Peach State College from the South."

"Which hotel is hosting the conference?" Jeremiah asked, glancing at Wallace's notes.

"*Hotels*," Kirby corrected. "The National Communications Conference is too big for one. The main headquarters is at the Washington Marriott Wardman Park, where I was the keynote speaker last…"

"And?" Calhoun interrupted.

"There is also the Omni Shoreham Hotel to the South, and the Woodley Park Guest House, between Georgetown and the Washington Zoo, all downtown. Our quarry will present their work in the Thurgood Marshall Ballroom in the Marriott."

"Well." Jeremiah paused meaningfully. "Pull everyone from their positions to the ballroom in the Marriott at least an hour before they speak. We'll make sure that not *one* of those Peach State College folks says a *word* in that room."

CHAPTER 48:
Friday, April 11

"Doctor Kirby, this conference is a madhouse!" Jeremiah Calhoun gasped. "Why didn't you tell me this event was so disorganized?"

Kirby laughed. "This is what an academic conference looks like!"

The Convention Registration Center by the foyer was even more of a mess, with men and women crowded in front of the haggard-looking volunteers who were dispensing schedule books and lanyards to the participants.

But what concerned Calhoun the most was that the Peach State College team was nowhere to be found.

The Spider settled in at the business center, next door to where the communications conference organizers located their headquarters. Calhoun ordered those who weren't scanning the bridges to swarm the conference hotels, especially the Marshall Ballroom, where the undergraduate competition would take place.

"What will we do when we spot them?" Hap asked.

"Contact the rest of the team through Spider," Calhoun informed them. "You'll be wearing those security uniforms. Wait for reinforcements to show up with the vans. Make sure all six students and their professors can be viewed. Then, at the right time, make the arrest, drag them to the vehicles, and we'll have them. We can then get them to the rented boat. But whatever you do, *don't* let them give that big presentation before the press, under *any* circumstances!"

By morning, it seemed half the journalists in D.C. were jammed in the Marriott ballroom. From Yale to Oregon, the students presented to the crowd. More seats than usual were filled, but everyone was waiting for the big event later that afternoon. Already, the networks were rolling in their cameras and fighting for laptop plugs.

Calhoun scanned the crowd, looking for a face, *any* face, that looked even vaguely familiar. Like his PPP employees, he had committed the photos of the professors and students to memory, but nobody looked familiar. Even as lunchtime approached, few reporters dispersed, not wanting to give up their coveted spots. PPP's CEO used the lunch hour to check in with his team. None of them had seen a white van with ABAC on it, or anyone who matched the facial images of the PSC students or professors.

Waiting… waiting.

After lunch, with every seat in the Marshall Ballroom taken, LSU and Michigan took their turns. Some of the broadcasters asked questions in the panels, while reporters with pens and pads interviewed attendees about what they thought about the missing students and professors.

Though a break was called at 3:00 p.m., few seemed ready to leave. Calhoun summoned everyone from the Potomac bridges to come to the hotel without delay. Even most of the teams from the prior presentations were sticking around now. It was standing room only. Three new teams with name tags and school identifiers entered the doors: one from USC, one from Pennsylvania, plus one from Wisconsin, each preparing for their turn. Covering the table on the end of the raised platform was a large label for Peach State College, but no participants took the chairs behind that table. *Where were they?*

Calhoun looked around. The fire marshal probably had the day off; there was such a large crowd that he could barely move among the attendees.

"This is like Woodstock for a conference," one aged hippie-looking attendee told a colleague half his age. She laughed, evidently getting the reference.

The minutes were ticking down, with no PSC team in sight.

The panel chair huddled with the discussant, and eventually the conference president, as the clock ticked down to 3:30 p.m.

"Ladies and gentlemen," the elderly leader of the conference began. "We shall begin the last panel with at least three of the four panelists, and see if the fourth school shows up. Perhaps they have been delayed by traffic."

There were murmurs of laughter, but Jeremiah Calhoun wasn't smiling. His prey was still missing. What if they got scared and were hiding? That was always a possibility. *Would it make his situation better*, he wondered? Well, the press wouldn't get word of it, which was a start. The PSC folks couldn't hide forever. Sooner or later, The Spider or another of his workers would track them down. Perhaps their absence was a blessing after all. But he had to stay and see this operation through until the end. He had to know where those professors and kids were to ensure such information *never* leaked out.

Pennsylvania went first. Their topic covered college speakers who had been disinvited, and where they were disinvited. *So Jackson, this is what you find so interesting*, Jeremiah thought. He felt like he understood his adversary better, though it hardly seemed worth risking one's life over such research.

Wisconsin went second. They took several events: a terrorist attack, a natural disaster, and a coup in Peru, and compared how the press in several countries covered the events. Now, Calhoun fervently watched all the doors to see if the Peach State College team had arrived. But nobody looking like Elena or Jackson, or any of their students, had entered.

By the time the USC team concluded their work on who shared what media stories on Instagram and Snapchat, Calhoun could barely pay attention. *Where are they?*

It was the moment of truth.

There was a quiet pause, and then a man with a thick black beard and ponytail stood up, walked to the platform, and ascended it. No, it wasn't Pierce, even in disguise. The Conference Chair intercepted him. The man spoke a few words to the chair as well as the discussant, showing them something. The two professors nodded, though they looked surprised. The man replaced the laptop with one of his own, and a full image appeared on the screen behind the panelists.

It was Professor Jackson Pierce and Professor Elena Pierce, flanking Sylvia Wright, John Marshall Bradford III, Nat Holman, Paul Herrera, Taira Malek, and Alicia Ina Sheehy, for a virtual presentation.

CHAPTER 49:
Friday, April 11

"Hi, my name is Sylvia Wright. I'm a senior at Peach State College," the aspiring lawyer began. "And I'm the lead presenter for our research project, with the title 'Next-Gen Product Placement'. I'm sorry we can't be there in person, but when you hear the whole story, you'll understand why."

Jeremiah's jaw dropped. Quick action was needed.

"Spider!" he hissed into his Miracle device. "Can you trace the signal?"

Static brayed back into his communication device.

"Mr. Dixon! Mr. Turosz!" He almost had to yell.

Their voices came in and out, so he only understood every third word. *Damn this Miracle piece of sh-...* He kept getting shushed by those sitting around him, making it harder to hear.

"Uh… can't trace…. time soon, Mr. Calhoun," his resident hacker finally replied. "Looks like… scrambled… good. By… pinpoint… location, they'll… gone…"

At least he was getting the gist of the message. It was like following broken Spanish.

"Yes?!" Hap replied.

"Get ready to go to the vans!"

"Go…. say… again?"

Calhoun threw down the Miracle. The critics were right about them. He wished they had gone with Bradford, makers of a much better communication device. Speaking of the devil, there was Trey, the Bradford brat, giving examples of product placement on the big screen.

The heir to the Bradford Corporation walked the audience through several historic cases of high-profile products being mentioned in the media, from the White Ford Bronco chase in the O. J. Simpson story, to the Tylenol poisoning cases in the Chicago area, to E.T. and Reese's Pieces.

Naturally, the audience recognized most of these. But Trey made sure they knew what was happening.

"Sometimes the company pays for the product to be visible in the TV show, or movie, like Hershey's did for the E.T. film. Other times, it's just bad luck to be targeted by a serial killer, as the Johnson and Johnson Company was in the Tylenol case. And sometimes, a company lucks its way into having its product covered in the news…vas the Ford company was, when their Bronco was making headlines, even as the company prepared to phase the vehicle out. They sold out of White Ford Broncos that year, and for several years afterwards."

Trey waited for his audience to absorb his words before proceeding. "Of course, one is not supposed to be able to do for the news what Hershey's did in the E.T. movie. And not everyone can be lucky, or unlucky, when their product becomes headline news. But what if someone decided to push the envelope, so to speak, going from having their product mentioned in the news to *making* the news?"

"Does that mean someone today could arrange for O. J. to be in that White Ford Bronco, and orchestrate the entire event?" asked a veteran CNN reporter, breaking protocol by not waiting for the Q&A.

"Exactly," Trey concluded.

"And that would also mean that maybe someone could pay to have their competitors get bad news?" the perky reporter from ABC News inquired.

"That's what we sought to investigate," Trey contended.

Instead of going to the vans, Calhoun watched Oeznik move toward the guy with the black ponytail and beard. Jeremiah shook his head. The guy was a cut-out, a messenger at most, and going after him would waste time and make a very public scene they didn't need. He tried Hap again.

"Get to the fire alarm!"

More static. *Mother of…*

"Say again."

"Fire alarm!"

"Fire," then a loud squeal that drew heads. "Fire what?"

"Alarm!"

"You want… me… fire alarm?"

"*Yes!*"

Now even some in the media looked over at him, and then returned to watching that kid, who The Spider said was their hacker, stutter her way through explaining the algorithm she used, which showed the Pierces and their students how PPP was hawking products through USBC. It was all coming out in front of the press. *This was bad. They needed to act fast!*

Once the fire alarm cleared the room and no one saw any more of their presentation, The Spider could pin down their location. Hap, Oeznik, Vinnie, Larry, and Ray could still shut them down. If only…

Where the hell was Hap? Why wasn't there a loud screaming siren? That football player Nat was already getting into the statistics.

"When we saw the numbers, A.I… I mean Alicia had come up with, we fed them into our computer stats program," Nat said. "At first, they looked random, like there was no connection to anything."

"But we applied the stats lessons that Professor Jackson Pierce taught us," Holman continued. "It was like the numbers were jumping off the page, forming patterns. That helped us see that some companies were statistically more likely to be mentioned in the news, and especially on the USBC network. And those companies whose products were mentioned the most were clients of the Preston Powell Partnership, or what some call the Product Placement Partnership."

———

There was a scuffle at the door. Jeremiah couldn't see what was happening, but he knew what he couldn't hear… the alarm. There was also what he *could* hear… which was the presentation. They were spilling a ton of evidence on PPP to the press. Where did the Pierces find these students? He would have to pull the fire alarm himself.

As he reached the wall, a pair of hands grabbed him from behind. "Jeremiah Calhoun, you're under arrest," announced a second person, while a third snapped a pair of handcuffs on his wrists. By now, he could see that Hap was being treated the same way, while Oeznik wasn't in sight.

"What the *hell* do you think you can charge *me* with?" Calhoun snapped.

An officer pointed to the screen. "Just keep watching."

———

"We later discovered that environmental lawyer Reginald Wald's death wasn't the result of an accidental overdose of sleeping pills," Sgt. Paul Herrera explained. "Instead, his death came at the hands of those who wanted to discredit Kipenium and promote SRD, after the company donated a tidy sum to PPP for the negative attention directed at their sleeping pill rival."

"And hockey star Pierre Bujols' car crash into that New Jersey River wasn't all that it seemed to be either. You were treated to a lengthy car commercial for the Gyrfalcon, made by Talladega Motors."

Gasps emerged from the crowd. Several whispered, "Really?"

"And you've probably heard about the hack of a politician who used Bradford Communications' Edict, designed to help PPP client Miracle Communications gain market share from their rival," Trey jumped in.

"Trust me… as a member of the Bradford family, I know." That earned a few laughs from those who knew his last name from the introductions.

―――

"This is full of it!" Jeremiah exploded. "I hope you know my lawyer will sue the hell out of whatever government agency you're with."

"I'm with the Justice Department," the male officer introduced himself. "D.C. Police Officers are arresting your boys in the vans below and on this floor, as well as your second-in-command by the front door."

"And I'm with the FBI," the female agent added. "Is your lawyer Dewey Symington?"

"Why?!"

"You didn't have him make your threats to newspapers, did you?"

Calhoun didn't say anything.

"He may be joining you at the defense table, but not as your attorney."

The CEO's outburst drew attention from some of the reporters. A few cameras swung to his scowling visage.

―――

"Remember when actress Giselle Robideaux was kidnapped on the set of the film 'Strong and Free'?" Taira Malek finally had the attention she craved from the media. *One day, I'll be the one with the microphone, asking the questions*, she thought.

"We thought it was Dale Travis, but turns out it was all 'an act,' shall we say," she joked. "Oh yes, the leading lady was abducted, just not by her co-star. She was nabbed by employees of PPP, who framed Mr. Travis for the crime to get a lot of attention for a floundering film, as well as plenty of focus on what was used to gag and tie up poor Giselle… the Knotty Scarves." Taira flashed her accessory, a little prop that earned a few hoots and whistles from the crowd.

"On a serious note," Paul put his hand on Taira's shoulder. "You'll remember the shooting on our PSC campus not long ago. The shooter was armed with the notorious 'Rebel Yell', a Richmond & Webb product. R&W is a PPP client as well. And we were the target!"

Some of the gasps turned to shouts of anger over the company's role in those killings. The press was sure to crush PPP in the news.

"I know our story is almost unbelievable," their top presenter, Sylvia Wright, pressed on. "And we would have a hard time believing it ourselves. But don't take our word for it. Hear the words from a PPP employee, or should I say, a *former* PPP employee."

She pushed a button, and an edited version of Kimber Elliot's words describing her firm's practices came out over the screen, terminating any lingering doubts.

The budding attorney clicked off the audio.

"We wish Ms. Elliot could be here, as well. She died in a suspicious crash just after she spoke those words to Bob Carlson, a reporter from the *Savannah Herald-Post*. PPP is suing that paper. Both reporter and PPP employee perished in the flames, but not before Carlson sent out this video of his interview with Ms. Kimber," Sylvia elaborated.

Murmurs escalated to loud accusations.

"The two were in a Marshall Pioneer, a rival in truck sales this year to the Talladega Jalisco. And Talladega is a PPP Client." Sylvia concluded.

At this point, those in the crowd wouldn't have been more surprised if the PPP company was behind JFK's Assassination.

Calhoun glared at the Pierces" on the screen, mustering the will to make the husband-and-wife professors see his reaction. He mouthed, "*I'll get even one day.*"

"Any comment about all of this disturbing evidence, Jeremiah?"

Among all of the calls for quotes and shouts of fury from the crowd, one voice sounded familiar. To his dismay, he saw the smirk on Britt Adams' face as the *Forbes* reporter was going to get her revenge, at his expense, by covering this top story.

Did the Pierces smile too as they saw Calhoun led from the room?

Outside the Thurgood Marshall Ballroom, the hallway was crawling with agents from a variety of bureaucracies. Several headed down to the lobby with Jeremiah in handcuffs, joining Hap Dixon and Wallace Bragg. Vinnie Moro, Larry Murray, Juan Fernandina, and Ray Maillon, all dressed as law enforcement officers, were arrested as well. Chip McLane was being brought in from outside the building. Calhoun was happy to see The Spider had evaded their web, and probably Darcie Matthews, too. It was important to have someone escape who could help rebuild the Preston Powell Partnership.

Later, he would learn that The Spider saw the officers and agents racing through the lobby on the security cameras, and made a quick exit after the Miracle failed to connect him to Calhoun. Darcie also spotted arresting officers early on. She ducked into a cleaning supplies closet, swiped a maid's uniform, and slipped away from law enforcement.

Oeznik Turosz was not so lucky. He was the one in the body bag on the stretcher, being wheeled away. He had shot a security guard and made it down the stairs to the back exit, just as a well-positioned D.C. police officer was ready, and didn't miss.

Jeremiah at least had one thing to smile about. The arrogant Dr. E. E. Kirby was being hustled along out of the Marriott, loudly protesting his detention. He was happy to see that his scholar-consultant would at least be in the same predicament.

Across the street from Washington Marriott Wardman Park sat The Spider, who watched the United States law enforcement agents rush in. Minutes ago, he too was at the conference, monitoring the situation.

At the firm, he'd spoken out against using The Miracle, but Jeremiah Calhoun and Wallace Bragg had brushed off his concerns, wishing to keep the almighty Esther Ruth Harding happy. Besides, they were pursuing unarmed kids and their teachers. How much damage could they do?

Plenty, Evan Gordy mused, especially if they made contact with police. Even before the Miracles all failed, as he predicted, he had his escape plan sketched out. The computer hacker swiped a maintenance worker's uniform. He changed in a bathroom stall and walked out, undetected, as soon as he saw the Peach State College team emerge on his computer screen.

Nobody paid him any attention. They never did for such low-level workers in this country. He still had his laptop locked into surveillance at other hotels. Evan Gordy, known as Ivan Gorsky in his native country, smiled as he saw the maid with long blonde locks slip around the officers storming past her. It was Darcie Matthews, of course. She'd been the only other person at the PPP meeting to express any skepticism of the "beloved" Miracle at the same meeting.

It looked like she kept an Edict as well. She was the only one to get the alert he'd sent on his own Bradford Communications device. Darcie made no eye contact as she slipped away, a smart survivor as well.

But because the Russian had kept his own Edict, he could still track her. And he would, since he needed her for his new operation, the next phase of his plans in the coming months.

———

In the Thurgood Marshall Ballroom, attention turned back to the Peach State College team, now showered with questions from professors and reporters, earning jealous looks from their competitors from California, Wisconsin, and Pennsylvania, who were being ignored in the wildest discussion section from a National Communications Conference panel in history.

"Looks like they have to give you first place," Elena Pierce gestured to her husband.

"Not really," he countered. "It's the students who will earn the award."

"Well, you better get something for all of this trouble," she snapped. "Our house has been burned down, we've lost half of our stuff, and who knows what they've done while we've been gone. Maybe you might get tenure at the end of this mess?"

Jackson shrugged, seeing his students celebrate, and watching PPP taken down by law enforcement.

He hugged his wife.

"For the first time in years, tenure isn't what I'm thinking about now."

CHAPTER 50:
Saturday, April 12

On Saturday, the National Communications Conference concluded its three-day event in Washington, D.C., with an awards ceremony scheduled for noon in the same Thurgood Marshall Ballroom where Friday's excitement took place. But there would be no morning panels or workshops for the Peach State College students or their professors. They were downtown in the auditorium of the Executive Office Building, next to the White House, extras in a press conference where the media peppered the FBI, ATF, D.C. Police, and the US Attorney, a veteran prosecutor of white-collar crime cases and terrorism financing convictions, who would be leading the investigation of PPP and fellow companies.

The Pierces and their students found themselves at one of the tables on the stage. They answered questions from the *New York Times*, *Washington Post*, and *Politico*. They fielded queries about how they uncovered the scheme on product placement in the news. Jackson and Elena were happy to deflect most questions to the students so they could answer.

As the press conference wound down, a man with thinning sandy hair wearing a suit, came over to the PSC table.

"Is Sylvia Wright here?" he asked.

Her eyes bugged out as she recognized Joe Douglas, the leader of the Civil Rights Division at the Justice Department of the United States. He had won several convictions in Alabama for bombings and assassinations during the Civil Rights era.

"I watched your video last night of the presentation you gave at the Marriott," he said in his thick Southern drawl. "I heard from your professor that your pursuits after graduation are geared toward the legal profession."

She could barely nod, a rare silent moment for the outspoken undergraduate.

He handed her a business card. "Call me about our summer internship program in Washington, D.C., unless you have a better offer."

"Yes… sir… Mister Douglas…" Then she tamped down her shock. "Actually, could I tell you right now about my hometown of Clifton, Georgia?"

As the two spoke in hushed tones, a *Sports Illustrated* reporter snagged Nat. Paul and Trey went over to talk to the Pierces. They were with A.I. while she shared a flash drive with the U.S. Attorney Rajiv Thangaraj, who was assigned to the case. Taira weaved her way through the throng of news broadcasters, answering questions and handing out business cards she had made before the trip.

———

The six students and their professors were whisked away to the Marriott just in time for the National Communications Conference awards ceremony. Then came the highlight of the post-lunch reception: the winner of the undergraduate research competition. The students from USC were named the third-place team, followed by the University of Pennsylvania, who captured the runner-up award. The Peach State College students looked around excitedly, even expectantly.

"And the first-place award goes to…"

"… The University of Wisconsin, for their work on…"

Jackson Pierce's students looked around. Shock was apparent on all their faces. After all they went through, and what they had accomplished, to finish dead last in the finals. Nearly every attendee shared their surprise, and more than a few shouted their displeasure at the outcome.

"Our apologies to the team from Georgia," the aged conference president announced. "The rules specifically require an in-person presentation to qualify for the award, regardless of the circumstances. But congratulations on *all* that you accomplished."

The angry muttering about the announcement persisted, but the PSC students, having been the darlings of the media and prosecutors that morning, eventually took it in stride.

Elena whispered something about what they had learned and what they had achieved. She added something about what mattered more: A plaque or trophy, or exposing a massive, dangerous cabal of corruption, perhaps saving lives and bringing about justice?

As the reception continued, LSU's James LeBlanc won the award again for best undergraduate research professor.

"It should have been you, Dr. Pierce," hissed Sylvia Wright. Elena and Jackson looked at each other.

"Which one of us?" Elena whispered back, earning a few laughs.

Professor LeBlanc held up his hands for silence after he received his medal.

"I know it's not on the program, but the Executive Committee of the National Communications Conference met last night. We feel that the extraordinary events of yesterday deserve special recognition by our organization. Will the Peach State College students and their professors please accept this token from the committee?"

On eight framed objects was a picture of the news story. Each featured a photo of their group presentation, taken by the conference historian. A team of graduate student volunteers provided the students with a different published article from that morning's press. In addition to the *Washington Post* for Elena and the *New York Times* for Jackson, each student got an article from a different network that covered the panel. These ranged from MSNBC and CNN to Fox and ABC, with one from CBS and the other from NBC.

"You'll notice that USBC conspicuously chose to cover something else," LeBlanc mused to the laughter of the professors and students.

═══

After the reception, the students elected to head back to see Fr. Figueroa, thanking him for helping them out and giving them a place to stay. That evening in North Carolina, Elena and Terry patched up their brief hostility and cooked Chicken Korma for those staying in the mansion, though they still quibbled over whether to use onion or garlic. Later, Atari invited the students to his basement bar, and those over twenty-one helped themselves to a drink.

"So, Mr. Holman, I know you hope to become the next Julio Jones," Atari began with a Cuba Libre in one hand, and everyone laughed, "And I suspect Ms. Sheehy will become the most notorious hacker since WikiLeaks. But what are the rest of you doing after you graduate?"

Sylvia sprang up to tell everyone the news. "The Justice Department Civil Rights Division offered me a summer internship. You never know… that might persuade one of the schools to give me a second chance."

"I'm going to work for my dad at Bradford Communications," Trey admitted. "But I'm thinking of going on the legal side, after this little adventure."

Taira shrugged. "PPP shut down all my broadcasting opportunities. But my luck might change. At that press conference, reporters and one news anchor gave me their business cards. So, who knows?"

"I hope to go to graduate school, get my PhD in Communications, and take Dr. Pierce's job away from him!" Paul smiled.

Everyone laughed.

"You had better not!" Elena shot back. "Do you know how hard it is for a pair of married academics to find work at the same school? And he'd better get tenure after this!"

"Just kidding, of course," replied Sarge. "But I struck out on the graduate student search, thanks to PPP. Dad wants me to rejoin the military, so that might be an option."

Jackson Pierce pointed at his student. "Remember what I said about the Alexandria Library? We might find a research assistant position for you in the program."

Nat looked for A.I., but didn't see her anywhere. He knew she wasn't a drinker, but he was surprised that she disappeared, just when she was getting used to socializing. Earlier, she had even played their humorous version of vacation bingo and Paul's trivia games in the van.

"Probably too shy for one of these parties," Taira reasoned.

Nat went on a search in Atari's eclectic mansion. After ten minutes, he spotted her on the terrace, headphones on, feverishly typing away on a laptop.

Nat knelt next to her to see what she was working on. "Is this another research project?" He asked. Then he leaned in for a closer look. "Hey, are these football stats?"

A.I. squeaked and slammed the laptop down. Then, she saw who it was. "Oh, Nat… I'm sorry! I… I… ah…"

"I didn't know you were a sports fan!" the PSC football star blurted.

She blushed. "Yeah—I almost nevermiss a football game. Dad, mom, andmyAunt took me to Florida State football games when I was a kid."

"Why didn't you go to FSU?"

"What happened tomyparents… bad… memories," she struggled to hold back the sobs. "And I heard thatPSC had a reallygreat Math and Comp Sci program. I… started going to games at PSC…"

"Are these our stats?" Nat asked as she reopened her laptop.

"Yours, actually," she pointed to the numbers on the screen. "I was goingto surprise… you… y-you're really good… 'n allthose teams were canceling your tryouts."

Nat could only stare at her work, mesmerized. "So what do you have?"

"YACs… or yardsaftercatch… broken tackles, defenders fakedout… targets uncatchable… yards andTDs called back because ofsomeone else's penalty, pass interference cases notcalled…" A.I. stumbled through the list, but it was clear she had stats that could easily be considered NextGen.

"For m-my whole career?" Now it was Nat's turn to get a little tongue-tied.

"Yes," she explained. "I just need your first two Freshmen games. Then I'llbedone in anhour."

"Can… can I send this… to my agent… ASAP?" he begged.

"Yes… it was my present to you… you know, for being like a friend to me this year…"

"You *are* a friend! I don't know how to thank you enough," the receiver managed. Then, in the most impulsive moment since he'd run a kickoff out of the End Zone, he gave her a bear hug.

"Thank you… thank you so much."

"Y-you're welcome." Was she trembling because of nervousness, or excitement?

"A… Alicia, after we get back, would you like to go to Paragon for a cup of coffee?"

Barely able to reply, A.I. nodded enthusiastically.

After the two stepped down the stairs, Taira glanced over to see Nat and Alicia's hands intertwined. She smacked her hand over her mouth to avoid screaming in shock. Once her palm was disengaged from her mouth, she picked up her cell phone, eager to tell the social media world the news of the latest couple.

But Nat shook his head. "Let the two of us tell everyone," he whispered. His classmate reluctantly agreed, though she did pull aside A.I. to hear the details.

CHAPTER 51:
Friday, April 18-Saturday, April 26

On late Friday afternoons, Peach State College faculty, staff, and students escaped for an early weekend, but not this time. Instead, all were crowded into the Hawkins Arena for a special academics and athletics ceremony. There was a lot to celebrate. The Women's Basketball Team recorded their first-ever Final Four appearance. Professors, undergraduates, and even a few in the evening college were given awards for papers, artwork, performances, and poster presentations, all delivered earlier in the day. As expected, the Communications Department received the undergraduate research group award, with Sylvia and Paul going to the podium to accept the honor, giving a shout-out to both Elena and Jackson Pierce. The announcement of Jackson receiving tenure almost seemed anticlimactic by comparison.

After the assembly, the students, their parents, other professors, and staff met at Paragon for a prearranged department celebration. Sylvia was a little late, and when she arrived, the others soon learned why. Trembling, she stumbled toward Jackson Pierce, holding out her cell phone. She hit the speaker phone and played the message that had come through during the assembly, when everyone's cell phone was muted.

"Sylvia, this is Cheryl Cochran, President of the Walter F. George Law School at Mercer University. You've been given full acceptance at our law school, covering all tuition. I hope you'll be pursuing the Cox Fellowship to pay the cost of tuition and books; it provides a small stipend to help you with housing. Your recent research and honors will make you a very competitive candidate."

Sylvia embraced both Pierces in a group hug.

"Are you going to take the offer, Ms. Wright?" Elena asked. The undergraduate nodded her head vigorously.

"And I'm going to join that Summer Internship with the Justice Department… in Georgia."

Jackson raised an eyebrow.

"It's a good thing, Dr. Pierce. You see, Attorney Joe Douglas reviewed our case about Clifton, Georgia, and institutionalized racism in the city government. He's assigning it to the U.S. Attorney for Southern Georgia, Woody Maxwell, and I'm going to help work on it over the Summer and while I'm at Mercer!"

She proceeded to tell Elena about the case, which Jackson already knew about, and how important this moment was.

Paul came over.

"Professor Pierce, could I get a letter of recommendation for the Alexandria Library job if that research assistant position is still open?"

Jackson nodded. "It is still open. But I thought I'd tell you about another option you might consider."

"Okay…" Herrera shrugged. "But it's too late to go to some of the others like USC, as they've already given out their awards for funding, and I can't afford graduate school on full tuition…"

Pierce handed him a letter.

"What's this?" the undergraduate gasped.

"You accidentally sent one of them with our department's address, so it came to our office yesterday instead of your inbox."

It was from Georgia State University. It wasn't a thin letter either.

The note at the top of the packet began, "Mr. Herrera, I wish to congratulate you…"

"YYYYYYESSSSSSSSSS!!!!!" Paul appeared to jump several feet in the air. "Oh my God… I'm going to GSU's graduate school! Communications!"

"It's not a doctoral program, but they do offer a master's degree, as well as full funding. You'll work as either a research assistant or teaching assistant…"

"Oh man!" he replied. "Can I do both?"

Jackson laughed. "Not at the same time, but you'll be there for four semesters, so you can be a TA in the fall and an RA in the spring…"

"Hey guys!" he announced, waving the envelope above his head like a signal flag. "I'm going to grad school!"

His classmates smiled at him.

"We know… Sarge." A.I. announced, which led Nat to fall over, guffawing. She was the last person anyone expected to use Herrera's nickname.

"Professor Pierce told us before you came in," Trey explained.

"I called in a favor with the brand-new graduate director at GSU," Jackson added.

"Another former classmate from Tulane?" Paul inquired.

Jackson shook his head. "She's one of the first students I ever taught here at PSC. She's been following your progress, and they're trying to build up their program to national prominence."

"And I won't be that far away from you all," Paul observed.

Elena and Sylva rejoined the group. "I bet Trey will be working for his dad at Bradford Communications."

"Me too!" A.I. announced. "Trey's dad even sent me a contract. I'll work for their IT department, going after those hackers who infiltrated the company. It'll help pay down the student loans."

Trey shook his head. "Sorry, Sylvia, but I'm not working with my dad."

She cocked her head, and then she dropped her coffee. "You-you're going to Mercer Law too?" she gasped as she saw his letter of acceptance.

"All of these legal adventures got me thinking." Trey smiled sheepishly, accepting an enthusiastic hug from Sylvia. "Besides, it would be better to go through the first year of law school with someone who would make a good study partner!"

Sylvia slapped her hands to her cheeks in shock.

"Any word yet, Taira?" Nat interrupted.

The Lebanese student rose up, flashed a smile, and turned her cell phone on speaker as well. It played a series of messages.

Beep!

"Taira, we're with WSB-TV. We hope you're still interested in our summer…"

Beep!

"Miss Malek, this is WATL. Our network would be glad to have you join our team…"

Beep!

"We here at WRBL know you're a top target of ours for our Summer…"

Beep!

"Taira, this is your mother! Why haven't you called…"

Click! She blushed furiously.

"Oops."

"Speaking of your folks, what's their status?" Jackson switched gears.

"I talked with the US Attorney working the PPP case, and played the conversation that DHS had with my parents. That bureaucrat who messed with their immigration case has been canned, and they're investigating someone named Nick Bradley, who may have been behind all of our problems with the government. Our legal status is still good. The new bureaucrat is drawing up the paperwork so no one else can pull this stunt again."

After cheers went up for the Malek family, the conversation shifted to Nat.

"Any chance of making the pros, 'Sports Center'?"

The star wide receiver for the Sabers shrugged. "Coach Darnell is trying to get me a tryout with the Montreal Alouettes."

"Who are they?" Taira asked.

"Canadian Football League," Nat responded. "My agent is also trying to get me signed as a non-draftee free agent and into a camp somewhere. But you're all welcome to my 'Draft Party', of course."

"We'll all be there," Jackson promised.

Jeremiah Calhoun frowned. He didn't know what was worse… having to defend against a mountain of charges from the Justice Department or the tacky orange jumpsuit they put him in. He'd plead guilty to something just to get out of this horrible outfit.

Instead of a cozy minimum-security facility like the moneymaking titans of the 1980s, they had him in the U.S. Penitentiary in Atlanta. The prior guest list had a lot of notorious lawbreakers, too. Mickey Cohen and Al Capone had done time here, along with Whitey Bulger and Carlo Ponzi. Criminals from Goodfellas, The French Connection, and "Catch Me If You Can" also made their residence at that facility over the years.

He was ironically only a few hours away from that infernal Peach State College. If only that Randall Rodes had come through and eliminated their entire team on campus with that "Rebel Yell" gun, Calhoun would be signing up more clients, with the Feds none the wiser. It was stupid to use such a loud gun that had enabled a security guard to shoot him down.

Yesterday, Preston Powell had jumped from his high-rise apartment in New York City, pessimistic about his defense of ignorance of what the PPP company was doing. His estranged daughter, a philanthropist, promised to use her dad's legacy to help the victims of the partnership's alleged crimes.

Juan Fernandina remained loyal, but that could only last so long. Vinnie Moro and Ray Maillon flipped on Calhoun. Murray was not so fortunate, as prosecutors could tie him to Rodes and that kid's shooting spree. Thanks to the others' confessions, Murray wasn't needed to nail the PPP higher-ups. His quarters were considerably more confined.

Dr. E. E. Kirby kept insisting he had nothing to do with PPP's business dealings and was merely a consultant. He was free on bond, but gone were those lectures and distinguished chair positions across the country. Chip McLane avoided being a fellow prisoner in Atlanta by agreeing to become the US Attorney's star witness in what was becoming known as the Product Placement Case. Wallace Bragg was still with Calhoun, but as the charges piled up and the years in prison looked longer, that could change. Only The Spider and Darcie were free.

SRD stock plummeted, and the *Wall Street Journal* speculated that Kipenium might ironically purchase the company, given that Howard Evans had been ousted from the board in a vote of no confidence. Jed Morgan of Talladega Motors was nabbed on his way to a British Caribbean Island with limited extradition and was being added as a defendant. Foreign buyers were already circling like vultures to scoop up the remnants of his company. Summit Studios made a bundle on 'Strong and Free', but most of those profits were being used to cover settlements with Giselle Robideaux and Dale Travis, who was now free to make more bad movies.

Richmond & Webb, the makers of the "Rebel Yell", had already declared bankruptcy and shuttered all operations. Esther Ruth Harding of Miracle Communications was fighting all charges, intensely claiming she was trying to gather information on suspected criminal activity by PPP.

She-Devil, Calhoun thought.

Her crappy communication system kept him from working with his employees to shut down the PSC team.

He looked up from his prison laundry duties at the television screen that was showing an ad. It was Giselle, smirking back at him on screen, touting the "Knotty Scarf" around her neck.

"Help capture that special man in your life with one of these," she grinned.

"Hey, Prisoner 60124, no throwing the laundry at the screen," one of the guards barked.

Nat was watching the same commercial, as well. It was his third day of sitting by the television. He had been watching the other players get picked, patiently waiting for his turn. The first night, Thursday, it was just him and his family, coach, a teammate or two, and A.I. A cot was set down in the living room so his dad, Willie, could watch it.

Friday night, the number of teammates doubled, and even Jackson and Paul popped by to watch the progress. Saturday morning, the small Holman house was packed, and half the attendees slipped out into the yard to visit the BBQ grill. Rounds four through five seemed to fly by. Shortly after noon, halfway through the sixth round, Nat made the top seven list of "Best WRs Available", which brought the biggest cheers from the house.

But the enthusiasm soon died down. Only two from that list were drafted. Halfway through the seventh round, the Sabre star had his hands clasped in prayer. Coaches, teammates, all of his communications class-mates, and especially family members were offering encouragement. But there were more players on that list of best available than spots left. With the seventh round almost over, there were only the free agent compensa-tory picks remaining. And there weren't many of those.

"Just remember," said Coach Darnell. "Montreal said…"

Everyone froze as Nat's cell phone rang. The wide receiver picked it up. "We'd like to talk to you about your vehicle's extended…"

Nat hurled the phone across the room, where it banged off the wall.

"With the 251st pick," former NFL star Ron Garrick announced a minute later, "The Atlanta Falcons select… Nat Holman, Wide Receiver, Peach State College…"

But that's all he heard as his mom hugged him from one side and A.I. grabbed him on the other. His older brother Rick slapped his back while coaches, Jackson, the others from his research project mobbed him, and his dad offered a hand-squeeze from his cot. Images on the screen highlighted his Gator Bowl exploits, including the catch and run against Tennessee that earned him the Number One Sports Center moment of the Bowl Season, and the campus nickname.

"This is James Reston," Holman's agent answered as he picked up his Edict. "Sorry you couldn't reach Nat… he had a problem with his phone.

"Now, let's talk specifics. You got the statistics I sent…"

EPILOGUE:
May 10

Few colleges could top Peach State for their graduations. Set on the intramural field, early in the morning where the hill overlooking ceremony was shielded from direct sunlight, attendees were treated to the Sabers' marching band, led by Dwight S. White, a stirring address by Civil Rights Icon Rev. Louis DeLindley, and a speech by Valedictorian Tommy Nguyen, a computer science major who challenged his fellow graduates to embrace social media in the service of others. The President of PSC tapped Sylvia and Paul to provide an overview of the year.

Jackson would normally sit with the other professors, but he opted for a reserved spot behind his graduates. Elena said she'd understand. She disappeared among professors who marched in, so they couldn't sit together and joke about the middle names of the graduates.

"Normally, the Higher Education Dean would be reading off the names of the graduates," President Sullivan began, which led to several groans from the audience. "However, Dean Franklin Arbell has resigned from Peach State College. So, to announce the names of the graduates, I'd like to turn the ceremony over to our new acting Higher Education Dean, Elena Pierce!"

The roar of the crowd showed this surprising decision was met with their approval. Elena walked from behind the stage to take the president's place at the lectern. She winked at Jackson, whose jaw dropped so far it looked like he was having dental surgery.

"Awesome!" Nat pumped his fist in the air.

"Dr. Pierce is now going be *Dean* Pierce!" Trey laughed. Then he told Jackson "You can go back to being Professor Pierce now."

"Did you know?" A.I. asked.

Jackson shook his head, struggling for words.

"We couldn't have gone to nationals without her," Taira admitted. "Or you, of course."

All four rose to wave at their classmates, Sylvia and Paul, up on stage. Jackson recovered from his shock and pulled out his camera phone. But as he did so, a man tapped his shoulder.

"Professor Pierce, can we speak for a moment?"

"I've got to…" but Viv and Isaac jumped up with their cell phones. "Don't worry Dad. We'll take the photos," Viv promised.

"Er… okay, but our chat has got to be quick," Jackson responded. "My students are…"

"My name is Bob Vance, and I work with General Burgess Hurdle," the gray-suited man whispered in a low tone.

"I've never heard of him."

"Perhaps not," Vance admitted. "But in the next few days, you and the rest of the country will."

307